Somewhere Beyond the Sea

Amanda James

W F HOWES LTD

LP

This large print edition published in 2014 by
W F Howes Ltd
Unit 4, Rearsby Business Park, Gaddesby Lane,
Rearsby, Leicester LE7 4YH

1 3 5 7 9 10 8 6 4 2

First published in the United Kingdom in 2014
by Choc Lit Limited

A CIP catalogue record for this book is available
from the British Library

ISBN 978 1 47126 655 3

Typeset by Palimpsest Book Production Limited,
Falkirk, Stirlingshire

Printed and bound in Great Britain
by TJ International Ltd, Padstow, Cornwall

MIX
Paper from
responsible sources
FSC
www.fsc.org   FSC® C013056

For Brian – My lighthouse.

CHAPTER 1

I folded my clothes neatly and placed them with the precision of a drill-sergeant on a flat rock by the shore. I positioned the letter in its blue envelope carefully on top and weighed it down with a round white pebble. Standing before the moonlit water, I felt the caress of the breeze like salt kisses over my naked skin.

I walked nearer to the sea. Firm sand cushioned my steps and, despite my weight, each footfall barely left an imprint. Surf foamed in, tickled my toes, and encouraged me further. Out on the island, the glass eye of the lighthouse winked as if it knew my secret, and a gull wheeled above in day-bright moonshine. I spread my arms wide, tilted my head to the dazzling stars and inhaled. I belonged to the universe. I relished the sense of freedom, the oneness with nature.

Ironically, I had never felt so alive.

Lowering my arms again, I turned to have a last look at the clifftops. In my mind's eye, beyond them I could see the Cornish village where I had lived for the past sixteen years. I could see every little street and lane, every little country garden. Most of the

1

buildings were now in darkness, of course, apart from the light of a lamp or two.

There was no light in my mother's house.

Turning back towards the waves I stepped forward. One, two, three long strides. No hint of hesitation fettered, nor apprehension restrained.

This was it. This was what came next.

The weight of the incoming tide was my only barrier, but even as a breath caught in my throat, I gritted my teeth against the cold and plunged headlong.

I would tire of course . . . soon. But for now, with adrenaline pumping in my veins, legs and arms powering my body through the waves, for now I was strong, free and in control of my destiny.

CHAPTER 2

Tristan stopped in the cobbled high street and scratched his head. Sweat beaded his brow and he jabbed his new glasses back up the bridge of his nose for the umpteenth time. It occurred to him to pop into the opticians on the way back from the shops and ask about alterations. They were far too loose, and now in this heat they were practically impossible to keep on. The trouble was he never seemed to have time to do anything apart from work. And run errands for his wife. Thinking of which, he couldn't for the life of him remember what he had to get from the damned shops.

He scratched his head again, partly because he was thinking, and partly because he'd managed to get some bloody insect bite when he'd taken a short cut across the meadow. The midges at this time of year were relentless, homing in like tiny Junker bombers, emitting that high-pitched screech until they found a meaty target. Tristan wet his finger, dabbed at the little lump that felt like a mountain, and loosened his tie. He'd heard about the new variety of bloodsuckers migrating here from the Continent due to global warming. Well, it was certainly warm today.

A few more steps took him to the high street and, shrugging out of his jacket, Tristan found himself under the stripy awning of Jackson's butcher shop and blessedly in the shade. Harold Jackson, round, ruddy and robust waved through the window, wiggling his sausage-like fingers at Tristan. Tristan raised his hand briefly in response and then prodded his glasses up his nose again.

The image reflecting back at him in the shop window did lift his mood a little. With his heavy, square, black-rimmed glasses – already on their downward slide – perched on his nose, he thought he resembled a film star that he'd seen in a romantic comedy recently. Karen had it on DVD . . . now what was he called? He looked at himself in profile. Hmm, the guy's hair in that film had been dark, much darker than his messy tawny mane. His chin sported a covering of Tristan's 'I was too late to shave this morning' look, rather than designer stubble, but if folk thought it was the latter, who was he to argue? Nope he couldn't remember the name of the actor or the film, but what did that matter? The main thing was that he looked, dare he say it in this heat, *cool*.

Wrinkling his brow, Tristan peered mole-like at the glass and pushed his fingers through his heat-induced floppy fringe in an effort to tame the mane. He sighed. Dear God, stop preening and put your thinking cap on. What exactly was he supposed to pick up for Karen?

A tray of steak thrust at him by Harold at the other side of the window startled him out of his contemplation. Harold mouthed something, pointed at the steak and grinned. Tristan sighed and shook his head indicating he didn't understand, so Harold beckoned him inside.

Having no wish to be bored stupid by yet another story of how no finer cut of meat could be found in the whole of Cornwall, Tristan shook his head and pointed at his watch.

Harold shook his head in return and bustled out of the doorway, just as Tristan was making his escape. 'Are you popping in here later then, Doc?' Harold asked, frowning.

'No, not today, Harold. I have to run an errand for Karen and then get back for afternoon surgery.' Tristan smiled apologetically and set off again.

Harold's voice stopped him again after only a few steps. 'Oh, so you don't want this steak that she ordered?'

A Homer Simpson type 'D'oh!' sounded in Tristan's brain. He only just managed to avoid slapping his forehead to complete the picture. That's what he'd come into town for – steak! Steak for the barbecue, the very same barbecue that seemed to be taking over his wife's every waking hour this past week.

The number of times she'd asked him whether the Prestons would be comfortable eating out on the patio because even though it was June there might be a nip in the air, didn't bear thinking about. Or, did he think that the best china at a barbecue might look as if they were trying too hard? And, was her homemade coleslaw too cabbagey? Too cabbagey? What was he supposed to say to that? What he *had* said was 'stop fussing about it all, Karen, it will be grand!' She had replied that it was all right for *him* to say, but it wasn't *his* cooking that was going to be judged by the vicar and his wife.

Tristan had wished at least half a dozen times that he hadn't asked Reverend Michael to dinner sometime. He hadn't really meant it, just said it in passing when he was examining the vicar's injured knee a few weeks ago. In fact, he should have known better given Karen's condition, but he'd blurted it out and that was that.

Michael had snatched his hand off. 'We'd be delighted, Tristan,' he'd said with a beaming smile, tucking his long wavy blond hair behind his ears. With his tanned skin, cool blue eyes and white smile, he looked more like an A-list celebrity than a vicar. The congregation had doubled its female intake since he took over St Mary's.

He surfed every morning too – that's how he'd got the injured knee – and he always had an audience. This audience was exclusively female, a few ladies who 'just happened' to be walking their dogs along the beach.

'In fact, we are free Friday week if that's any good?' Michael continued, pulling his trousers back up. 'And a barbecue would be just the thing for this weather.'

Tristan had little choice but to say that would be fine. He hadn't suggested a barbecue but Michael seemed set on it, so a barbecue it would be. But now, he had almost sent the entire plan into free fall by forgetting the main part of the meal. Karen would have murdered him, marinated him in the new herb dressing she'd raved about and put *him* on the barbecue instead.

Outside the butcher's shop, Harold was still looking at Tristan as if he'd suddenly sprouted another head.

He took a deep breath and painted on his tried and tested 'trust me I'm a doctor' smile. 'Of course I want the steak, Harold. Just joking with you!' he said, stepping forward and ushering Harold back into the shop.

Harold looked a bit nonplussed, but grinned in return. He went to the other side of the counter and busied himself weighing and packing up the steak. 'How are the babes?' he said.

'They're grand thanks. Sebastian is hardly a baby though, he's nearly two and a half, and Bella's walking now.'

'Is she really? How time flies. And the good lady wife? I've only seen her from a distance the once and you've been in Kelerston, what, about a year now haven't you, Doc?'

Tristan nodded. 'She's feeling a bit stressed at

the moment, Harold, as we're having guests over for a barbecue tonight. But she's much better in general. I'm trying to get her to agree to come down to the Rose and Crown one evening for a drink.'

'That would be nice.' Harold laughed heartily. Harold was one of those people who laughed heartily for no apparent reason. Tristan would never get used to it. It made him feel uncomfortable. Apparently it was a sign of insecurity, but Tristan had a sneaky suspicion it was a sign of a vacuous brain. He tipped the butcher a weak smile and rummaged in his wallet.

Harold stopped laughing. 'Being an agorapheebric can't be much fun,' he said and arranged his face into a suitably sympathetic expression. Slapping the bag of steak on the counter, he held out his meaty paw. 'That'll be twenty pounds to you, Doctor Tristan.'

Tristan handed over the money and wondered why people said that 'to you' nonsense. 'Thanks, Harold. And like I said, her agoraphobia is much better, just a matter of time before she's out shopping for herself.'

'Well, I wish her all the best. Make sure you pass on my best wishes, mind. And while you're here,' Harold said, disappearing under the counter, 'take this chicken for her. I'm sure she could make use of it on the barbecue with perhaps a nice marinade?'

Tristan nodded and smiled. 'Oh, that's very kind

of you, Harold, and I know just the marinade she'll use.'

As he made his way back to the surgery he felt a little sheepish. Even though Harold seemed a bit disingenuous with the hyena laugh and all, he was good at heart. In fact most people in Kelerston were. Perhaps he needed to be a little less on his guard about his wife and more accepting of their concern. That aside, it was in his nature to keep his private life private – he was a public figure after all. It didn't do to let folks know too much about his personal affairs.

A doctor needed to be friendly yet professional; too much information could lead some people to assume they could call on him day or night just to look at a boil on their arse. He hadn't hidden the reason for his wife's absence, however. Tristan was a firm believer that awareness of mental health conditions was the key to understanding.

He had to admit to himself though that it wasn't true that she was better. She had *been* getting better, but over the past few weeks she'd retreated back into her shell. Karen's agoraphobia had started when they moved here from Swindon a year ago. She'd never been an outgoing person at the best of times, but living here had triggered the first anxiety attacks. Karen had been dead set against the move ever since he'd told her of his desire to return to his Cornish roots.

Tristan had grown up in Porthcothan, the next

village to Kelerston, and when a post came up at the local surgery, he'd leapt at the chance. He'd been surprised at Karen's less than luke-warm response, what was not to like? Tristan thought that she would warm to the idea once she saw how much better it would be for the kids to grow up in a small friendly village by the Atlantic Ocean, with its windswept coastline, open spaces and sense of freedom, rather than trapped in the pollution and confines of a city. But he had been sadly mistaken. Once or twice he'd seen glimpses of the old Karen, but mostly she had remained withdrawn and pale, like a snowdrop under the winter frosts.

Upon reaching the meadow, Tristan's arms waved about like a demented windmill to deter the Junker bombers, while his head ran through the discussion he'd had with his wife that morning. It wasn't like him to say things to her about her condition without thinking, but his throwaway remark about her trying to get out of the house more, had resulted in hostilities.

'I'll come out when I'm good and ready, Tristan. Even though you're a doctor, you don't seem to understand how I feel. You say you do, but you don't, not really,' Karen had said, trying to wipe jam from Sebastian's mouth as he toddled towards his father.

Tristan picked up his son and stuck his tongue out at him. Sebastian's solemn little face lit up

10

and he returned the gesture, pointing a finger at his father's mouth as if to say 'do it again, Daddy'.

'I do understand, Karen, it's just that you seemed a lot better a few weeks ago. You even came off the medication . . . but now you've gone back to where you were a few months ago. And I don't really understand why. I mean, what's happened to set you back?'

Karen pushed her honey-blonde hair out of her eyes and lifted their daughter Bella from her high-chair. 'There doesn't have to be anything in particular, it just happens,' she snapped, balancing Bella on her hip and busying herself collecting the breakfast dishes.

Tristan noticed that she avoided looking at him. She always did this when she felt unsure. Perhaps she wasn't telling him what was really on her mind. He knew better than to push it though and he was late for surgery. He walked over to her and Sebastian put his tongue out at Bella and then the children started to pull at each other's curly chestnut hair. 'There normally is a trigger, hon,' Tristan said softly and stroked her cheek. 'But if you don't want to say, then let's just leave it.'

Karen moved her head away impatiently and set Bella down. 'Yes, let's just leave it. You go to work and leave me to get on. The only thing that would help is for us to go back to Swindon, but that won't be happening will it? No, as long as Doctor Ainsworth is happy, that's all that matters.'

That last comment had really hurt. Everything

he ever did, he did for her and the children. And it wasn't like Karen to be quite so nasty. Yes, she was always on edge lately, and often snapping at him, but that comment had been the worst yet. If being in Kelerston was damaging her that much, perhaps it was time to throw in the towel and go back to the city.

Tristan turned into a narrow street and the welcome shade. The surgery was only a few yards away so he needed to get his orderly head on, as he called his professional persona. Then a picture of Karen's anguished eyes surfaced in his mind. Perhaps he was as selfish as she'd indicated, ploughing ahead regardless, imagining he knew what was best for all of them. His past had taught him some hard lessons – never give up and never rely on others. But was this both a strength and a weakness?

Tristan wished with all his heart that Karen would sing again. She had an incredible voice, but only sang when she was happy and mostly when she thought nobody was listening. She did sing in front of him sometimes, but always got embarrassed when he praised her. To save her blushes, he had crept up to the bathroom to listen at the door while she sang in the shower. Her soaring notes held his heart captive and brought a knot of raw emotion to his throat. Since moving to Kelerston, however, her voice had been solely reserved for barbed comments hurled in his direction.

Stepping through the surgery door and hanging his jacket in the lobby, Tristan resolved to entice his songbird back to the nest. And, he thought for the second time that day, if that meant a retreat to the city away from his beloved Cornwall, then so be it.

CHAPTER 3

Was I dreaming? I felt again the stubble of an unshaven face brush my cheek and then the pressure of a mouth over mine. My lungs expanded under the force of a breath from alien lungs. My stomach twisted, I rolled on my side and retched a spume of salt water onto the beach. I coughed and sucked at the chill night air. A hand rubbed my back, another grasped my forearm, trying to control my shaking body. A man's rough voice in my ear.

'I knew you'd make it. That was the seventh breath I put in you. Seven's a lucky number . . . thank God you're alive.'

I had made it? I was alive? Then I remembered what had happened. Despair flooded through my heart like a rip tide. A brace of rabbits lay on the sand a little way off, the moonlight glinting in their dead eyes. They were lucky.

'Here, let's get you warm, young 'un. Put this on,' the man said, covering my nakedness with a heavy coat. The stink of rancid sweat and nicotine filled my nostrils. I heaved again, but my stomach was empty.

Tears rolled down my face as I looked up into his. A broad brow, long nose, pinched mouth and grey, shaggy hair. I guessed him to be about fifty. Even though the only light came from the moon and his torch, I thought I recognised him. He was one of the Travellers I'd seen selling potatoes round the village in the last few weeks.

He wiped my tears away with a calloused finger. 'So, were you tryin' to do yerself in? I 'spect you were . . . being naked an' all.'

I shrugged, nodded.

'And a young 'un like you? Such a waste. Nothin' is ever so bad as to try to take away what's most precious to us all. Now, let's get you off the island and 'ome safe.'

Island? I couldn't be on the island. That was too far out. I knelt and raised my head, looked over the sand dunes to the sea. A 'now-you-see-me-now-you-don't' flash of light shone a path across the waves towards the coastline. I turned to look at the light-house behind me, a little way off.

'I swam a long way,' I said, almost to myself.

'You did that,' said the Traveller. 'Now, give me your 'and. My boat's just down round this 'ere cove.'

'No. I'm not going back. Never going back.' I pulled his coat closer around my body. It was a little too small, but despite the stink, it felt comforting.

'Well, that's as mebbe, but you can't stay 'ere all night.' He ruffled his hair and peered at me owlishly. Perhaps his eyes weren't as good as mine in this light.

He stood and scooped up his rabbits. 'Ain't you got no family?'

I smiled humourlessly. 'Not anymore.'

He sighed and offered me his hand again. 'Well, my wife will be glad to put you up for a few days, just 'til you feel more normal like.'

Normal, that was a joke. I wasn't normal. That was half the trouble. I took his hand anyway and stood. I had to hold on to his arm as a wave of nausea rippled through my belly.

'You're going to need lookin' after, kid. And what's your name? I can't keep callin' you young 'un or kid, can I?'

'I don't have a name,' I said, and meant it. Right then I felt that I was nothing – nobody. I should be floating dead on the waves somewhere, wished I was.

'Right, well I'm Bob.' He guided my shaky legs towards a small rowing boat high up on the shingle. 'And I'll call you, Bobby. Not very imaginative, but it'll do.'

As Bob cast us adrift, I watched his sinewy arms take the strain as he dipped the tips of the oars in-out-in-out of the water. His steady rhythm rowed us away from the island, and back. But back where and to what? My life was supposed to have ended. I had planned no way forward. In-out-in-out-in . . .

I looked at the ink-black sea and wished I was beneath it.

CHAPTER 4

'Are you sure they're asleep? There's no point in me putting the chicken on if I have to leave off in a minute,' Karen said, threading the last chunk of chicken onto a skewer.

'Yes, sound asleep. And if they do wake up, I can sort it,' Tristan said, stepping up behind his wife to encircle her in his arms. She sighed, exasperated by this move and made an exaggerated stretch to retrieve a plate on which to put the skewer. He made no move to free her and kissed the back of her neck.

'Tris, for God's sake let me get on with this. Michael and Jenny will be here in a minute.' Karen momentarily regretted her tone as she saw her husband's face fall, but it was his fault they had to have this stupid barbecue in the first place. What with that, and having the children on her own all day, it was a wonder she could think straight.

She could feel his eyes on her as she raced around the kitchen pulling this and that from the cupboards. 'Okay, garlic, chilli oil, what else

17

do I normally put on the prawns?' she said cheerily, hoping to make up for snapping. He didn't answer, just walked over, pulled the bag of prawns from her and took her face in his hands. She frowned and sighed, 'Tris, I just told you—'

'Shh. Listen to me, this won't take a minute,' Tristan whispered, a sad little smile playing over his lips. 'Next week I'm going to start looking for a post elsewhere. I'm not sure if it will be Swindon, but I'll try my best to get us nearby. I should have listened to you, and like you said this morning, I should have been more concerned for your happiness, instead of making you leave your home town and everything. I just thought I knew best. I love it here so much, and I thought you would . . . I was wrong.'

Karen felt her throat thicken and tears prick her eyes. Tristan was such a wonderful man and looking into his soft green eyes full of love for her, she thought her heart would break. He wasn't wrong, wasn't wrong at all, but she could never tell him her true feelings.

She blinked back her tears and looked away. Beyond the patio doors the table was set up for the barbecue. The lush green lawn rolled away to join the fields and the heady scent of lavender mingled with sea air wafted in on the evening breeze. Idyllic. She looked back at him. 'I don't know what to say,' she muttered. At least this was the truth.

'Don't say anything, my love.' Tristan kissed her forehead. 'And you always add lemon juice.'

'Lemon juice?'

'To the prawns.' He grinned and went to the fridge.

So far so good. Karen smiled as she handed the salad bowl to Jenny. She had been nervous about meeting the Prestons but it had been a lovely evening so far and they were great company. They had complimented her on the food and, for the first time in ages, Karen was starting to relax and enjoy herself. As long as she didn't relax too much and let her guard down she'd be okay. Tristan was having fun too. He hadn't had much of that lately, and all because of her.

'So, Karen, what did you do before you met the good doctor and had the kids?' Michael asked, helping himself to more wine.

'Oh, I worked on a farm. I loved the outdoor life,' Karen said, holding her glass up for a refill.

'A farm, how lovely!' Jenny said, her elfin face lighting up. 'Before I met Michael I just worked in an office. How boring was that!'

'And now you are a boring vicar's wife.' Michael laughed, kissing his wife on the shoulder.

'You are many things, my love, but boring isn't one of them,' Jenny replied with a grin, and kissed him on the cheek.

'That's where we met,' Tristan said, forking chicken from his skewer. 'I went to the farm to

19

attend to a worker who'd got his wrist trapped in one of the machines and broken it. The surgery was just down the road and Karen ran to get me. I was late for my rounds, so she was lucky to catch me. We might never have met if I had left a few minutes early.'

'So was that in Swindon, then?' Michael asked, stuffing a hunk of steak into his mouth.

'No, a small village on the outskirts. We both lived in Swindon but worked in the village. We love open spaces and fresh air, don't we, Karen?' Tristan said, and then looked at her apologetically. 'Um . . . well, we used to . . .' his voice trailed off.

Karen knew that he'd not meant to bring attention to her agoraphobia, but he had anyway. The Prestons looked a bit uncomfortable, so she decided to meet it head on. 'Not to worry, Tris.' She smiled, patting her husband's hand. She looked at Michael and Jenny. 'I am getting better, and I might even try to go clothes shopping in a week or so.'

'Well, that's great,' Jenny said, her hazel eyes full of sympathy. 'If I can do anything to help, just let me know. I'd be more than happy to come with you.'

'Oh no, don't let my wife loose in the shops, she'll buy the whole town before you can say Gok Wan,' Michael said, playfully tugging his wife's long dark ponytail. That made everyone laugh and the awkwardness disappeared.

★   ★   ★

A chill wind from the ocean had driven them inside and they now sat around the log fire nursing brandies. It was nearly ten o'clock, but the conversation showed no sign of stalling. They had touched on the weather, commenting on how baking hot it had been in the day and how strange it was having to light a fire at nine in the evening, the state of the economy, local events coming up and everything under the sun. Karen hadn't felt so good in a long time, she actually felt normal for once. But then Michael asked a few questions and everything changed.

'So were you both born in Swindon?'

'Karen was. I'm from round here, the next village along actually.'

'Ah, right. We're both Londoners but we just adore it here, don't we, Jen? Fresh air, country life, and the sea. I feel like I belong by the sea. It's kind of in my blood somehow if that makes sense?' Michael thumped his chest for emphasis. 'There's no way we'd ever go back to city life now. Would you, guys?'

Tristan jumped up and held his finger to his lips. 'Was that one of the children?'

The Prestons cocked their heads to one side. Karen thought they looked like a pair of puppies listening for the return of their owner. She knew they would hear nothing, however, apart from the strengthening wind in the eaves. The children were sound asleep. Tristan had said that just to interrupt the conversation.

21

'Nope. All quiet on the western front.' Tristan beamed and pointed at the brandy glasses. 'Another?'

'No thanks. We'd better be making our way back in a bit. Choir practice in the morning, isn't it, Jen?'

Jen uncurled herself from the sofa and nodded enthusiastically. 'Yes, I can't wait. I just love to sing. We have a great choir now; a real mix of folk, older and young ones, too.'

'Do either of you sing?' Michael asked, then drained his glass.

Before Karen could signal her husband to keep his mouth shut, he said, 'I have the voice of a frog, though when I was a kid I apparently had the voice of an angel, but Karen's voice is stunning, I mean *really* stunning.'

'Wow!' Jenny said, clapping her hands together in excitement. 'You must join us!'

'I really mustn't. My husband exaggerates, and anyway I'm not sure if I could manage a church hall right now.' Karen could feel a flush creeping up her neck like acid up litmus paper and her heart hammered in her chest.

'Her husband does *not* exaggerate. She reduces me to tears every time,' Tristan said, somehow oblivious to her discomfort. Must be the booze. Karen had noticed him topping up his glass quite a few times earlier. He'd had one too many, but she hadn't stopped him enjoying himself, probably because she'd had one too many too.

'I'll reduce you to tears again if you don't stop

harping on,' she said jokingly, though her smile cemented in a grimace.

'Good job that the sessions are held at my house then. You could manage that, couldn't you?' Jen asked hopefully.

Karen looked at her and shook her head. 'I doubt it, and anyway, I'm not much for hymns.'

'It's not just hymns; they do lots of contemporary stuff, too. The youngsters would lose interest if they didn't,' Michael said.

'Even, so . . . I just don't think I could face . . .' Karen began, but was stopped by Michael.

His blue eyes flashed and he held his finger up in the air, eureka style. 'I think I might have the answer! The choir could meet here. There's plenty of room and it would mean that you didn't have to leave your own home.'

Karen sighed and bit her bottom lip. Then at last Tristan seemed to realise that everyone was putting too much pressure on her. 'Hey, guys, I know you mean well, but I think Karen needs a bit of time to think about it.'

Michael and Jenny nodded sagely.

'Of course. We should have known better. Sorry, just got a bit overexcited, didn't we, Jen?'

Karen looked at the three sympathetic faces smiling towards her and suddenly could bear it no longer. Perhaps it was her way of making amends to Tristan, perhaps it was because she'd had a drink, perhaps it was because she loved singing so much, or a combination of all three, when she said, 'I'm game if you are. Not tomorrow though, the week after maybe? I need a little time to get my pipes working!'

The chorus of, 'yay' and 'good on you' and 'that's fantastic' almost raised the roof and Karen flapped her hands at them and pointed to the ceiling.

Jenny put her hand over her mouth and stepped forward to hug Karen. She whispered in her ear, 'Sorry, don't want to wake the babes, but *so* pleased you agreed to sing. I can't wait to hear you.'

As Karen and Tristan watched the Prestons walk off down their drive and into the country lane, their torchlight bobbing in front like a will-o'-the-wisp, Karen sighed and leaned her head on Tristan's shoulder.

'Well, that was a great evening, and I can tell you I was very pleasantly surprised that you agreed to sing next week,' Tristan said, taking her hand and leading her inside. 'In fact, I thought I'd be in the doghouse after landing you in it.'

Karen filled the kettle and shook her head. 'No, you're in the doghouse too much lately . . . and you weren't half as surprised as I was. God knows what possessed me.'

'Well, whatever it was I am so happy that it did. You coming to bed?'

'Yep, in a minute. I'll have a cuppa and just gather my thoughts a bit. I feel like I might have turned a corner, you know?'

'It certainly seems like it, my love,' Tristan said, 'but don't be too long though, the bed's too big without you.' He blew her a kiss from the kitchen door.

Karen smiled and blew one back.

Half an hour later Karen checked and locked the back door. She wished she'd done the same with her mouth earlier. What the hell had she been thinking? Tristan hadn't been exaggerating when he said she could sing. When she opened her mouth, people were gobsmacked and as a girl she had been the star of the local church choir. But then she'd stopped singing as the light had gradually dwindled and disappeared from her world, snuffed out by a chill wind of fate. Karen never expected to see the light return, but then she'd met Tristan.

Tris was like the sunlight creeping over a barren field, encouraging new shoots of trust, laughter and love in to her icy heart. Over the years she'd sing now and then, but though she enjoyed it, thoughts of her past often muscled in, taking the edge off. Bedsides, once the babies arrived, she'd had no time to consider serious singing. But now, now all that might be set to change.

A big fat problem sat heavy on her shoulders though. What if her singing attracted too much attention in this small town? Too much attention was the last thing she needed. Karen wandered to the foot of the stairs and snapped off the light.

If she'd turned a corner, why did she feel as though she'd just hit a brick wall?

CHAPTER 5

The sky was blue, the sun was yellow, the sand was brown and the sea foamed in and out, chopped by a white-horse breeze. A midweek late afternoon trip to the beach was so rare for the Ainsworth household that finding the teeth of hens would be more common. In fact, any trips to the beach had been few and far between lately, especially with the whole family.

Tristan looked along the beach and marvelled that the cows in a field along the top of the cliff didn't just fall into the sea. From this angle they looked very precarious. And the other side of the beach was framed with an identical cliff complete with little dots of colour moving along the top. These were folk walking along the coastal path that stretched for miles along the Cornish coast, zigzagging and undulating its way past secret coves, over fields, through woodland, and winding down to sleepy harbours.

One day Tristan planned to walk the whole of the North Cornish coastal path and hopefully Karen and the kids could come too, when she was properly better and the kids were older, of course.

He arranged the picnic rug carefully and then hammered the parasol post into the sand with a rubber mallet. As he stooped to fix the yellow and red striped parasol shade into the post, he glanced at Karen and the kids paddling in the shallows. The three of them looked like an advert for Cornish tourism. She, tall, willowy, long-legged, striding along, her golden hair streaming out behind, followed by two little, chubby, chestnut-haired children bouncing along like ducklings after an exotic mamma bird. The children took after him in hair colour and stature; he'd never been particularly slim, especially when he'd been in his teens. Theirs was baby fat, but at thirty-four Tristan couldn't put his little paunch down to that.

The night of the barbecue had seen a real transformation in his wife. Tristan couldn't for the life of him think what had happened to help Karen turn a corner, but a corner she had definitely turned. Her mood had become calmer and not once had she mentioned going back to Swindon since he told her they would on Friday night. He'd raised it again a few days ago and she'd just put a finger to his lips. 'Let's just leave plans of moving for a while. At the moment I feel better . . . we'll see how it goes,' she'd said and kissed him tenderly. And then she'd suggested they had supper on the beach today. He'd thought she was joking at first.

Tristan sat down under the shade and rummaged in the picnic basket. Sausage rolls, chicken legs, salad, quiche, my goodness what a feast. He looked up to see his family hurrying back up the beach towards him. Sebastian held a bit of seaweed in his hand and called, 'Daddy, I got weedsee!'

'Seaweed, wow!' Tristan ran to meet his son and swung him up into the air. The seaweed slapped against Tristan's head like a wet kipper. 'Yuck!' he said and pulled a face. Sebastian laughed and slapped the seaweed again.

Karen picked up Bella and ran over to them. Bella tried to grab the seaweed from Sebastian, and a full-on tug of war ensued, resulting in Tristan getting covered in slime amid much laughter from all four.

'Will you keep an eye on them while I put the food out?' Karen asked, slipping under the shade.

'Yup, indeed! Now who wants to build a sand-castle?' Tristan yelled and did a crazy dance in the sand. The children looked a bit surprised and then Sebastian danced too, giggling. Tristan felt closer to Sebastian's age than his own right at that moment and dared to hope that these happy times would continue.

Supper consumed, the children played chase and then happily dug in the sand.

Tristan sighed contentedly and rested his head on Karen's lap. He smiled up at her. 'Sand, sea, family and scrumptious food. Who could want for more?' Tristan pulled his T-shirt up and prodded his belly. 'Do you think I'm getting too fat?'

Karen sighed and ruffled his hair. 'With that six-pack? Why do you always stress about your weight and the way you look? You're gorgeous. I'm sure half your female patients make appointments for no reason.'

Tristan frowned at his tanned belly and had to concede that there was some definition there. But a six-pack? Perhaps a four, at most. 'Don't know about that . . . and I suppose it's due to childhood insecurities. You ought to have seen me when I was fifteen, sixteen or so. I bet you wouldn't have fancied me then.' Karen tutted and flicked his nose. 'Ouch. So have I put weight on, do you think?' Tristan persisted.

'For goodness sake, Tris. A few pounds maybe, but life's too short to watch every mouthful. I love you exactly as you are.' She ran her cool fingers over his abdomen.

'Mm, thank you for that, kind lady.' He pulled her hair. 'Praise indeed, especially coming from one who never has an extra ounce to worry about, even though you eat for England and have had two kids one after the other.'

She tapped him on the shoulder playfully. 'Eat for England, charming! And I don't have to worry because I run, as you well know.'

'Hmm, perhaps I should start running.'

'I run because I enjoy it, it's not a chore . . . and I might even start running outside again soon. That treadmill is *so* boring.'

Tristan's heart flipped. If Karen was contemplating running outside, then her agoraphobia must really be under control. The condition wouldn't allow for a sufferer to be miles away from the safety of their home with no way of escape. That they were here on the beach this evening was miracle enough, but then their house *was* only five minutes over the dunes.

An impulse to cheer and make a big fuss came over him, but the casual way she'd told him of her intention to run outside again kept him calm. She obviously didn't want to make a big thing out of it and Tristan knew that if he did, she might feel under pressure to prove that she could. There was no way he was going to rush her into it. 'That's great sweetheart. Perhaps I'll join you one day if you can run at a snail's pace.' He grinned.

Karen grinned back. 'We'll see. Now I don't know if you have noticed, but your son and daughter are halfway down the beach. It would be marvellous if you could go and play with them while I have a bit of "me time" to read my book.'

'Aye aye, Cap'n, orders is orders.' Tristan knew that his pirate accent needed work, but Karen laughed anyway. As he jogged down the beach towards the kids, all he could think about was how quickly things had turned. The old Karen had come back to him it seemed, or at least was on the return journey. He had no idea why, but he decided that he wouldn't over-analyse it. Lately he'd had to be more of a doctor than a husband to Karen, but now it was time to just be there, love her, and be thankful that she was getting better.

★   ★   ★

The useful thing about wearing sunglasses was that they masked the eyes. Tristan could always tell what she was thinking by looking into hers. Karen balanced her book on her knees, watching her husband running to the children and blew out a long breath of air. The brick wall she'd smacked headlong into on Friday night was beginning to crumble, but she felt it would be a while longer than she was pretending to Tristan before it finally tumbled to the ground. And, in her heart of hearts, she expected there would always be a few blocks lurking, just awaiting the hand of fear to build them up again.

It was heavenly here on the beach, but the pressure of having a load of strangers round on Saturday morning was already sending little fingers of apprehension tickling up her spine. Nevertheless, she knew she had to stick to the plan for Tris's sake. He had put up with her moods and anxieties for too long.

The main thing keeping her on track was the warm glow that had been reignited in her soul. A fire of passion sprang from it that for many a year had been extinguished and reduced to cold grey ash – the joy of singing.

Once she'd made the decision to have the choir round last Friday, singing had given her spiritual release and physical rejuvenation. It was just like the old days again. To her, singing was as natural as breathing.

And now she was going to have an audience,

something that thrilled and terrified her in equal measure. Apart from Tristan, nobody had heard her sing properly since . . . she pushed away unwelcome memories and picked up her book. Karen wet her finger and flicked through to the right page. Her eyes rolled over the words but she wasn't taking them in. Instead she was thinking about the move to Kelerston and her life over the past year. Her self-inflicted imprisonment.

Last week when Tristan had asked her what had triggered her setback, she'd said nothing in particular. When he'd asked her why she had turned a corner again the other day, she'd replied the same. And to an extent it was the truth. She guessed that it was just the pressure of her feelings dropping and rising like some crazy emotional barometer.

On the other hand, Karen knew full well the origin of the pressure and she wished with all her heart that she could share her burden with the man she loved. She also knew that was out of the question. If she did tell him, she was certain that she'd lose him forever.

CHAPTER 6

I followed Bob up the steps into the dark caravan. The floor creaked under the weight of our footsteps and I heard a muffled snore coming from another room. Bob pushed open a door. 'Maureen . . . Maureen, wake up.'

'Hmm? What time is it? It's still dark, Bob.'

'It's about 'alf two, but you 'ave to wake up, we 'ave a visitor,' Bob whispered, switching on a standard lamp.

I watched, still numb inside, as Maureen's tangled mop of peroxide blonde hair appeared over the blankets and a tattooed arm stretched out, flicked on the bedside light. I could now see that the caravan was so filled with every bit of tat and bric-a-brac, that barely a wall or shelf space could be seen. When Maureen sat up, I could see that her body had suffered a similar fate, hidden as it was beneath the colourful tapestry of tattoos displayed along both arms and around her neck.

'What the bloody 'ell?' Maureen rasped.

'This is Bobby, Mo, and we are goin' to make sure we show our usual 'ospitality, aren't we?' Bob said, nodding and pulling a face at Maureen as if to say 'don't argue and I'll tell you later.'

34

Maureen pulled her arms into a dressing gown that had seen better days and slipped out of bed. She walked over to me and breathed stale beer breath into my face as she gave me the once over. 'Bobby, eh?' She sniffed narrowing her dark brown eyes. She turned back to her husband. 'And what are we supposed to do with this 'ere Bobby? Just what the 'ell are you doin' bringin' a kid 'ere at this time o' night, Bob?'

'Questions will keep for mornin', lass. Let's just say Bobby is goin' to stay for a few days. There's plenty to be done round 'ere, and we could use an extra pair of 'ands.'

Maureen turned back to me and folded her arms. 'You gonna 'elp round 'ere are you?'

I shrugged. I just wanted to sleep, escape from this waking nightmare.

'So what will your folks 'ave to say about that then, mm?' Maureen poked me on the shoulder.

Bob stepped between us. 'Now just shut up, Mo. I told you we'll discuss it in the mornin'. Just get some spare blankets and make up the bed in the other room.'

Maureen sucked her teeth and swished past. I could hear her banging cupboards and shaking blankets out. I felt even worse now I knew that I was obviously an unwelcome guest, but I wanted to sleep more than I wanted to leave.

I left Bob's coat on and slipped under the blankets on the sofa bed. It was comfortable and despite Maureen's bark, she had been careful to tuck sheets and plump pillows. It was more than I deserved or desired. By rights I should have be sleeping on the seabed, so why the hell wasn't I? The fear of death was nothing to the terror I felt at being alive. What on earth would become of me now? I drifted off to sleep listening to the sound of muted voices rising and falling in the next room.

The next morning I was rudely awakened by a chipped white mug being slammed down onto the table by my bed.

'Tea, for you,' Maureen grouched.

I opened one eye and watched her shuffling about the caravan grabbing pans, bread and eggs from various cupboards. In the daylight she looked to be around forty-five, short, sinewy and had the skin of an alligator. I guessed years of smoking and outdoor work had eroded any trace of peaches and cream, and replaced them with farm tracks and crow's feet.

''Ave yer tea and get up. We ain't got time for slackers round 'ere,' she snapped pointing a bread knife at me.

'Hey, Mo, give Bobby a chance to come round,' Bob said, coming in with an armful of clothes. He placed them on the bed next to me. 'These should fit you; they were mine when I 'ad a bit more weight to me. You're a plump 'un right enough.' He grinned at me, but not unkindly. He was just telling it like it was. Plump was an understatement. Five foot eight and nearly eighteen stone – that was a lot of plump.

'Not 'ealthy for a young 'un to be so chubby. A bit

of 'ard work pickin' taters will soon see the back of it,' Maureen said.

I gathered the clothes to me and got up.

Maureen nodded to a door along the corridor. 'Go in the bathroom and get dressed. 'Ave a wash too and comb yer 'air. You look like a sack of shit tied up in the middle.'

If I wasn't mistaken she had a twinkle in her eye and smile of encouragement on her leathery face. Perhaps she wasn't as bad as she liked to make out.

The clothes fitted, more or less. A red vest, a huge checked green and white shirt, and a pair of black joggers. All the items had seen better days but they were clean. I washed my face and cleaned my teeth with my finger; there was no way I was going near either toothbrush in the holder. I found a pink hairbrush on a shelf and tried to do something with the coarse, salt-coated mat that passed for my hair. When I was finished I returned to the main living area.

Maureen and Bob sat at the table eating scrambled eggs on toast and a place had been set for me. Bob pointed at a chair with his fork. 'Sit down, then. Glad to see you lookin' a bit more 'uman.'

I sat and Maureen brought a plate of eggs for me from the hob.

'Eat that, then we'll think about shoes.' She leaned down, looking at my bare feet under the table. 'I think it will have to be Bob's old boots. I'm a five, there's no way your pasties will fit into any of my trainers.'

I took a sip of tea and pushed the eggs around my plate. For once my appetite had abandoned me.

'Eat up then. Beats me 'ow you got to be so big if you don't eat,' Bob said, pushing a round of toast towards me. Even though I knew he was just speaking in his normal plain way, I couldn't hold it together any longer. I opened my mouth and a silent scream heralded a tidal wave of tears.

''Ere now, don't cry. Bob told me 'ow he found you and there's nothin' so bad as can't be fixed. I should know, I've fixed a few in me time,' Maureen said, standing and patting my back.

I looked up into her face now full of concern, and try as I might, I couldn't staunch the hysterical outpouring.

'Come, come now. We'll 'ave you as right as rain and back 'ome in no time.' She continued hugging my bulk to her slight frame.

This show of compassion from such a prickly character made me even worse. 'I . . . I can't go home. I have no home . . . not anymore.' I sobbed.

Maureen wiped my face with a cloth and tilted my chin up. She looked into my eyes and to my shock, hers shone with moisture. 'Then until you decide summat else, this is your 'ome, Bobby. As long as you pull yer weight, of course,' she said with a wink.

I stayed with Maureen and Bob for two years.

CHAPTER 7

'Dearly beloved, we are gathered here today to join this scone and this coffee in perfect union,' Tristan said. He tossed a freshly baked scone in his hands, blew on it and took a bite. 'Mm, lovely, but whooo hot, hot, hot.' He ran water into a glass and gulped it down.

'You'll never learn. I told you to leave them for ten minutes,' Karen said, taking the plate of scones and placing them on the large kitchen table. 'And no more until everyone gets here or there'll be none left.'

'There won't really be enough for twenty people, so I think I should eat some more. You could just put out some of that cake from Sainsbury's instead.' Tristan grinned and tiptoed over to the table.

Karen turned from the sink and caught him in the act. 'Stop right there! I have another batch in the oven *and* we're having the cake. Now, go and check on the kids. They're too quiet for my liking.'

Tristan huffed and took the remains of his scone and his coffee into the living room. 'It's okay,' he called over his shoulder. 'They've only painted the walls and set fire to the carpet, no need to worry.'

★   ★   ★

Karen smiled to herself and gathered up the mugs to place on the table next to the scones. Tristan was so much like his old self at the moment, but she guessed that was because she was like *her* old self. The apprehension she'd felt the other day on the beach was still lurking low down in her gut, but the thrill of singing again was getting the upper hand.

The kitchen clock chimed ten. The choir would be here in fifteen minutes. Just time to check her appearance for the hundredth time.

The hallway mirror seemed to make her look thinner than the one in the bathroom. Perhaps she was getting a bit too skinny. The figure hugging green T-shirt used to accentuate her curves, but her boobs looked a bit flatter today. She turned to the side and pulled at her black jeans bagging around her bottom. Yep, she'd definitely lost some weight. But then was it surprising with all her worries recently? Karen loosened her hair from the scrunchie and ran her fingers through to add a bit of volume. Yes, that made her face look softer, less severe.

Her mouth twisted to the side. She'd never get used to these green contact lenses. It seemed like a good idea to change her eye colour when they'd moved, and at first she'd loved them, but now she wasn't so sure. Leaning closer to the mirror she pouted and then bared her teeth to check for spinach. Why did she always do this when there wasn't even the remotest chance of the telltale green leaf clinging to her pearly whites?

Now, the big fat hairy-legged question was, should she put a bit of pink lip-gloss on, or would that look as if she was trying to impress? She'd already got some light eye make-up on as it was. Karen tossed her head and grabbed her handbag. *Oh, for goodness sake, stop worrying, just do what you feel like doing, woman!*

Lip-gloss applied, she walked back into the kitchen just in time to save the second batch of scones from burning. A dose of calm and collected was obviously needed more than lip-gloss. How the bloody hell could she have forgotten the scones?

'Sounds like they're here, shall I let them in?' Tristan asked, popping his head round the door.

'No, just let them stand on the doorstep, Tristan,' Karen answered, adding a withering look. He frowned and went to the front door. Karen sighed. Being nasty to Tris wouldn't help her nerves. He'd been lovely lately, so why had she snapped at him? *Perhaps because of the stress of the big fat secret you're hiding, Karen?* She took a deep breath and smoothed imaginary crumbs from her jeans. Her stomach was rolling like the waves outside and she wished she'd never agreed to the whole stupid idea. Why couldn't she have just said no?

'Hey there, you look nice!' Jenny came in a few seconds later on a bright and breezy cloud and a noisy gaggle of strangers followed in her slip-stream. Karen's heart rate galloped up the scale

41

as she cast her eye over them all, but Jenny's cheerful manner soon put her at ease. Instead of introducing them formally, Jenny shouted their names as if they were a class of schoolchildren. One shouted back, 'Yup, here, miss!' which caused a ripple of laughter and the ice to be broken.

Karen waved to them all and shook hands with the ones nearest, and moving round the group concentrating on trying to remember names, her anxiety eventually disappeared.

'Don't suppose anyone wants coffee and scones do they?' Tristan asked casually, when there was a lull in the hubbub. Mutterings to the contrary met his poker-faced stare. 'Well, that's good, because I had to go out and buy eight extra mugs yesterday!' He laughed.

Twenty minutes later, the last scone had been eaten, the last coffee mug drained, but the party atmosphere continued unabated. Karen smiled and nodded her reassurance at Tristan's quizzical expression. She knew that although he was clearing plates, that look silently asked her if she was coping. Karen was more than coping, goodness knows why she'd been so nervous. She was in her element, and soon she would sing.

On cue, Jenny stood, clapped her hands. 'So, let's get to it, we haven't got all day!'

As everyone made themselves comfortable in the large conservatory, and Tristan busied himself setting up the backing CD, 'helped' by Sebastian,

Jenny spoke softly to Karen. 'I thought we'd start with "I Can See Clearly Now". I thought you'd know that one. If not, don't worry, I have the lyric sheets with me.'

'Yes, I do, I love it . . . and the lyrics are very appropriate for the way I'm feeling today.'

Jenny squeezed Karen's arm and then walked to the front of the group. 'Okay, the first song today will be "I Can See Clearly Now".' She nodded at Tristan to start the track. 'Right after three, nice and loud, guys. Let's shatter the glass in this conservatory!' She winked at Karen and counted them in.

As they sang, Jenny conducted and then walked around listening to the voices. Karen was predictably standing as far back as she could, so Jenny gently took her elbow and guided her to the front row. Jenny raised her voice to be heard over the choir. 'Nice, very nice, Karen, but you're not open full throttle yet. Just relax and go for it.' Jenny returned to her place and waved her arms enthusiastically, her ponytail swinging as she nodded encouragement at them all.

It was true what Jenny had said. Karen wasn't singing to the best of her ability but she didn't want the others to think she was showing off, it was enough to be singing again. Adrenaline pulsed through her veins and her face flushed with happiness as she saw Tristan grinning and the children waving at her.

She felt Jenny's eyes urging her on during the last verse. Karen nodded and smiled and raised her volume slightly, but Jenny held her right hand palm upwards and wiggled her index and middle fingers at her in a 'come on, give me more' gesture. Taking a deep breath Karen launched into the chorus, pulling out all the stops and singing from the heart.

After a few seconds, she was aware that hers was the only voice in the room. The rest had stopped, were staring at her open-mouthed. Jenny steepled her fingers to her chin and her eyes were moist as she listened intently. After a few more seconds, Karen, now the colour of a stop sign, came to an abrupt halt.

A round of applause from all there almost did shatter the glass in the conservatory and then everyone talked at once, patting her on the back, asking questions like had she been professionally trained, and had she thought about entering talent competitions or putting herself on YouTube? Overwhelmed, all Karen could do was grin and say no to all.

Jenny clapped her hands. 'Right you lot, back to work, and Karen, if you wouldn't mind, would you be the soloist in our next song?'

Everyone looked at Karen expectantly. She felt a bit of a wobble return to her tummy. 'Hmm, not sure, what is it?'

'"Hallelujah", do you know it? It made the charts again a few years back because of X Factor,' Jenny said, handing out the song sheets.

'Yes I know it . . . but I've only heard it on the radio, never sung it. I'm not sure I will be able to manage it.'

'She's not sure that she will be able to manage it, folks.' Jenny returned to the front. 'What do we think?'

A resounding yes from everyone lifted Karen's spirits and banished the wobble. Wobbles were for the past; this was what she'd dreamed of for years. To be able to sing properly like this was something she'd thought would never happen again, and now here she was. The fears of the past year seemed ludicrous to her now. If she kept her head and continued to be careful, there was no reason for her secrets to be uncovered.

Karen looked around at everyone and her eyes locked onto her husband's. They were so full of love and pride that hers grew moist. She blinked, cleared her throat and looked at Jenny. 'Um . . . if you want me to, I'll give it a go.'

CHAPTER 8

The nightmares never left. Even now, sometimes I wake up sheathed in sweat believing my mother to be in the dark corner of the room, wardrobe, or perhaps under the bed. Years ago, images of her twisted mask of hatred hovering over me as I slept were so real I could scarcely breathe.

I'd count to ten and then shoot my hand out to the switch on the bedside lamp flooding the room with a pool of yellow light. I'd creep out of bed, wary of the caravan creaking, trying to be silent as I examined the wardrobe, corners and then taking a deep breath, every nerve ending strung out as taut as a violin string, I'd peep under the bed.

My mother was never there, of course. How could she be?

I was so lucky to have the protection of Bob and Maureen. Without them, I know I wouldn't be here today.

Two days after Bob saved my life, he returned to the caravan with the local newspaper. I'd been helping Maureen with the washing and we were just having a cup of tea. Bob slapped the paper on the table and pointed his finger at the headline. 'Looks like we'll 'ave to move on up north to our Jack's earlier than we thought, Mo.'

My heart lurched as I read the headline. 'Local Teenager Missing Presumed Drowned.' Under that was a picture of me in my school uniform. It had been taken in happier times, before I had ballooned into a walking whale. I remembered the way I'd felt on that day. A bit self-conscious in front of the camera as any teenager would be, but largely happy. My life had been ahead of me, sunny and full of promise. Little did that kid know, smiling out at me from the newspaper, that in a few short years there would be no future.

Maureen picked up the paper and followed the text, laboriously tracing each line with her finger. Her mouth worked as she spelled out each word and now and then, she'd look to Bob, her brow furrowed. 'That says, "suspicious",' he said. And later, 'circum-stances.' Maureen would look up at me occasionally, her eyes full of pity. I quickly read the piece over her shoulder and felt my stomach twist. Before my breakfast could make a reappearance, I stood up and pushed past Bob on the way to the bathroom.

'Don't you fret, kid,' he called after me. 'We'll be up north by this time tomorrow, nobody will find yer!'

Bob had been as true as his word. The Traveller camp near Swindon welcomed me as one of their own. I remember it was my birthday the fifth week of arriving and I actually thought there was a point in celebrating it for the first time in years. No questions were ever asked about who I was, and what I was doing travelling with Maureen and Bob. Well, at least they never asked me directly. Bob's brother, Jack, was happy to find work for me and though I missed the sea, and my beloved Cornwall, I settled fairly well, or at least as well as any seventeen-year-old on the run from a terrifying past could settle.

Gradually I began to think there might be a point to living after all. I had more affection and care from strangers there than my mother had ever shown me, especially over the last few years. They judged me on my merit and focused on the good. My self-loathing diminished along with my enormous bulk as a result of my physical daily chores. I felt I was really contributing to the community, and, in some small way, repaying Bob and Maureen. I knew I could never really repay them, however, what they had done for me was priceless.

They had five children all grown, and looking back, I guess I became the sixth. They never actually referred to me as their child, of course, but I don't think they could have given me more love and care if they had actually been my real parents. Maureen especially never splashed her affection around freely. But I knew without any doubt that she loved me even without a public declaration. And I loved them. I miss them every day.

CHAPTER 9

The wind nearly undid all Karen's hard work. As she kissed her children gently and closed the door to their room, the breeze coming in from the landing window sucked the handle out of her grasp. Just in time, she grabbed it and gently pulled the door shut. Realising she'd been holding her breath, she tiptoed away and blew a sigh of relief. It had been one of the best days in her life, but God was she knackered.

She found Tristan in the living room watching television. 'Did they go off?' he asked.

Karen noticed that he'd poured himself a whisky and the remains of a sandwich sat on a plate by his chair. She couldn't help but feel a bit miffed. Where was her sandwich? Even a cuppa would have been nice.

'Yes, but the door nearly slammed and then I would have spent the next hour getting them off again.' She flopped down on the settee and closed her eyes. 'You'd think that they would have just conked out after all the excitement today.'

'Yeah, but they were probably overtired I think. It's not every day that they realise that they have a singing star for a mummy.' Tristan shot her a huge smile. 'Oh, you're going to sleep?'

Karen opened one eye. 'No, I'm tired but I need to eat something. Looks like you have sorted yourself out.' She looked pointedly at his plate. 'No thought for the poor old singing star trying to get two little monsters off to sleep for the last hour *on her own*, eh?'

'Oops, sorry, love. I was a bit peckish and couldn't wait for dinner. You were ages upstairs. What is for dinner anyway?' He patted his tummy.

Karen jumped up. 'Oh, I'm sorry, I'm slacking in my duties as a cook now, took too long getting the kids to sleep, obviously. I'm just a crap mother and wife, must do better.' Karen saluted at Tristan and marched off into the kitchen. She stopped short. On the table was a bottle of champagne, flowers and a card. She put her hand to her mouth and felt a flush of shame creep over her face. What a cow she was sometimes.

Tristan came up behind her and folded her into his arms. 'Just a little surprise for the wonderful singing star, wife and mother,' he said, kissing her on the shoulder.

She turned and kissed him full on the mouth. 'Oh, I'm such a bitch sometimes. Thanks Tris, but I'm not sure I deserve these after being so snappy.'

'You weren't to know and I *was* winding you up just a little bit,' he said with a cheeky twinkle in his eye. 'But seriously, never say you're a bitch or crap mother. I had one of those . . . she wrote the book on it.'

Karen held him at arm's length. 'I wish you'd talk about her. I'm sure you'd feel better if you told me why you hated her so much.'

Tristan handed her the card. 'I don't think it would. No point in raking over the past. Let's just say she cared more about herself than anything else,' he muttered, taking her arm and sitting her down at the kitchen table. 'Now open that card, drink champagne and chat to me while I make my signature dish to round off this momentous day.'

Karen laughed. 'You mean your only dish?'

'My lasagne is not an "only" dish, it is an incredible dish, a "fit for a queen" dish.'

'Oh . . . incredible!' Karen put a hand to her head dramatically. 'Sorry, for a minute there I thought you said "inedible".'

'Watch it, matey, or you'll get bread and jam.' Tristan poked her on the arm and went in search of glasses for the champagne.

Slipping her finger under the envelope flap, Karen pulled out the card. On it was a seascape. A striped lighthouse stood centre stage, gulls flew overhead and a yellow boat bobbed on a bright blue ocean. Karen's hands trembled with emotion, as inside Tristan had written:

You are my lighthouse, I am the boat. You saved me from life's rocks the day you said 'I do.' I was so proud of you today; and I have no

51

words to describe how much your voice touches my soul.

Thank you for being my wife and the mother of our babes.

Love always and forever,
Tris xxx

The card fell from her fingers as a wave of emotion smashed into her. Tristan returned from the dining room to find her sobbing her heart out. He set the glasses down and ran to her side. 'Hey, hey, what's the matter?' He pulled her to him.

'The words . . . the words in the card . . . so lovely.' She sobbed.

'They were supposed to make you smile, not cry,' he said, hugging her tighter.

'I guess it's everything that's happened. The singing today, the fact that I'm getting better . . . the words about the lighthouse . . . just every-thing.' Karen sniffed into his chest.

'Glass of champagne help?' Tristan asked, handing her a tissue and kissing her forehead.

She dabbed at her eyes and blew her nose. 'Perhaps, but the kissing is working wonders too,' Karen murmured, opening the buttons on his shirt and caressing his chest, relishing the way his smooth tanned skin felt under her fingers.

'Do you think we might leave the lasagne for a while?' Tristan ran his hands down her back and lingered on her bottom.

She looked into his eyes and saw desire kindle them a deep jade. Her fingers twisted through his tawny hair, now lightened with gold from walks on the beach, and his slow sexy smile started a flame of desire low in her belly that quickly grew into a fire. As she felt his cool hand slip under her T-shirt and over her breasts, she gasped. 'I think that would be a very good idea indeed.' Then Karen smiled and pressed her mouth to his.

Thursday, a few weeks later, was another landmark for Karen. The sky painted itself blue, the birds sang, and the people of the little town of Kelerston bustled like ants in a nest. The clock tower atop the war memorial marked a common meeting place for the townsfolk, and it was under this that Karen waited for Jenny. Tristan worried that she might panic, alone, away from the safety of their home as he'd dropped her off. She did have a few worries herself, but it wasn't because she was in an open space. Not being able to share them with him, she just kissed him goodbye and told him she would be fine. She had her mobile and if she needed to, she'd call.

In the shade of the tower Karen watched the comings and goings. A fat man in a bloodstained apron came out of the butchers. He bent over to write on the blackboard propped on the pavement. *Best leg of lamb – finest in all Cornwall.* Karen smiled when she remembered the tales Tristan had told her about Harold Jackson. It was great to finally see him in the flesh.

Harold dusted his hands off, placed them on his hips and gazed down the street, a wide grin on his face. Following his gaze, she saw that he was watching a dog cocking its leg against a fruit and veg stand outside the greengrocer's shop. Karen giggled inwardly and had an impulse to shout and wave to him, but that might be a bit much. She was supposed to be taking it slowly after all. Besides, she looked up at the clock, Jenny would be here in a few minutes and a conversation with Harold would take considerably more than that.

A few moments later Jenny hurried around the corner by the chemist, and waved her arms to and fro upon seeing Karen under the clock. A smile sprang immediately to Karen's lips and her heart filled with warmth. Jenny was just one of those hot water bottle people. Anyone who met her couldn't fail to feel the force of her optimistic personality. Joy clung to her like a second skin, the mundane seemed to be an adventure to her, and even the smallest bit of good news would set her pretty hazel eyes alight and her elfin face wreathed in smiles.

Karen waved back and hurried across the road. 'Hey, there. How are you?' she called closing the last few steps between them.

The two women embraced and laughed as people do when they are genuinely pleased to see each other.

'I'm fine, it's how you are that's the main question,' Jenny said, slipping her arm through Karen's and guiding her down the high street. 'Any, you know . . . wobbles?'

Karen giggled and patted her flat stomach. 'No, apart from on my belly.'

'You don't have an inch of fat on you! Me on the other hand . . .' Jenny grinned and pointed to hers.

Karen noticed the other day that although tiny in all other respects, Jenny *had* got a bit of a tummy; but she certainly couldn't be called overweight. There was no way she'd mention her observations to her friend, of course. 'Nonsense! You aren't fat. Do you fancy having a coffee somewhere before we hit the shops?'

'Yes, and we could have cake, too, considering we need feeding up!' Jenny laughed.

The table by the window was perfect for people watching. As Karen waited for Jenny to order, she watched what she imagined was a typical summer afternoon scene in Kelerston. There was something a little old-fashioned about it that she found strangely comforting. Even though people were dressed in contemporary clothes and modern cars punctuated the flow of pedestrians now and then, the narrow street and brightly-coloured Victorian shopfronts jostling for elbow room belonged entirely to the past.

'A penny for them?' Jenny said, sitting opposite.

'Really, are you sure? My thoughts can be a little unorthodox at times.'

'I think I'll cope.' Jenny laughed.

'Okay, I think that we have all been transported back in time,' Karen said solemnly. 'And if we were to wander outside the boundaries of this little town we'd just find a void . . . and on the periphery of that void, there would be a whirling mass of stars in an ancient galaxy.'

Jenny's rosebud mouth fell open, her brow knitted together and she fiddled with the end of her dark ponytail. 'Er, are you okay?'

Karen could keep a straight face no longer and laughter erupted like water from a burst dam. It felt good to laugh like that: it had been too long. She explained her thoughts to a quizzical Jenny in a more conventional way and then said, 'Sorry, I couldn't resist. Your face was a picture.'

Jenny, obviously relieved that Karen wasn't having a 'wobble' of some kind, returned to her normal pixie-like self. 'Phew, that's good! Now, I have ordered cappuccinos and carrot cake, is that okay?'

It was more than okay. Every morsel tasted like heaven and the cake was soon demolished, leaving not even a crumb as evidence of its existence. They talked mostly of the choir and the next rehearsal and how much Jenny had loved Karen's voice. Karen began to get a bit embarrassed with all the gushing praise Jenny was heaping on her, complete with typical Jenny type gesticulations and exclamations, especially as she'd noticed a few eavesdroppers here and there in the café. One such listener had even inched her chair closer to their table and had practically stopped her own conversation altogether.

'Enough about me . . . anything interesting happening in your life?' Karen spoke softly and indicated the reason for her lowered tone with sign language and mouthed messages.

'Eh? What do you mean she's listening? Who's listening?' Jenny attempted a whisper, but failed miserably. It did the trick though. The woman eavesdropping pulled her chair back to her own table and stirred her drink noisily. Karen shook her head and giggled. Jenny was certainly an original.

A few moments later, Jenny rested her elbows on the table, laced her fingers and rested her chin on them. Her eyes sparkled with excitement and she grinned at Karen. 'There is a bit of exciting news actually,' she whispered, more successfully this time. 'Promise you can keep a secret?'

Karen nodded and put one finger to her lips in a 'shh' mime and jabbed the other towards the woman.

Jenny glanced at the woman and shuffled her chair round close to Karen's. 'I'm not supposed to say anything as I only found out myself on Sunday, and it's very early days yet, but guess what?'

Karen put her head on one side and looked at her friend. The twinkle of excitement in Jenny's eyes coupled with the recent thought that Jenny had 'a bit of a tummy' and Karen's finely honed intuition added up to, 'Oh my God, you're pregnant aren't you?'

Jenny's face fell. 'How did you guess? I wanted to surprise you.'

'You did. I only just guessed in the last second or two. I'm so thrilled for you. What did Michael say?'

'Oh, he's over the moon, he can't wait to tell his and my parents, but I said we should wait until the twelve weeks. I'm only about seven at the moment.'

'Yes, good idea, and was it planned?'

'No, we thought we'd wait for another year, but God had other ideas.'

Karen just smiled at this. Her belief in God had been buried not long after her father. 'So, did you plan yours? They are really close together aren't they?'

'Yeah. Just thirteen months apart. And no, we didn't plan Bella. I'd heard that breastfeeding would act as contraception, and Tris and I were careful.' Karen rolled her eyes. 'But I fell pregnant again, just four months after Sebastian was born.'

'Blimey, that must have been such a hard time. Did that add to your illness?'

'It was, very hard.' Karen hesitated. Her 'illness' wasn't something she wanted to talk about if she could help it, but she could see from Jen's enquiring expression that some response was needed. 'I don't

58

know if the situation added to it, it wasn't easy as I've said. But my children are such a joy, Jen, and I'm sure yours will be as well.'

'Oh, I'm sure too. Just can't wait to shout the news to the parents and the whole community. And I bet that yours and Tristan's parents dote on the kids, spoil 'em rotten?'

A black cloud blew in with those words and threatened to rain on the sunny news. It was a natural remark by Jenny, but one that brought untold sadness to Karen's heart. Her dad would have adored Sebastian and Bella, her mother . . . she sighed and shook her head. 'I'm afraid both sets of grandparents are dead, Jen. They never saw the children, and in fact never saw Tris and I get together.'

Jenny's pretty face crumbled and her hand shot out to cover Karen's. 'Oh, I am *so* sorry, love. I never thought, just rambled on not thinking—'

'Why should you? It was a natural comment; it's just unfortunate that's all.'

Jenny sighed. 'So how did they . . . you know?'

'I'd rather not talk about all that now, Jen. It still hurts too much,' Karen said, standing up. And then in a voice loud enough to make sure the eavesdropper heard she said, 'Now, I guess we should get off to these lovely clothes shops. I intend to buy a tiny skirt and a revealing top. My husband loves me in sexy things you know.'

Jenny raised her eyebrows and then twigged on quickly. 'Oh and mine!' She giggled. 'He's certainly not what you'd expect from a vicar in the bedroom department, if you know what I mean?'

The two women left the café arm in arm and in fits of laughter.

CHAPTER 10

Apparently I was the reason that my mother's life was a mess. My fault that she drank, slept around and locked me in the attic. I had never been the child she wanted; I always wanted to do the opposite to what she told me, so petulant and unruly. Too clever by half. And before I was even born I'd ruined her figure. Her tummy had never been the same after the birth, and the welt of stretch marks were an embarrassment. Bikinis had been out ever since.

And, as if that wasn't all bad enough, I was still such an embarrassment to her now. How could someone as pretty as her admit that she had a hulking monster for a kid?

My father, of course, was nearly as much to blame. He doted on me at her expense. She said he'd changed that first day he held me in the hospital. There she'd been, so weak with pain and exhaustion, her vagina feeling like a rare joint of beef and there he'd been, paying her no attention, yet full of love and admiration for a 'little cabbage-faced ball of shit and tears'.

It got worse as I grew up. I could do nothing wrong

for Dad. We two were inseparable, always down by the beach or talking about crap of some sort or another. Well, we were separated now, by the grave and my mother was bloody glad that he was dead. That would be the end of all the namby-pamby mollycoddling. It was about time I stood on my own two feet, got a job like other teenagers, instead of sitting on my fat arse doing fuck all. What did I think she was, a bloody idiot? Why should she work in the pub all hours to keep me in chips and cake?

Though she'd never been particularly pleasant to me, and often spewed torrents of verbal abuse as just described, the months of torture only began about six months after Dad died. Once I woke to find myself choking, gasping for air, my lungs full of acrid smoke. My mother had set fire to the rug in my room while I slept and then crept out, locking the door behind her. I could hear her howls of laughter out on the landing as I hammered on the door, begging to be let out.

She opened the door just as I was passing out and threw a bucket of water on the rug. As I lay coughing and retching on the floor, she kicked me hard in the kidneys and told me to 'clean up the fucking mess' before I went back to bed. Whenever I smell smoke now, fear twists my gut. I really thought that she'd leave me to burn that night.

Other less physical torture happened on a regular basis. For example she thought it was funny to pretend she'd put ground glass in the meal I'd just eaten and would explain in gory detail what would happen to my insides as a result. Another time when I got home from school she said that we'd won the lottery and she'd bought tickets to Disneyland. Of course it was all a lie.

She even watched me pack a suitcase and told me to hurry up and get in the car. Climbing into the driver's seat she turned to me, a huge smile on her face and said, 'Right you all ready?' I'd nodded hardly able to believe how exciting everything had suddenly become, and how nice my mother was being to me. Then the red lipstick smile turned into a snarl. 'Just joking,' she growled. 'We haven't won anything at all. If we had won the lottery I'd dump you in an orphanage and bugger off to Las Vegas.' Then she watched me cry while she howled with laughter.

My misery seemed to give her a kick. One of her favourite things was watching me cry and seeing me crumble under the realisation that the one person left in the world who was supposed to love and take care of me, actually delighted in being inhumanly cruel.

As the years wore on, I deprived her of that pleasure. Even though I often wanted to draw myself into a tight ball of sadness and weep for hours, I'd concentrate all my emotions into a shield of hatred and defiance. It made her furious that she couldn't reduce me to a quivering mess of snot and tears anymore. But no matter what she did to me, when I reached the age of fourteen, I never cried in front of her again. Tears were reserved for the wee-small hours of darkness under the covers as I held my dad's photo to my chest and sobbed until my eyes were sore.

The very worst memory I had of her before the end came was when I'd woken to the sound of shouting. Tiptoeing down to her bedroom I realised she had a man in her en suite bathroom and he'd apparently vomited on the floor. I couldn't see either of them through the gap in the door, but Mother was calling him a drunken, shit-faced bastard and he was slurring back that 'she could fucking talk'.

Deciding to make myself scarce, I turned to go back up the attic stairs, but the landing floorboards creaked badly and that noise alerted her. She ran out after me delivering a resounding slap across my head and dragged me into her bedroom.

The man was naked, had his back to me, and was splashing his face with water. She punched me on the arm, pointed to the vomit and said, 'Sort this out you useless tub of lard. Me and Jeff have more interesting things to do, don't we, honey?' She grinned lasciviously at him and ran her hands over his bottom.

Seeing her behaving so disgustingly and obviously unashamed in front of her own child turned my stomach and fuelled my defiance. I said that I wouldn't clean up after them and turned to leave again. Mother said something along the lines of teaching me a lesson and then both of them grabbed my arms and threw me into the vomit, laughing like maniacs.

I scrambled to my knees and it took all my resolve not to add to the vomit I was covered in. I watched them go back to bed and start having sex as if I wasn't there. I honestly think they had already forgotten about me.

I crawled into the shower in my pyjamas and showered his filth off me. I had never felt so humiliated, alone, and totally alienated from my mother. I sank down into the corner of the cubicle and because I was sure they couldn't see me, as the water pounded on my head, I cried for my dad, I cried for me, I cried for the want of a mother's love. I cried as I had never cried before.

CHAPTER 11

Six weeks had gone by since the first rehearsal in the conservatory and four since Karen's trip into town with Jenny. Tristan realised it was still early days, but he could almost say that the Karen he fell in love with was well and truly back. As he stood at the bottom of the garden looking out over the dunes to the coastline beyond, he sipped his coffee and sighed. It was a cliché but it felt good to be alive.

Here he was on a beautiful July Saturday morning, the breeze bringing sweet scents of the sea, lavender, newly mown grass and cow pat. These aromas were the very essence of the country coast, of Cornwall and the epitome of happy childhood days. Closing his eyes, an image of his father running on the beach surfaced. And there Tristan was, about six years old, running behind, but never quite catching up. He remembered he'd said later collapsing on the sand next to his father, 'You can run much faster than me, Dad.' His father had turned to him and said, 'Yes, but you can run for much longer than me, Tris.'

Tristan turned to check on his own children.

Not for the first time did he wish that his father could have seen them, and yes, even his mother, bitch that she'd been. She was his flesh and blood when all was said and done and perhaps she would have been different with grandchildren.

The kids were playing in the Wendy house on the lawn. Sebastian popped his curly head through the window and shouted, 'Daddy, I want my bike!'

'Okay, I'll get it.' Tristan walked over and stuck his head in the door. 'Do you want anything, Bella?'

'Want dink,' his daughter said, and for reasons known only to her, tried to squash a teddy into a saucepan.

Karen came out of the house just then with a tray of drinks and snacks for the kids. Tristan's breath was taken away as he watched his wife walk barefoot towards them over the lawn. The new red maxi dress with shoestring straps that she'd bought on her trip to town with Jenny, billowed out on the soft breeze, and her hair, newly washed, floated around her like a golden mantle. He had always realised what a lucky man he was, but since she'd started to get better, Karen seemed to grow more beautiful every day.

'Hey, you saved me a job. Bella has just asked for a drink,' he said, kissing her on the cheek. 'I'm popping to the shed to get Seb's bike and then I'll be back. You look good enough to eat by the way. Any chance that when the little guys have their nap we could . . .?' He slipped his fingers under her hair and massaged the back of her neck.

Karen wrinkled her nose and shook her head. ''Fraid not. Maybe this evening. I'm going to the vicarage for lunch and then practice, had you forgotten?'

He had, damn. Returning with the bike a few minutes later he joined them on the grass. He grabbed a handful of raisins and a slice of melon. 'No biscuits?' He pulled an injured face and rubbed his tummy.

'No, there is not, Tristan. I want to encourage the children to eat healthily,' Karen admonished, biting into an apple. ''Sides, thought 'oo 'er cuttin' down?'

'Sorry, I can't understand a word you said. Don't you think speaking with your mouth full is a bad example to our children?' Tristan teased.

Karen swallowed her apple. 'I said, besides, I thought you were cut—'

'I know what you said, you daft mare.'

'Daft mare is it?' Karen threw a plum at him. 'What happened to "you are my lighthouse" et cetera?'

'You are my lighthouse, but you're also a daft mare.' Tristan grinned launching himself at her and pinning her to the grass. The kids squealed with excitement and jumped all over their parents too. Helpless with laughter, Karen looked up into her husband's eyes. He looked back at her and smiled. The children were busily climbing onto his back yelling 'Giddyup!' and wriggling so much that he had to release Karen to steady them.

A few minutes later they sat side by side watching their children playing chase and whooping like Howler monkeys. Tristan felt so much love in his heart that he wondered if it were possible to get much happier. He put his arm around Karen. 'Are you happy, my love?'

'Unbelievably so,' she said, stroking his forearm.

'Ditto. Have you decided that it's better here than the city?' He held his breath in case she said no.

'Oh, yes, you can safely say that.'

'Phew, so you're not going to run away back to Swindon and leave me then?' He laughed.

'Of course not. In fact I worry that you'll leave *me* one day,' she mumbled and knelt to gather the remains of the snack.

Her hair curtained across her face and Tristan couldn't see if she was joking or not. She certainly didn't sound as if she was. 'What do you mean? I would never leave you, silly.'

'Oh, you might . . . If I had done something terrible.' Karen picked up the tray and walked towards the house.

He called after her, 'Eh? What are you on about?'

'Don't mind me. I'm just being daft.' She turned and blew him a kiss from the patio doors. 'I'll see you later; Jenny will be wondering where I am. Bye, Bella, bye, Sebastian!' The children waved at her and then carried on with their game.

Tristan raised his hand too and then turned his face to the sea breeze. Sometimes he just couldn't

69

understand his wife. One minute she seemed fine and full of the joys, the next she'd turned melancholy and distant. He knew that depression was often part of agoraphobia, but she'd shown no signs of that for weeks. And to change so quickly like that? Still, nobody could call her predictable, and that was a plus in his book.

A cloud floated across the sun, casting Tristan into shadow. But what had she meant by *something terrible*? A chill crept through him, not from the shade, but from an unwelcome suggestion that kicked him hard in the gut. Had she been seeing another man? The thought of someone else's hands, mouth on her revolted him.

Tristan closed his eyes and remembered the way they had made love the other night. She'd taken the lead, stripping him, gliding her tongue down his body and then straddling him on their four-poster bed. He smiled when he remembered how he'd teased her, bucking her off onto her back and returned the favour dropping hot kisses all over her breasts and then trailing his tongue across her stomach and lower. That had driven her crazy and she'd had to turn her head into the pillow to make sure she didn't cry out and wake the kids.

Tristan thought about the *something terrible* puzzle again. If she was seeing someone else, would she be so passionate, tender and loving with him? Since the night he'd given her the card, their sex life had been better than it had been for years. He ran his hands through his hair and shook his head.

He couldn't see it himself. And even if she was, he couldn't picture life without her.

Sebastian closely followed by Bella came hurtling up to him and flung themselves on his lap, giggling fit to burst. Tristan tickled them both and said, 'Your mummy must be crazy if she thinks I'd ever leave. Now, what do you say to a paddle, eh?'

The vicarage, large, Victorian, and imposing, hulked at the end of a long gravel drive. As Karen crunched along it, her flip-flops threatening to twist on the hard stone, she thought that the character of the house was out of kilter with its inhabitants. Michael and Jenny were young, colourful and full of life; they would be better suited to a white country cottage with roses round the door, or a stone built barn conversion like hers and Tris's. Still, it came with the job and there wasn't much they could do about that she guessed.

Jenny appeared at the door and waved. 'Hey there! Gosh you look stunning in that dress.' She hugged Karen and ushered her inside.

'This old thing?' Karen laughed. She stepped into the house and was pleased to find that the inside was considerably more cheerful. The hallway had original stripped oak floors and lemon walls littered with photographs of the Prestons and presumably friends and family. A carved wooden sculpture of leaping dolphins stood in an alcove and a collection of seashells sat nearby in a deep burgundy bowl.

71

The rest of the house was done out in a similar vein, but the massive sitting room was Karen's favourite. It was very simple but stunning for all that – white walls and high ceilings were complemented by a dark wood floor. A Native American rug in turquoise and yellow graced the hearth before the open fireplace, and more carvings of sea creatures stood proudly in each corner. Two dark turquoise three seater settees sat invitingly in the centre, and lots of natural light flooded the room from floor to ceiling windows.

From the windows, Karen's breath was taken by the rolling lawn, the blaze of colour from the shrubs and flowers and overall, the nearness of the ocean. The sea could be viewed from her own garden, but she had to walk right to the end and even then, it wasn't as dramatic as this. She turned to Jenny who was plumping the cushions on one of the settees. 'Oh my God, I want this house!'

'It is rather lovely, isn't it? We brightened it up big-time and had those windows put in.' Jenny indicated that Karen should sit on the settee. 'When we arrived it was so dull and tired. The previous vicar had lived here for about forty years and had done bugger all to it in that time.'

'Well, it certainly isn't dull now. How's Michael?'

'He's grand, ta. He'll join us for choir practice after lunch because he's not heard you sing yet.'

'Oh, that will be a treat for him.'

'It will. And I wish you wouldn't be so modest, you are incredible. Also I thought we'd sing in church today. The acoustics are great in there . . . that's if you still feel okay about . . . you know.' Jenny made a face.

'Thanks, Jen, I think my agoraphobia is well under control now. In fact, I haven't felt so good in years.'

Goose pimples played over Karen's arms as she stood in the church later. This was partly because the new red dress was not the kind of thing to wear in a cold church and partly because being in a church choir brought back happy memories of childhood.

'You look perished, love. Do you want my jacket? I've got a cardi in my shopping basket, so I don't need it,' one of the choir members said. Karen thought her name was Gillian, and if she wasn't mistaken, the postman's wife. She looked like she could be an extra in *Midsomer Murders*. Sensible shoes, pleated skirt, all fussy and wittery, but nice with it.

'Oh, I think I'll be all right . . .' But a quick glance at the plain black jacket over Gillian's arm and the fact that her arms were turning blue changed Karen's mind mid-sentence. '. . . Actually could I?'

'It would be my pleasure. Now slip your poor little arms in.' Gillian shook out the jacket for Karen while still wittering on. 'There, that's better . . . a bit big, but we can't have you freezing to death, can we? Mind you, you should always have a jacket or cardi handy, especially in a cold old church on a warm afternoon. I find that it's always a lot colder inside when it's warm outside, don't you?'

Karen said that she hadn't known that they wouldn't be rehearsing in the vicarage, or she would have brought something to put around her shoulders. Gillian barely seemed to hear and went on and on about the weather. Thankfully, another choir member, Linda, who had told her last time that she worked in the bookshop, came to her rescue.

'Hey, Karen, Jenny asked me to borrow you for a minute. She wants me to talk to you about the order of songs today.'

Karen excused herself from Gillian and went over to Linda, who whispered that she'd only said that to allow Karen's escape. Karen giggled, immediately warming to Linda, and they chatted for a few minutes until Michael walked through the door, stunning many of the women there into adoring silence.

Michael was undeniably good-looking, and today, tanned and dressed casually in black jeans and a denim shirt that reflected the blue of his eyes, he couldn't fail to have caused many women to do a double take. But Karen didn't fancy him. She liked him, of course, and thought he had a very attractive personality, but she was a one-man-woman, and always would be.

At the opposite side of the church, Jenny was

74

going over the song order with a few of the choir members. Michael eventually caught his wife's eye, nodded, gave her the thumbs up sign and pointed to the pews.

'Right ladies and gents, take your places please!' Jenny called.

A few songs in, Jenny beckoned Karen forward to do the solo as they'd agreed previously. Karen smiled and stepped forward a few paces, thrilled by the beautiful sound their voices were making in the lovely old building. Michael stood a little way behind his wife who conducted them with her usual vigorous enthusiasm. While Michael had a huge grin on his face, clearly enjoying every moment, Karen noted that he kept looking to the door as if he expected someone to walk in.

Jenny gave her the signal for the solo and Karen forgot about Michael, forgot about everything except the song. She opened her heart and closed her eyes as her melody soared up to the rafters. But upon opening them again, her heart nearly stopped. Next to Michael knelt a man snapping photographs of them as though he was paparazzi. He held a big professional camera and it whined like a hundred mosquitoes as he flashed one shot after the other.

Karen stopped singing, and froze in her place.

'Don't stop, love, I'm getting some kick-ass shots,' the photographer said, impatiently moving this way and that, clearly waiting for Karen to begin again. His ID tag said *Cornish News*.

'Surprise!' Michael beamed and did jazz hands. 'St Mary's fantastic choir is going to be in the paper! A lively choir might bring in even more parishioners.'

Karen looked around desperately, feeling her whole world shrinking, closing in on her. Her heart thumped against her ribcage and her breathing became ragged. Everyone's eyes were on her, puzzled as to why she'd stopped singing; she probably looked like a frightened rabbit, she certainly felt like one. All she knew was that she had to get out. She heard herself say, 'I . . . I don't want this!' She shot an anguished look at Jenny and ran down the aisle. Michael put his hand on her arm, but she shrugged him off and escaped into the sunny afternoon.

Having no real thought to her direction, Karen ended up back at the vicarage just along the country lane from the church. She leaned her head on the cool wall at the bottom of the drive to get her breath. It would be a twenty-minute walk to get home, fifteen if she cut over the fields, but she desperately wanted to be there now. She felt sick, lost, alone – she needed Tristan.

Trying the tactic he'd taught her in case of panic attacks, she breathed in through her nose and out through her mouth. It felt funny to be doing them for real after all the fake attacks she'd pretended to have over the last year. A hand on her shoulder made her jump.

'There you are. What happened? Is the agoraphobia back?'

Karen turned her eyes to Jenny's anxious face and shrugged. She didn't trust herself to speak, and besides, lying to such a lovely woman grated on her conscience. After a few seconds she said, 'I felt self-conscious. There I was in the spotlight, which still feels odd to me, *and* I was wearing Gillian's jacket, which is much too big for me. I must look a fright on the photos. I had no idea that a reporter—'

'I had no idea either! I'll be having words with my husband later. He should have told me what he was up to. I could have asked your permission at least, then.'

Karen dashed away tears and got her head together. She was glad she'd avoided lying outright, but just wanted to get home. 'Not to worry, I'll be off now. I'll ring you tomorrow.'

'Nonsense, wait here and I'll get the car. We'll have you back home in five minutes.'

Karen shook her head, slipped off the jacket and handed it to Jenny. 'No, don't be silly. I'm okay now, really. The choir will be wondering what's happened to you. See you soon.'

And before Jenny could reply, Karen turned away and set off for home as quickly as the damned flip-flops would allow.

CHAPTER 12

The mist was still over the land, the sun just a suggestion on the horizon as Karen made her way across the meadow next morning. A brisk walk across the dew-soaked countryside would hopefully give her some answers about the way forward. The debacle at the church yesterday had left her reeling. Tristan had been told that she'd just had a wobble, what with being in an unfamiliar place, the photos, being the centre of attention and so forth. It was more or less word for word what she'd told Jenny.

Tristan had held her tight and she'd rested her head against his chest, while he'd spoken words of comfort. The feel of his arms around her and the steady thump of his heartbeat had sent her demons running for cover. At last she felt safe, protected. Karen wasn't sure how much longer she could keep her secret, however. If her photo was splashed all over the *Cornish News*, the likelihood was it wouldn't be very long. Didn't Tristan deserve to find out from her, rather than a stranger?

A fox darted across her path, halting her thoughts and her footsteps in their tracks. She watched the beautiful creature trot through the rising mist and over the silver cobwebbed fields – a burnished copper dash in the grey morning. As she watched the fox grow smaller and disappear into the distance, she allowed calmer thoughts back into her head.

The photos might not be the end of everything. After all, she did look very different now. A wry smile played over her lips. Even her own mother wouldn't recognise her. She looked down at her dew-covered Wellingtons and noticed a beetle upside down in the grass, its legs waving manically as it tried ineffectually to right itself. That's exactly how she'd felt since yesterday – upside down and out of control.

Bending over, she poked the beetle upright and smiled as it scuttled away between the blades of grass. Releasing the beetle from its predicament seemed to help hers. More rational thoughts joined the calm ones. A rash decision to tell Tris everything might just throw her whole life into jeopardy. No, best let sleeping dogs lie for now. *You didn't come this far just to chuck it all in at the first hurdle, did you?*

With a lighter heart, Karen followed literally in the fox's footsteps, as the path it had taken was clearly visible in the wet grass. It seemed to be making for the cliffs, and Karen decided that was as good a direction as any. She might even climb down to the beach and pick up some pebbles for the children.

It was hard to see properly as the sun was rising

spectacularly over the sea and cast everything into a haze, but as she drew nearer, Karen thought she could see a figure standing near the edge of the cliffs. The figure walked even closer to the edge, then stepped back again. It repeated this action twice. Karen's stomach turned over. Quickening her pace, she could tell the figure was a woman, nearer still and she thought she recognised her.

Not wishing to startle the woman, she instinctively changed her direction slightly until she was out of her peripheral vision. At this angle Karen was almost sure that the woman was Linda from the choir – the one who had rescued her from Gillian yesterday. They were of a similar age and they had got on really well from the first time they had spoken a few weeks ago. Patting her pockets, Karen realised that she'd forgotten to pick up her mobile phone. In her mind's eye she could see it sitting on the kitchen counter. No bloody use there was it?

Linda took a step to the edge of the cliff again and put her hand to her mouth. This time she didn't move back. Karen shuddered. What should she do now? If she called out, Linda might be startled and slip. She noted that the woman wore no shoes and had an old grey jumper pulled over yellow pyjamas. The pyjama legs were soaked and covered in grass seeds. Free from its usual neat plait, Linda's long amber hair lifted on the breeze to reveal a red welt on the right side of her face. She took another step to the edge.

Karen swallowed a scream, she had no choice, this was a now or never moment. 'Linda, it's Karen. Fancy you being up here on this lovely morning, too.'

Though Karen's voice was soft, Linda whipped her head around as if she'd suffered an electric shock. She stared wild-eyed at Karen and shook her head as if to physically dispel the image. Linda said nothing for a few moments, then her lips parted slightly and a high-pitched keening rent the air.

It sent a shiver down Karen's spine. She had never heard a sound so utterly desperate. Holding out her hand, she moved forward.

Linda shook her head vehemently. 'No! Don't you *dare* come near me!'

Karen tried to make her voice calm. 'Okay . . . I'll just sit here; I need to rest for a while.' She took off her raincoat, lay it over the damp grass and sat down slowly.

'Why don't you just go?'

'I told you I need to rest, and because I'm worried that you'll jump.'

'Nothing to live for, so why not?'

'Why don't you tell me what's wrong? I might be able to help.'

'How can *you* help? You're looking at me like I'm crazy, but you're bloody mental too! Not being able to leave your house for ages, and then running out of the church yesterday because a photographer came.'

Karen noticed that as Linda yelled, she stepped closer to Karen than the cliff edge. So far, so good. 'Yes, I can see your point,' she said, looking away from Linda and out over the sea. 'But people who have problems can sometimes help others with theirs. Surely nothing can be so bad that you want to kill yourself?'

'Yeah, well you have a nice little life, don't you? Lovely husband, and two lovely kids.' Linda's eyes filled with tears. 'What have I got, eh?'

Karen remembered that Linda was married to a policeman. 'Is it your marriage?'

'Marriage, that's a laugh! He's married, but to his job. I never see him. Always in bloody Truro working all hours to try and climb the ladder, and what for?' Linda raised her arms in an angry gesture and stepped backwards.

Karen's heart was in her mouth, one more step and Linda would be over the edge. 'Look, come and sit by me, and we can talk properly. You are making me anxious standing there.'

Linda looked at the raincoat under Karen and then turned back to the sea. 'How old are you, Karen?'

'Thirty. Why?'

'You've got two kids; I'm thirty-four and have none. Luke always promised we'd have them before I turned thirty, but then the job took over. That's what we rowed about in the early hours when he eventually deigned to come home.'

'But you have time yet. Lots of women have kids in—'

'No, I don't! Because guess what?' Linda's eyes shone with anger. 'He's been shagging a work colleague!'

Karen felt her heart sink like a stone. What should she say next? She was just about to open her mouth when Linda volunteered more.

'That shut you up, didn't it? Only found out because I was getting my hair off at him coming in so late. Then I started on about having kids, as usual.' Linda turned to Karen again, her face ashen. 'That's when he told me. He's been seeing her, loves her apparently and he's leaving me . . . and have a guess what else he dropped on me?'

Karen hoped she didn't know, but she had a gut feeling that she did. What would she say? 'Um . . . I don't know,' she managed, ineffectual but at least benign.

Linda's face crumbled around the words that she spat from her mouth. 'She's fucking pregnant! Eight years younger than me and pregnant with HIS child.'

Karen's gut feeling had been right, and the anguish on Linda's face as she sank deflated to her knees brought an egg-sized lump of emotion to her throat. But at least one good thing came of Linda's outburst; she was crawling away from the cliff edge. She seemed apparently directionless, however, subsumed as she was in despair, and soon turned in a full circle until she was facing the sea again. *Distract her Karen; for God's sake get her over here!*

'So what happened to your face? It looks sore, come over here and let me have a look.'

Linda didn't take notice until Karen repeated her words in a louder voice. She stopped crawling and looked over at Karen, a long strand of snot hanging from her nose. 'My face?' She put her hand to her cheek and winced. 'Oh, that's when he pushed me away and I hit my cheek on the banister. I was beating the cheating swine across the head with a frying pan.' Linda started to laugh hysterically, but then it turned to sobs again.

Something inside Karen told her that now was the time to act. Without thinking too long she got onto her knees, crawled quietly over to Linda and wrapped her arms tightly around her shoulders. 'Oh, I'm so sorry, love . . . so very sorry . . . but he's not worth your tears and definitely not your life.'

Linda pulled away slightly, but then returned Karen's hug, sobbing so much that Karen could feel every tremor travel through her chest.

Blinking back tears of her own, Karen eventually pulled Linda to her feet and led her slowly away from the cliff and down into the meadow. Linda didn't resist as Karen explained that she was taking her back to her house for a hot drink and perhaps a nice bath. She could stay as long as she liked until she got her wits about her. Karen couldn't be sure that Linda had understood. She remained silent, her face expressionless, but she kept putting one foot in front of the other, zombie-like, until they reached Karen's front door.

Once inside, Linda became hysterical again when she saw the children having breakfast. All she could say between sobs was that she wanted her mum. She did eventually agree to have a bath and Tris gave her sedatives. Karen phoned Linda's mum who lived an hour away.

Mrs Gordon was understandably distraught and said she'd leave straight away. She was also extremely angry with Linda's husband. 'I always knew that Luke was a philanderer. He has those shifty eyes. I *did* tell her that he would bring her unhappiness . . .'

Karen listened quietly to the woman's rant, and rolled her eyes at Tris. She interrupted after a few minutes and explained that she thought a calm approach was needed when Mrs Gordon arrived. 'Linda is in a very fragile state, Mrs Gordon. I know you are angry, but if you can possibly let Linda do the talking? What she needs now is someone to listen . . . and, of course, a mother's love.'

Once he'd settled the kids in the playroom, Tris came over to Karen and hugged her. 'I am incredibly proud of you, my love.'

'Why?'

'Why?' he said, looking at her in surprise. 'Well, it might have something to do with the way you talked a distraught woman out of jumping off a cliff before breakfast . . . or it might be that you remembered to buy some apples. Take your pick.'

She smiled and shook her head. 'I have no idea how I did it. I was terrified.'

'Wouldn't anyone be?'

She kissed him on the cheek and broke their embrace. 'I just worked on instinct I guess,' she said airily.

'Exactly! You're a natural. That was obvious with the way you dealt with Mrs Gordon just now. I think you'd make a fantastic counsellor. Of course, you'd have to have training, but you're halfway there.'

'Counselling?' Karen looked up from the washing-up. 'Have you forgotten I have enough problems of my own?'

'But that's why you would be good. People who have had problems are more likely to empathise.'

Karen didn't tell him that's exactly what she'd said to Linda earlier. She had to admit she was very proud of herself, but counselling? When would she have the time for that with the kids? 'And what exactly would I do with our children while I'm off counselling?' Karen asked over her shoulder, as she put cornflakes and Marmite back in the cupboard.

Tristan rubbed the stubble on his chin thoughtfully. 'Well, you could do a course at night school and then perhaps work part-time when the kids got bigger . . . but only if you wanted to, just an idea.'

'I think I need a bit of time to get on top of my own feelings before I think about helping anyone else, but thanks for the vote of confidence, love.'

'At least you didn't say no outright. There is a shortage of good counsellors. I know I couldn't have come back from my depression without mine,' Tristan said.

Depression? Karen turned from her chores and looked at her husband. There was something not right about the timbre of his voice – it seemed strained, like a violin string ready to snap. He was staring out of the window with a faraway look in his eye and his arms wrapped tightly around his body.

'I knew you went through a bad patch, but didn't realise you saw a counsellor for depression, Tris. Was it about your mother?' Karen had always known that he had a bad relationship with his mother but he'd refused to open up about it all. She was surprised, therefore, when he came over and sat at the kitchen table, his head in his hands.

'It brought it all back today when I saw the broken look on Linda's face. My dad's face looked like that on a regular basis because of his bitch of a wife. He could never please her, never do anything right. God knows why, but he adored her. She treated him like some lapdog. Me and Emma, we kind of looked after ourselves when Dad was at work. He would work six days a week, sometimes seven to keep her in shoes, handbags, and whatever else she decided she "must have" that week. I think the local hairdressers and beauty salons could have retired on the packet they made out of her . . . no, not her, Dad.

'Mother "worked" at the local pub sometimes, up the road in St Merryn, but it was just so she could flirt with all the men from the village. My uncle told me recently that she even squandered a few thousand left to me by my granddad. He knew I wanted to be a doctor and thought it would help when I was a medical student.'

Karen wanted to ask him questions but she was worried that if she interrupted, the flow would stop. Tristan seemed almost oblivious of her presence. He just talked and talked, one word almost running into the other. Then he'd stop and rattle off a machine gun fire of short stilted sentences. Moving to the opposite side of the table, Karen pulled out a chair and sat down.

Tristan took his hands from his face and looked across at her with haunted eyes. 'She killed him in the end you know, killed them both.'

'Killed them both? What do you mean?' Karen reached across the table for his hands. They trembled under her fingers.

'They'd been to a champagne "do". One of my mother's so-called friends. Bitched about her all the time even so. Dad was tired and didn't want to go, but she more or less forced him. She was stinking drunk by all accounts. My dad had a few, too. People at the party said she harangued him until he had a drink. Said he was just a boring old fart, in front of everyone. They were arguing when they left the party, leastways, she was . . . screaming and swigging from a bottle when she got into our car and my poor dad trying to calm her down.

'Anyway, nobody knows for sure, but it's thought that she must have got out of control on the way home, perhaps grabbed the wheel or something. They came off the road. Police found the car wrapped around a tree in the early hours.' Tristan's voice broke and he put his hands over his eyes again.

Karen rushed round to his side. He pressed his face into her stomach and she felt him stifling a sob.

'I'm so sorry, Tris,' Karen whispered into his hair after a few minutes. 'Who looked after you and your sister that night while they were out?'

Tristan wiped his damp eyes. 'Nobody. I was sixteen, old enough to look after myself and her. Emma was two years younger, of course. Poor little sod, I'll never forget the look on her face—'

'My God, it must have come as a terrible shock to you, being told by the police?'

'Yeah . . . yeah it was.'

Karen thought he looked as if he wanted to say more, but then a shadow fell over his face and he blew heavily down his nostrils. She hugged him again and kissed a tear from his cheek.

After a few minutes, Tristan looked into her eyes and saw that she was crying too. He shook his head. 'I'm sorry for upsetting you. You lost your parents to cancer, not as quick as a car crash, but it must hurt just as much. And I haven't gained anything by spilling everything like a soppy idiot.'

'You aren't a soppy idiot, Tris! Men *are* allowed to show their emotions too you know, despite outdated chauvinistic views about toughness that are still around today. And it's about time you told me all about it . . . you kept it inside for too long.' Karen kissed the back of his hand. 'Keeping things hidden never helps. Believe me, I know.'

Tristan looked at his wife, puzzled. 'What have you kept hidden?'

Karen heaved a heavy sigh 'Oh, Tris—'

At that moment Linda appeared at the kitchen door, her face a snowflake in a tangle of auburn hair. 'Sorry to interrupt. I wonder if I could have a drink.'

Karen, glad of the diversion, hurried over to fuss over Linda and took her into the living room. Tristan never received his answer.

CHAPTER 13

The most humiliating incident that ever happened to me haunts my dreams lately. Three nights this week I dreamt that I was sixteen and back in school. It was three months before my suicide attempt and I was on the running track in the June sunshine trying to do something about my weight at last. I was determined to shed the pounds and try to get my life under control, because if I lost the weight I was sure I'd feel more confident when standing up to my mother.

I had never told the teachers about how vile my life was after Dad died. I had thought about it, but what would they do? They'd tell social services and I'd get shunted from one foster carer to another. Perhaps it would be for the best, but perhaps it would be as bad as staying with Mother. I'd heard stories about kids going into care and being sexually abused and all sorts. No. The plan was to stick it out until I left school, then get a job and share a flat or something. And if I looked half-decent, I'd find it easier to cope in the big, bad world.

You would think that the vomit in the shower incident that my mother inflicted on me would be hard to top, but this one does it. As the afternoon sun beats down, there I am plodding round the track sweating like a pig and looking like one. My hair was plastered to my head and my skin grew pink from running in the heat. I should have known better than to run in the sun, but I didn't want to put it off any longer. It was after school, so there were relatively few people about to see my efforts.

I was used to the bullying, of course. Since I ballooned into the walking whale, as my mother called me, there was no shortage of nasty comments and disgusting messages passed around the classroom. Sometimes these were behind my back; sometimes they were face to face. Andrea was the worst. She was one of the most popular girls in school, not just among the girls but the boys too.

We were quite friendly at one time, but when I got depressed after my dad's death, she blanked me. And when I put the weight on, she became hostile, taking great delight in making fun of me in front of her entourage. I tried to explain to her one day that I stuffed my face because I was comfort eating, but she just shook her head and walked away.

Anyway, eventually after completing three laps, I staggered into the changing rooms and wiped my face down with a towel. The only sound in there was my laboured breathing and the drip, drip of a shower head. In my dream, the drip is unfeasibly loud, joining with the rhythm of my heartbeat as the incident's relived again.

Usually showering was a luxury I couldn't afford

after games' lessons in school. I was far too ashamed of my naked body to reveal it in front of my peers. On this day, however, I decided that I was just too sweaty to get dressed and walk home. There was nobody around, and if I was quick, I'd be showered and gone in ten minutes.

Almost finished and giving my hair a final rinse, I thought I heard a noise. I turned off the shower and grabbed my towel. Peeping around the corner of the tiled shower wall I was relieved to see the changing room empty, but my heart sank as I watched the door slowly closing. Shit someone was here and they had seen me naked! I flushed the entire length and breadth of my bulk, and dressed quickly. This would be all over the school by tomorrow. I couldn't believe my luck. I had been trying to make my life better by doing something positive, and now I had just made it a trillion times worse.

It was far, far worse than I could ever have imagined, however.

On walking into my classroom the next morning, I was greeted by silence and a notice board full of naked photos. Naked photos of me in the shower. Me in profile, rolls of fat and soapsuds. Me bending over to wash my feet, arse the size of a planet. Me pink-faced and round-bellied, me, me . . . me. Then the classroom erupted into howls of laughter and Andrea stood to take a photo of my face – a mask of horror – and my life started crashing and burning around my ears. I looked into her deep brown eyes and at her red lips peeled back from her perfect straight white teeth in a vicious snarl. How could someone so pretty have a soul so ugly?

I ran through the door and straight home, thankfully my mother was out. I knew I'd get no sympathy from her anyway, so I resolved to keep quiet about it. Somehow she found out though and took huge delight in taunting me upon her arrival home later that day.

As I looked at my puffy, tear-stained face in the mirror that evening I couldn't decide who I wanted to kill the most . . . Andrea or my mother.

CHAPTER 14

Karen looked at the green contact lens on her finger and then back up at the bathroom mirror. Her pale blue eyes looked back. It would be more accurate to say that one pale blue eye looked back. The right one was totally pale blue, the other had brown spots, or freckles as Karen preferred to call them, on the right side of the iris.

She let the contact slip back into its case and snapped the lid shut. Contact lenses were a damned nuisance, particularly when there was nothing wrong with her eyesight. Three months had skipped by since she had first joined the choir and she'd been out and about in public for ages now. The photo of her had been on page two of the *Cornish News* and not a dicky bird. It would be cool without the contacts.

Turning to leave the bathroom, she stopped suddenly, walked back to the cabinet and took out the case again. Nobody had recognised her . . . yet. But they might if she went back to her real eye colour. She opened the lid a fraction, then closed it. *Oh, come on, Karen, get a grip. You've worn them for a year, can't wear the bloody things forever.* She placed the case back in the cabinet and ran downstairs before she could take them out again.

'Hey, good lookin', what ya got cookin'?' Tristan sang, as he walked into the kitchen.

Karen flipped an omelette and nodded at the toaster. 'Can you butter the toast, hon?'

'Ooo an omelette, you spoil me.'

'I know, but you deserve it. You have to look after the children again this morning, so I thought I'd treat you.'

Tristan tossed the toast onto a plate. 'I thought that was this afternoon.'

'Nope. Jenny wants the rehearsal this morning as she's got her scan this afternoon.'

'A scan on a Saturday?' Tristan sat down at the table and bit into his toast.

'Yes, my love. Remember, she was ill for the last one, so they said she had the option of Saturday.' Karen put the omelette in front of Tristan. 'I'm quite nervous to be honest. We have an audience again.'

'Don't see why. You have to get used to singing in front of people if you are part of the town choir.'

Karen put her hands on her hips and narrowed her eyes at her husband. 'It wasn't so very long ago that I daren't leave my own house, so I don't think I'm doing too badly, do you?'

Tristan looked at her and grinned. 'You are so

easy to wind up, my darling.' He then did a double take. 'Hey, you've got your eyes back!'

'Yep. Took you a while to twig, didn't it?'

'I'm so glad. I didn't say so before because you said you wanted a change, but I never really liked them. I have missed those unusual eyes . . . one of the things that first attracted me to you.' He patted his leg. 'Come and sit on my lap and let me give you a big eggy kiss.'

'No can do. I have to pick Linda up. It's the first time she's been to choir since you know what.'

Karen blew him a kiss from the doorway and went into the playroom.

Bella was busy building a wobbly tower of toys in the corner. A large doll lay under a book, a cuddly elephant, a toy car, another larger book and a doll's house. The doll's house looked ready to topple, so her daughter was supporting it with one hand while she tried to prop it up with a doll's chair held in the other. Concentration wrinkled her brow and pursed her lips. Karen thought she looked very much like the garden gnome in next door's garden and put her hand over her mouth to stifle a giggle.

Sebastian was doing his favourite thing – hiding. Karen marvelled at his patience. He would hide for ages and never get bored. Even though he had a room full of toys he would shout, 'Mummy, find me, I'm hiding,' at least five times a day. Just the tips of his little Elmo slippers were showing under the curtains, so Karen went into the routine. 'I wonder where Sebastian is . . . is he outside?' She pretended to look outside. 'No, no he's not outside. Is he behind the settee? No . . .' After a few more 'is he's', she went over to the curtain where her son was standing so still she wouldn't have known he was there . . . apart from the slippers, of course. 'Is Sebastian behind the curtain?' Karen whisked the curtain aside and yelled, 'Yes! There he is!'

Sebastian giggled and said, 'Gen, Mummy, find me gen!'

Karen hoisted him up into the air and then hugged him to her chest. He smelt of satsumas and baby shampoo and she thought for the millionth time how very lucky she was to have him. Sometimes Karen felt so full of love for her children that she could hardly breathe. A miracle really, considering her own background.

'I can't find you again, sweet pea, I have to go out in a minute. We'll play later though and Daddy will find you if you ask him nicely.'

Daddy at that moment had just finished his toast and booted up the laptop. The seeds of an idea he'd had last night after he'd told Karen about his mother, had this morning grown roots and popped out of the soil. What he and Karen needed was a short romantic break away from everything. And he aimed to surprise her with it already booked. They couldn't go for long obviously, because of Sebastian and Bella – he could already see his wife in his mind's eye pulling a face and saying it would be impossible. But Tristan thought that if it was just one, or perhaps two nights in a nice hotel, he might persuade her.

It couldn't be far away either. Perhaps just Falmouth or St Ives – somewhere they could drive back from at the drop of a hat in case Karen had a few wobbles or she was worried about the children. Tristan rubbed his chin as he searched for hotels; he figured they needed some special time together without having to worry about being woken at 4.00 a.m. or creeping about in case they woke the cherubs. It had been far too long. A twinge of guilt tapped him on the shoulder as he heard Sebastian chuckling in the other room, but then he shook his head. There was nothing to be guilty about. The babes would be safe with his sister Emma, or even Jen might have them?

And just think of all that spare time you would have in the bedroom, Tris. A slow smile crept over his face as a luxury suite with jacuzzi bath and a stunning view of the sea spoke to him seductively from the screen. The price gave him a jolt though, but bugger it, you only lived once, or so they told him. Karen's voice from the doorway gave him a jolt too and he nearly trapped his fingers shutting the lid of the laptop down at the speed of light.

'What were you doing, looking at porn?' she said absently, searching for something under the table.

'Don't be daft,' Tristan said, feeling a slow flush creep up his neck. Damn, she would think he had been, when he couldn't explain why he'd

99

slammed the lid down. He couldn't tell her the truth could he?

'Have you seen my bag?' She popped back up and tossed her hair out of her eyes. God she looked sexy and he had missed those eyes. And thankfully she'd not asked him what he'd been looking at again.

'Um . . . nope.' He stood up and pulled her too him. 'You look incredibly sexy this morning,' he murmured into her neck, as his arms encircled her slim waist.

'You don't look so bad yourself either,' Karen whispered. She nibbled his ear, ran her hands down his back and gave his bottom a squeeze. 'Especially in just that T-shirt and boxers.'

Tristan felt his excitement growing and slipped his hands onto her bum too, pressing the heat of her thighs through her thin cotton trousers close against him.

Karen looked intensely into his eyes, moved her hand over his erection and kissed him quickly and deeply on the mouth.

A gasp escaped his lips. 'If you don't stop that right now I won't be responsible for my actions,' he said with a groan, sliding his hand under the waistband of her trousers and down over the smooth silk of her knickers.

Karen stepped away and hurried to the kitchen counter. 'There's my bag! Right, see you later, alligator.' She turned and blew him a kiss.

'Hey, you can't leave me like this!' Tristan scowled, noting the smirk of mischief on her face.

Karen eyed him below the waist and giggled. 'You told me to stop. And besides, don't you think that Tweedledum and Tweedledee in the playroom would be a bit nonplussed if we just skipped off to bed?'

Tristan sighed as the door closed behind her. The sooner he sorted out their romantic break away, the better.

Linda waited at her gate looking anxiously up and down the street as Karen drove up. Her unruly hair had been scraped back into a ponytail and she wore a heavy winter coat, armour against the buffeting autumn wind. Karen glanced at the clock in the car, was she late? Nope she was a few minutes early. She pulled up next to Linda and buzzed down the window. 'Want a lift, pretty lady?'

A ghost of a smile briefly haunted the corners of Linda's lips and then vanished. She hurried round the car and jumped in.

'You okay?' Karen asked, idling the engine. 'You looked a bit anxious when I pulled up.'

Linda shrugged. 'I'm always anxious these days. I think that people are pointing and looking at me. Gossiping, you know?' She didn't look at Karen, just off into the middle-distance.

'I'm sure they're not, love—'

'Yes, they *are*,' Linda said, her navy-blue eyes darkening in frustration. 'They'll be saying, "look, there goes that poor cow Linda. Her husband dumped on her big-time. Got some other woman up the stick and now Linda's doolally".' She twirled her index fingers in the air either side of her head.

Although Karen tried to assuage Linda's fears again as she pulled out into the traffic, she knew from her own experience that Linda was probably right. People were so quick to jump on any sniff of mental illness. Linda had given up her job at the bookshop and rarely went out. She was seeing Tristan for medication and he'd persuaded her to have counselling. Even though she had seemed to be a bit brighter the last few weeks, a good part of Linda was still on the cliff edge staring out to sea. Still, singing should do her good; it had been Karen's salvation.

Jenny hurried towards them down the path from the church. She looked like a nineteenth century heroine in a Brontë novel. Her raven hair billowed behind her, tugged by the September breeze and the hem of her blue velvet dress rustled the fallen leaves as she walked.

'You're looking gorgeous today, definitely blooming!' Karen said, kissing Jenny's pink cheeks.

'You wouldn't have said that a few hours ago when I had my head over the toilet bowl,' Jenny said with a laugh. Then she noticed Karen's eyes. 'Oh my goodness, your eyes have changed!'

'These are my real ones, well, they were *always* real eyes, of course. It's just that I fancied a ch—'

Linda stood a little way off and nodded towards

the church. 'I'll just go inside, girls. I'm feeling the cold.'

Karen and Jenny watched her walk away stoop-shouldered and huddled in a thick grey coat. They looked at each other and sighed. Here they were, laughing about morning sickness without a second thought for Linda's situation.

Karen shrugged and slipped her arm through Jenny's. 'Hey, we have to be more careful that's all, easily done, but bloody insensitive nevertheless.'

Jenny nodded and the two women began walking towards the church. 'Yes, poor love. So, now, tell me about your eyes.'

Even though it was only late September, the church had a Christmassy feel somehow. Karen noted that the brown cushions on the pews had been renewed in a deep crimson and everyone had brought the breath of autumn in on their coats. Wood smoke, apples and Karen thought she could even detect a hint of cinnamon wafting here and there. There had been talk of a Christmas concert already and she couldn't wait for that.

Last Christmas had been a miserable affair. She knew nobody due to her confinement to the house and she had been fearful of the future. Now, she was the lead vocalist in the local choir, had made some lovely friends, Jenny in particular, and also some at the playgroup that she took the kids to on a Tuesday morning. She and Tristan were the happiest they'd been for ages and Karen imagined that all being well, this year would be their best Christmas ever. The church started to fill up with the 'Saturday Singers' audience and Karen popped over to offer a few words of encouragement to Linda before taking her position in the front row.

Michael whisked in with his usual flamboyant air at the beginning of the last song of the rehearsal and leaned next to a pillar about halfway down the aisle. His sharp blue eyes danced over their faces and an impossibly wide grin stretched across his handsome features. Karen noted that such a grin would look totally false on anyone other than the vicar of St Mary's.

At the end of the song he led the applause and then hurried to the front of the choir. Jenny received a bear hug and peck on the cheek and Karen noted in amusement a few green-eyed stares from some members of the audience and choir alike. Michael turned to the choir and beamed, then back to the audience.

'Now, my wife and some members of the choir will probably murder me,' he said, turning briefly and shooting an apologetic smile at Karen. 'But I have rather an exciting announcement to make . . . I wanted to keep it secret a little longer, but I just can't.'

Jenny caught Karen's eye and shook her head to let her know she had no idea what her husband was up to. Karen smiled and pointed at Jenny's tummy to indicate it must be about the baby. She did feel uncomfortable, however. Why had Michael looked so pointedly at her?

'I'm sure you all remember the time when I asked a reporter to come here a few months ago to try and get our little choir on the map? Well, not long after the photo appeared in the newspaper, I got a call from the BBC.' Michael looked at Jenny, his eyes shining with excitement. 'They wanted to know if our choir would like to take part in a new TV series called *Voices of Angels*. It's a competition to see which church choir is the best in Britain. Well, you can imagine it didn't take me long to give an answer.' Michael took one of Jenny's trembling hands and squeezed it.

'You can tell from my lady wife's face that this is a bit of a surprise.'

The audience laughed good-naturedly, but Jenny didn't. She let go of her husband's hand and sat down on a nearby stool.

'Anyway,' he continued, oblivious to his wife's discomfort. 'We won't know until Christmas whether we'll be in the programme and then if we are they'll start filming us in the spring. They have to vote on the tapes I sent them too, but they said we stand a very good chance down to our Karen's beautiful voice.' He beamed at Karen and looked at her expectantly.

If last time when the photographer had been snapping at her feet like an excited puppy had felt like her whole world had been closing in on her, this news felt like the end of it. Michael had rolled up an Armageddon hand grenade and tossed it casually into her lap.

Karen glared at him and managing to draw breath into her constricting airways croaked, 'So you're saying that because of my voice there is a chance that we'll be on national television?'

'I am! Isn't that just fantastic?' Michael beamed at her and then turned to the audience. 'I think we ought to give this little choir a big hand ladies and gentlemen.'

The applause raised the rafters, bouncing off the balustrades and stone columns and then everyone began talking at once. Brendon Mason, chair-person of Kelerston Small Businesses Association, hurried over to Michael and pumped his hand vigorously. 'My goodness, Michael, what a boon for Kelerston! If the choir gets popular on TV just think about the tourism, and if they win, well . . .'

Karen watched his eyes shining with excitement, his mouth continue to form words but her ears had switched off and she felt as if she were outside her body somehow. Jenny's anxious face floated briefly and she lip-read, 'So sorry, I had no idea, Karen.' Then the whole scene swirled into a tunnel as she felt her stomach roll and heat rise through her body like wildfire. She had to get outside for some air before she threw up.

On legs that felt like they belonged to a newborn foal, Karen tottered along the aisle and pushed open the ancient wooden door. Leaning against the wall for support, she stumbled along the path and around the back of the church. Gasping for air she spat the excess liquid forming in her mouth on the ground and leaned forward placing her hands on her knees. *Please don't let me throw up, please not here!*

Karen's pleas were answered as the waves of nausea sloshing in her stomach gradually became ripples and the cool stone wall against her forehead eased the fire in her blood and the jumble in her brain. Bloody hell, it wasn't as if she'd actually *been* on telly yet and broadcast to millions, all she had to do was to leave the choir and that would be it.

Yes, of *course* it would be a shame, but it couldn't be helped and it was a damn sight better than the alternative. Standing upright, Karen leaned her back against the wall, closed her eyes and waited for her legs to feel a bit stronger before she went back in the church to make her excuses to Jenny.

How stupid was she? Thinking she could lead a normal life, do normal things. No. She had been very lucky so far and she should be thankful for what she had. And what she had was everything that people like poor Linda could only dream about. The main task ahead, as far as Karen could see, was making damned sure she hung onto it, rather than singing in a bloody choir.

A few seconds later the sound of a footfall on the gravel path snapped her eyes open, but she couldn't see anyone. Odd, she could have sworn? Feeling a chill creep across her shoulders she hugged herself and looked around. The wind whipped the autumn leaves into a skirmish of yellow and red along the path by the gravestones and the branches of a giant yew tapped a tattoo on the church gates. But apart from nature's rhythm, no other sound met her ears.

Jenny's head popped around the corner of the church. 'There you are!' she gasped and crunched up the path to put her arms around Karen. 'God, Karen, I'm so sorry. My idiot husband's done it again, hasn't he?'

'Er . . . I *was* thrown a little off balance but I'm all right now,' Karen managed, hugging Jenny back. She then stepped to the edge of the church looking to the right and left. 'Jenny, did you come round here a few seconds ago?'

'No, I went down the road thinking you'd fled back to the car but I couldn't see you. Then I thought you might have been in such a flap that you forgot the car and so I kept walking . . . anyway I've found you now, thank goodness. So you're okay?'

'Yes, I'll live, but I'm sure that I heard someone on the path just now.' Karen frowned.

'Well, I didn't see anyone. Come inside with me and we'll tear a strip off Michael. He needs to understand that he can't keep doing things like—'

'No, I can't go back in. I'd be faced with a barrage of questions and congratulations from well-meaning folk. Can you just tell Linda to meet me by the car in five minutes if she still wants a lift?'

'Of course. Look I'll ring you later after I have talked to Michael. We'll sort this out, don't worry about it.' Jenny smiled. Then she hugged Karen again and walked back to the church.

Karen took deep breath and took a few steps along the path. Her legs felt a little stronger and the nausea had settled into flat calm. Right, so far so good, things would look better once she was home and with Tristan. The sound of crunching leaves behind her stopped her dead. Spinning round, she saw a woman stepping from behind a gravestone.

At first Karen didn't recognise her, but then she realised that she'd seen her once or twice sweeping the church floor and cleaning the brass. They'd never been introduced though and Karen had never really taken much notice of her . . . until now. In the autumn sunshine her face looked strangely familiar, but she couldn't quite . . .

'So, now *she's* gone we can have a chat,' the woman said, narrowing her coal-black eyes and pushing her greasy grey hair behind her ears.

'You were here before and hid behind the gravestone?' Karen said incredulously.

'Yeah, I didn't want miss "sugar and spice and all things nice" to hear what I have to say . . . and neither will you.' The woman's mouth curled into a sneer.

Karen looked at that sneer and then a finger from the past jabbed her hard in the gut . . . but it couldn't be. Her heart pounded in her ears and the nausea returned on a tidal wave. 'I, er . . . what do you mean?'

'Penny dropped then? By the look on your face I think it has. Now if you don't want the lovely little life you've got going to disappear, meet me back here at let's say,' she looked at her watch hanging on her skinny tattooed wrist, '. . . eleven tonight.'

Karen stared slack-jawed. It couldn't be her . . . perhaps she was really losing it. 'No, I won't. I don't know what you're talking about!' Karen shrieked in panic.

The woman put a nicotine-yellowed finger to her lips. 'Shh, Melody. We don't want these good people to hear you . . . Eleven tonight, or I'll come knocking on your door.' The woman pulled her coat hood up and scuttled away down the path.

Karen fell against the wall and slid down it. Hanging onto everything she had now looked about as likely as a holiday on the moon.

CHAPTER 15

My dad would always sing the old songs as we walked along the beach. He used to say he was born too late, a child of the sixties loving the music of the forties and fifties. By the time I was five I knew most of the classics. Frank Sinatra flew me to the moon, I danced a **Mambo Italiano** with Dean Martin, and I sailed with Bobby Darin, somewhere beyond the sea.

Dad said that I sang that one just like an angel. I'd never heard an angel sing, but I expected that angels had nice voices, because Dad always smiled, got a bit tearful and swung me round and round in the air. I pretended I had wings when he did that because angels have wings and if I closed my eyes I could almost believe I was flying.

One day when I was eight as we walked back from the beach I asked him why he liked that song so much. He said that the lyrics reminded him of someone he knew years ago. She apparently emigrated to America and he never saw her again. 'Was she your girlfriend?' I asked, hoping that she had been, because even then I thought he had a pretty rough time with my mother. He looked down at me and I will never forget the haunted longing in his eyes.

Ruffling my hair, he said, 'Yes, she was my first love . . . thought she'd be my last too . . . but then she went and I met your mum, so . . .' He turned his face to the wind and walked on. That 'so' was the most desperate, sad and awful word – those two letters summed up years of lost happiness.

Dad had a huge collection of old vinyl records that were the fruits of his hours spent browsing collectors' shops. My mother never liked him to play them and always made fun of him when he did. 'Why don't you play CDs? You're like something out of the bloody Ark,' she'd say, or 'Don't you realise that you look like an idiot with that 1950s hairstyle. It might have been retro-cool when I met you, but now you just look like a reject from Showaddywaddy.'

Dad would just take it, a wistful little smile playing over his lips, perhaps thinking of happier times and he'd say nothing. The only time I saw him snap was when he came back from work one day to find her drunk and smashing his collection to pieces with a hammer. I was upstairs crying my eyes out. I was only nine but I'd tried to stop her. I pulled her away and slapped her arms, but I just got a pummelling as a result.

She was like some crazed animal, her eyes wild in her face, her mouth set into a grimace and through clenched teeth she hissed vile words about Dad. Some of the words I hadn't heard before, but I knew instinctively that they were the worst kind of swearing.

I heard Dad's anguished roar and I ran downstairs to find him towering over her with the hammer raised in his fist, his face a mask of hatred. She was on her knees mascara and lipstick smeared over her face, crying and laughing at the same time. 'I didn't really mean to, Dave. Just got a bit wasted, you know?' she slurred.

His mouth worked but no sound came out and then he just shook his head. Perhaps her pathetic response stayed his hand and he lowered the hammer, let it fall to the floor by her feet. 'Go ahead, you may as well finish the job, Sandra, you've smashed everything else in my life,' he murmured, and then he turned and saw me peeping round the door. 'Well, apart from this one here, God knows where I'd be without you, my child.' He held his arms out to me and I ran into them, mingling my tears with his as we held each other tight.

She dragged herself up, pushed past us yelling obscenities and left the room. I went over to the ruin of his collection and realised there were a few still intact. I held one towards him, 'Look, Dad, she didn't smash Amore.' I shot him a hopeful smile.

'Oh, but she did . . . she did,' he said, his face crumbling. It would be a few years before I realised what he'd meant.

CHAPTER 16

Karen looked at the clock on the TV for the hundredth time. 10.02 and Tristan showed no signs of going to bed. Typical. For the last three nights he'd been yawning his head off at 9.30 and suggesting that they'd go to bed by 10.00. Now, he was staring intently at an old documentary on TV about the raising of the *Mary Rose*. She stood up, stretched, forced the tremor out of her voice and said, 'You can go up and I'll lock the doors after I sort the washing out for tomorrow.'

Tristan looked up and frowned. 'Eh, it's only just gone ten and it's Sunday tomorrow, no need to get up early.'

'Er, I think you'll find we have our own personal alarm clocks upstairs in the nursery, my love.' Karen rolled her eyes and pointed to the ceiling. 'And I'm knackered to be honest.'

'Well, leave the washing, you go to bed and I'll come up after this has finished.'

Karen groaned inwardly. After the day she'd had, she wondered just how much longer she could hold it together. Then she remembered how much they had wanted each other that morning. Time for a little manipulation, she'd no choice. 'When I say knackered, I don't mean totally . . . in fact I think a little "us" time is just what I need,' she said suggestively.

Tristan jumped up and switched the TV off quicker than a speeding bullet. 'Race you upstairs then?' He chuckled.

'Keep the bed warm, I'll be up in ten.'

Tristan walked over and folded her into his arms. 'Make sure it's not a moment longer,' he murmured, kissing the corners of her mouth.

After he'd gone upstairs Karen flopped down on the settee. Her best hope was he'd get fed up of waiting and just fall asleep. If not she'd go up and say she had a headache. In her mind's eye she saw the woman's face again – greedy, grasping, evil. There was no way that bitch was going to turn up at her door. If she did, that would be the end of everything, of all of them. Despair flooded through her. *Please God, let Tris fall asleep*!

Ten minutes later she heard the floorboards creak in their room and Tris moving across the floor. Damn, he's coming to see where I am! Karen plumped a few cushions and threw herself full length on the settee. Wrestling her palpitations under control and slowing quick breaths into a deep rhythmic rise and fall, she faked for England.

Karen heard Tristan creep in and lay his hand on her shoulder. 'Karen? You asleep?' She continued to breathe deeply and added a little snore for good effect. 'Karen, come on, you'll get a crick in your neck sleeping on here all night.'

She mumbled incoherently and pushed her face further into the cushion. Tristan sighed and left the room. Minutes later he was back and she felt a blanket being tucked gently around her and his lips lightly brush her cheek. 'Night, my love,' he whispered, and then he snapped off the light and closed the door. A creaking of floorboards over head again and then silence prompted a deep sigh of relief. Karen sat up. Her watch said 10.25. To be safe, she should leave it another ten minutes or so to make sure Tristan was sound asleep, but she couldn't afford that luxury.

Karen pulled the conservatory door gently closed behind her and tiptoed down the path. Considering it had been such a crisp autumn day, the night had turned almost sultry and a harvest moon hid her yellow face behind a bank of dark cloud. That's all she needed, a downpour. Once on the road, she switched on her pocket torch and guided by its bobbing white light, hurried along keeping to the hedgerows.

Just before she arrived at Jenny and Michael's gate, she hopped off the road and scurried over the field and onto the bramble lined public foot-path that snaked past the church and into town. That route was slightly longer and even though it was now five to eleven, there was no way she wanted to be recognised on the main road by folk walking their dogs or coming home from the pub.

The drumming of Karen's heart in her ears sounded loud enough to wake the dead beneath the gravestones. The gravel path next to them seemed to shout her arrival to the entire village as each crunching footstep amplified in the quiet churchyard. The wind that had blown the leaves along with such gusto earlier, just sighed now and again as if it was fed up of the job and the moon decided to peep out of the clouds just when Karen could do without the spotlight.

Keeping to the church wall as much as she could, she glanced at her watch. Five past eleven and there was no sign of the woman she'd come to meet. Hell, had she set off to Karen's house already? A rustle of leaves to her left answered that question. Turning in that direction she watched a figure walk along the church path as bold as brass as if she were on a Sunday school outing. Karen turned on her heel and hurried around the back of the church away from the view of the road and waited.

The woman followed and stood just a few yards away from Karen, the moon now bright enough to reveal a face twisted with hatred, staring black eyes and a grin to curdle milk. ''Bout time, Melody,' the woman hissed.

Karen felt the ground move under her feet and she leaned back against the wall. Swallowing hard she said, 'My *name* is Karen.'

A dry rasp passing for laughter escaped the woman's throat. 'Yeah, and mine's Rapunzel. You know who you are as well as I do or you wouldn't be here, now would you?'

'I came because I was scared that you'd turn up at my house and say crazy stuff to my husband and—'

'Shut up and listen. I want fifteen thousand pounds by the end of the month or I ruin your life.' The woman folded her arms and stuck her chin out defiantly.

Karen's heart lurched. 'What? I don't have that kind of money, we're not rich—'

'Ha! You expect me to believe that? Hubby's a doctor, isn't he? I've seen your big fat house and car . . . no, you've got it all right.'

'I haven't . . .' Karen tried to keep the fear from her voice. 'And why do you want to ruin my life for God's sake?'

'Because you ruined mine, Melody, and it's time to pay up.'

'I ruined yours . . . I . . . I don't even know you.'

The woman stepped forward a few jerky paces like a puppet on shortened strings, her lips pursed, hand raised in a fist. Inches from Karen, she lowered her fist and looked into her eyes breathing heavily. Karen flinched from those beady eyes and the stench of her rancid nicotine and alcohol laced breath. 'Because of *you* I was chucked out,' the woman said through clenched teeth. 'Because of *you* I couldn't get a decent job as I didn't have a worthwhile qualification to my bleeding name and because of *you* I ended up on drugs, on the streets. I whored to fund my habit, and now you have the sodding barefaced cheek to say you don't even KNOW ME!'

Stepping quickly to the side, Karen just avoided a hard slap to the side of the head. She held up her palms in a gesture of surrender. 'Okay, stop, calm down . . . let's talk,' she said tremulously. Although the woman's face full of hatred struck terror into her heart, Karen kept her eyes on it, trying to gauge her next move.

Thankfully after a few moments the woman seemed to relax a little, the cold greasy smile slid back from under the folds of a grimace.

'So you do know me . . . admit it, Melody . . . 'cos I know you. Oh, yes, you have changed your hair and lost half your body weight, but I'd know those eyes anywhere . . . and that voice. You always could sing, I'll grant you that.' The woman prodded Karen in the stomach with a bony finger. 'I know you, and I know what you did.'

Karen put her hand to her mouth to prevent a hysterical scream breaking out from her depths. She couldn't speak, just shook her head, but in her brain she yelled over and over: *Make it stop, please, let this be a dream, please, make it stop. MAKE IT STOP!*

The woman prodded her shoulder more forcefully and then shoved her hard to the ground. A sob broke free as Karen scuttled backwards

119

crab-like and bumped her head on a gravestone. The woman laughed and picked up a handful of gravel. As Karen cowered before her, placing her hands protectively across her head, the woman pelted the sharp stones at her face and hands. 'Say my name, Melody, say my name!'

Karen shook her head and sobbed, rocking back and forth. The woman knelt beside her, grabbed Karen's hair and yanked her head back so that she couldn't fail to look into her eyes. 'Say-my-fucking-name!' Each word spat from the woman's mouth was punctuated by a vicious yank of Karen's hair.

Karen dashed tears of humiliation from her eyes, looked back up at the woman, took a deep breath and said it.

CHAPTER 17

Three weeks before I folded my clothes on the rock by the shore and walked out to sea, I walked out onto the stage at school. Mrs Goodhale, Assistant Head of Music and Drama, and also my Head of Year, had cajoled, flattered and practically bullied me (in a nice way) into taking part in the school concert. Ever since Year 8 she'd encouraged and taught me how to develop and perfect my singing voice, despite my increasing reluctance to attend her classes.

Dad died just as I went into Year 9 and by the end of the next year I had gorged myself three and a half stones heavier, and by the end of Year 11, I had added another three. So because of this and my ever-present depression, standing up in front of the entire school, fab voice or no fab voice, was hardly number one on my to-do list. Nevertheless, Mrs Goodhale was one of the few adults who really seemed to care about me, and I guess I did it for her more than anyone.

I had loved to sing in public when I was a kid and had often been in school concerts and in the church choir, because my dad had encouraged me. Dad swore I would go on to be a star. He'd always been so proud of me and under his encouragement I'd pushed myself, believing that the sky was the limit. But then he'd died and my world had grown dark.

For a time the joy of singing had been muted by sadness, as memories of Dad clung to every note.

I can see him now, in the audience beaming with pride, snapping away with his camera and clapping the loudest. Once he had put a couple of fingers at each side of his mouth and whistled so noisily that the vicar had shook his head solemnly and wagged his finger at him.

Ever since that day, if either Dad or I had done something a bit naughty, the other would shake their head and wag their finger and we'd giggle like a couple of loons. Mother hated that, of course, as it was just one more display of our togetherness. Instead of joining in or laughing along with us, she'd say something cruel and nasty, or just look at us as if we'd crawled out of a cesspit.

Funny how you remember certain smells isn't it? Lemon furniture polish had been used to shine the handrail by the steps leading to the stage and every time I smell that now I'm right back up there in front of the whole school. I was to sing a solo and the rest of the singers were going to troop on after I had done my bit, waving Union flags and sing the chorus. The concert was a medley of World War II songs, some significant anniversary of its end; I can't remember which one now.

We were all ready, but then there was some trouble with the sound apparently and I had on one of those microphones that's taped under your hair so that it stays close to your cheek and you can sing free of any encumbrance. I remember fiddling with it as it felt too tight and sweat was pouring down my cheeks from my hairline because of the heat from the stage lights. And then there was my weight. I didn't need much help in the sweating department and I was beginning to feel nervous, uncomfortable and totally ridiculous wearing a too tight 1940s outfit, (specially made by a textiles teacher) and shoes that pinched my toes and squeaked when I walked. I'm feeling jittery even as I write this.

Just as I was ready to do a runner, Mrs Goodhale appeared in the wings and gave me the thumbs up. The sound glitch was fixed. The band struck up the introduction to We'll Meet Again and the stage crew lowered a large banner behind me that read: We'll Fight them on the Beaches.

Just as I opened my mouth to sing, the audience began to mutter and shuffle and some of the younger children laughed out loud. I looked to the wings and noticed that Mrs Goodhale's face was no longer wreathed in smiles, but frozen in horror. I followed the direction of her eyes to a point somewhere over my left shoulder, and turning around I saw what all the commotion was about. The banner didn't read We'll Fight them on the Beaches at all. Someone had put a line of thick red paint through the first four words, replaced the 's' of beaches with a 'd' and added a few more words. The banner now read The Beached Whale Sings!

I felt as if someone had ripped my heart out. How much more of this could I take? I ran towards Mrs Goodhale as fast as the damned shoes would allow, but it wasn't fast enough. A jet of water hit me in the face from somewhere above the stage and within a few seconds I was drenched from head to foot. 'That's it boys, make sure the poor whale gets some water!' shrieked a familiar voice. I tried to escape again but slipped in a puddle of water and fell all my length. The kids in the audience by now were howling with laughter, perhaps they thought it was all part of the show . . . perhaps they didn't, who knew? All I did know is that I just wanted to die . . . then the curtain fell.

CHAPTER 18

The heavens opened ten minutes from home with a rumble and a crash – a storm unleashed. Karen's hot tears mingled with the cool raindrops running down her face and she struggled to keep her footing as she hurried along the dark country lane. She'd left the torch somewhere in her panic to be rid of the bitch at the churchyard. Thoughts whirled through her mind in a frenzy of scenarios all involving Tristan learning the truth about her and then he and the children walking away.

A calmer side of her nature tried to suggest that it could all work out, that Tristan never need know, that she could sort bitch-face somehow. But that suggestion was swiftly squashed. How the hell *could* she sort her? There was no way she'd drop her demands. Karen had already tried to talk her down to no avail, and she'd had to arrange to meet her two weeks from tonight. 'Same time, same place, be there or be-ware. Beware, good, eh?' Bitch had said, chortling as she'd left. In her head Karen just thought of her as Bitch. She refused to allow her a real name; she didn't deserve that human decency.

Fifteen thousand pounds just like that was a joke. They had, Karen thought, around six that she could lay her hands on, but not easily. Some of the money was in ISAs and because of Tristan's long-term planning, the basis of a nest egg for the children's university needs. There was an extra two in a joint savings account for any nasty shocks like a new boiler, or if the car threw a wobbly, but that was it, and that was all.

The recent barn conversion purchase had swallowed a huge chunk of their previous savings and even though Tris did earn a good salary, it would be a while before they could feel comfortably off again, especially as Karen had no paid work. She exhaled in exasperation. What on earth was she thinking? No matter if they had a hundred thousand saved, once Bitch had been paid some money she'd demand more. It would never end.

The conservatory door sliding gently into place sounded like that recent thunderclap to Karen's ears. Bugger, Tris better not wake up. She'd have a hard time explaining why she was just coming in from the garden at 12.30 drenched through and shaking with emotion.

Undressing in the kitchen she shoved her mud-hemmed jeans in the washing machine and towelled her hair vigorously. If she sneaked into their bed now she might wake Tristan and then he'd notice her damp hair, smell the night air on her skin and ask questions. No, she'd have to sleep in the spare room tonight, just when she needed the warmth of his arms wrapped protectively about her. She so wanted to wake him and tell him everything, but of course she couldn't. Or could she? He might understand, forgive her for lying . . . yeah right.

From the back of a kitchen cupboard she grabbed a half-full bottle of brandy. Pulling out the stopper she tipped back her head and downed a good few gulps feeling the liquid burn a fiery path to her stomach. She took another and then shoved the stopper back in. If she had more she'd end up swigging the bloody lot. And God knew she felt like it, but she knew that would be her undoing. This mess needed a clear head and calm nerves if she were to have any chance at all.

It was perhaps this kind of reasoning that had brought her this far in the first place. She felt comforted by this thought. It wasn't everyone who could have lived the kind of life she had before she'd met Tris and still be standing.

In slightly soggy socks she padded around the house locking the doors and switching off lights. An unwelcome thought floated. How much longer would she be able to call this home, to be called Mrs Karen Ainsworth, to be mother to her children? Swallowing a lump in her throat the size of a golf ball, she slipped into the spare room and crawled into bed. Closing her eyes Karen prayed with all her heart that tomorrow would look brighter and some miracle would have risen with the dawn ripe for the plucking. Despite her turmoil, in five minutes she fell into an emotionally exhausted sleep.

Down the landing Tristan was far from sleep and had been ever since he'd seen the light of Karen's torch bobbing away down the lane the best part of two hours ago. He'd just been to the toilet and happened to glance out of the window before returning to bed. At first he thought his eyes were deceiving him, but no, there had definitely been a light. Had someone been trying to break in?

A quick search of the house had revealed no burglary, no Karen, and a deep well of panic in his heart. That was it then. The enigmatic, supposedly 'throwaway' comment she'd made a month or so ago looked like it had substance after all. Also the memory of how she'd said that he might leave her if she'd done something terrible, and then said she was just being daft when he'd asked her what she meant, tumbled round his head on instant replay.

Now in the darkness of the bedroom, the idea that had burst through the soil this morning began to wither and die. Just the thought of the romantic break away he'd been planning made him feel like a sad fool. Tristan thumped the pillow and closed his eyes as if to block it all out, but he might as well have tried to stop the waves outside from crashing on the beach.

He just didn't get it. Karen had been so warm and passionate with him this morning. How could she *do* that to him? Lying in bed wide awake, Tristan went over various innocent reasons for why his wife had pretended to be asleep on the settee and then gone out into the night, but he found them all wanting. He had to face facts – there was probably someone else.

Under his hand, Karen's side of the bed felt cold and hard. He reached out, pulled her pillow to his face and inhaled the scent of her perfume. Tristan's stomach gripped into a knot of loneliness and he ached for her warmth and soft skin against his. Had she been pressing that soft skin to the body of another tonight?

Sitting up, he hurled her pillow across the room and gathered the duvet tightly about him. She couldn't even face being in the same bed as him now. Perhaps Tristan was a poor substitute for whomever she was shagging. Thoughts of Karen in various sexual positions with a faceless stranger made him want to heave. *How could she?* Karen was happy, wasn't she? Well, relatively since she'd overcome the agoraphobia. And what about the kids? How could she disrupt their happy little lives? Sebastian and Bella's faces surfaced and the knot of loneliness tightened. If she left him, they'd go too; he knew he couldn't bear being just a weekend father.

An hour later after turning similar thoughts over in his aching head, reason whispered soothing words in his ear. *Wait until morning, perhaps there will be a reasonable explanation staring you right in the face at the breakfast table.* While he didn't really buy it, it helped him to drift off into oblivion.

'Tris, hey, wake up sleepy head.' A brush of warm lips tickled his cheek. 'Linda's on the phone. She sounds really upset and insists on speaking with you.'

One eye flickered open to be met with the bedside clock's challenge of a 9.15 stare. Bloody hell, how did he sleep until this time? A memory of his insomniac ponderings and the reason for them slammed into his gut like a sledgehammer and the bottom of his world fell out. He pushed his fingers through his hair and sat on the edge of the bed to collect his thoughts. Hang on . . . hadn't Karen just woken him lovingly with a kiss as if there was nothing wrong?

Bleary eyed and disorientated, Tristan stumbled downstairs and took the phone from his wife. His head felt as if a steel band was using it as a rehearsal room and he needed coffee and a shower before he tackled Karen.

The very last thing he wanted to do right now, apart from perhaps jump under a moving train, was to talk to Linda. She'd been abusing the 'we were friends long before you became my doctor' card quite a bit lately and he was too soft to draw the line. Well, today she'd get short shrift; he had major problems of his own.

'Linda, yes, what's up?' he barked, all the time never taking his eyes from Karen as she put the kettle on and took a tray of scones out of the oven. She waved to the children who were running riot in the playroom and blew him a kiss. How the hell could she bake scones, make him coffee, look after the little guys and blow him a kiss just after she'd shagged someone else last night? Slow down, Tris, perhaps she didn't.

'Tristan? Are you there?' Linda asked.

'Hmm, oh, sorry, I'm miles away this morning. I didn't sleep well,' he said, looking directly at Karen. She glanced away and poured hot water into the cafetière.

'I was wondering if I could pop round. I've stupidly run out of my antidepressants and I forgot to ask you for a repeat prescription.'

Warning bells replaced the steel band as the doctor side of him kicked in. How the hell could she have run out already? 'But you had enough for another week at least, didn't you?'

'I know, but I . . . stupidly spilled coffee on them . . . they were on the side and the coffee melted them before I could . . .'

Tristan knew a lie when he heard one and this one was a whopper. 'Have you been taking more than you should, Linda?'

'No! I told you what happened. Look, Tris, can I come over and get some. I don't have any at all.' The sheer panic in her voice jumped down the line and into Tristan's blood.

'I'm not sure I have any in my bag . . . right, come over in about an hour. I'll see what I can do.'

Tristan ended the call, walked over to the kitchen table and slumped down on a chair.

Karen poured coffee and said, 'Poor baby, is she hassling again? I know she's going through a tough time, but I thought we could have a nice quiet family Sunday. She'd better not stay long.' She looked at Tristan and smiled. 'Do you want bacon and eggs?'

A nice family Sunday and bacon and sodding eggs? Was she mad? He had planned to causally drop into the conversation that he'd woken and found her missing last night so he could see what her reaction would be and if she'd make something up, but she'd made him so furious he just blurted, 'So where did you go last night? I saw you leave the house with a torch.'

Karen had her head in the fridge so he couldn't see her reaction immediately, but her voice sounded normal and there was no hesitation in her answer. 'Oh, did you see me? Thought you were fast asleep. I woke up with a crick in my neck and then heard a noise outside the conservatory door.' She turned to face him and held up a packet of bacon. 'Smoked all right?'

'What? Yes, whatever, I don't mind.' He waved his hand. 'So what noise?'

'It sounded like a squeal of a small animal, a vole or something, so I went out but I couldn't see anything.' Karen sighed and then busied herself with breakfast.

Tristan sat back in his chair and watched her

body language. She seemed perfectly normal and at ease. 'So right, you heard a vole that wasn't there; you grabbed a torch and went off down the lane?' *And didn't come back for nearly two hours . . .*

She looked at him and frowned. 'What's up with you? Are you angry with me?'

'No, it just seems a bit odd that's all.'

'Well, if you'd let me finish without pouncing on me. I heard what sounded like a kitten in the distance and thought an owl might have taken one of the feral ones and dropped it down the lane or something. I guessed that's what the squeal was.'

Tristan had to concede that this sounded pretty plausible. 'And so you went off down the lane in search of the kitten . . . Did you find it?'

'Yes, it had a bit of blood on the back of its neck but it seemed more shaken than hurt. If I had got there a few minutes later it would have been a goner. The owl swooped over my head just as I picked it up and put it in the hedgerow. I heard another cat meowing just there, must have been its mother.' She turned away and placed the rashers of bacon on the grill.

A weight started to drift off his shoulders but it was still anchored by a thread of doubt. Clearing his throat he said, 'I see. I did wonder what you were up to . . . I lay awake to speak to you when you got back, but I eventually fell asleep. Why were you gone so long then, love?'

She came over to him and slipped her arms around his neck. 'Well, the night was so lovely that

133

I decided to walk to the beach. Mad I know, but the urge just took me. Got drenched later on in the storm though. That's why I didn't come to bed all cold and damp.'

With her words the thread of doubt was broken and Tristan felt relief flood through him. She'd not been with anyone after all. Thank God! He hugged her tightly, inhaling the scent of her shower-fresh skin and ran his fingers through her silky hair. Why had he been so suspicious? He made his voice light. 'I could have warmed you up. You're such a crackpot.'

'That's been said before. Now let go, I'd better see to the bacon unless you want it burnt!' She giggled, broke free and hurried to the grill. 'Why don't you have a quick shower and it will all be ready when you come down. I'll find those tablets for Linda, too.'

'You are a treasure, what would I do without you?' he said, as he walked to the door.

'Oh, I'm sure you'd manage somehow,' Karen mumbled, turning back to the cooker.

CHAPTER 19

'Hope you don't mind me tagging along, Karen . . . but Tris did ask and I didn't want to be alone today.' Linda waved at Sebastian running up the beach towards them. The storm last night had washed the sky of clouds and the sun shone down from a cornflower-blue sky.

'Of course not . . . don't be daft.' Karen smiled, handing Linda a sandwich. She knew she shouldn't, because of the state poor Linda was in, but she did mind. Still, at least being forced to chat to Linda meant that she could block out the relentless pummelling that thoughts of Bitch had been giving her brain for the last few hours.

A picnic on the beach had been Tristan's idea and he seemed in very good spirits after his initial moodiness this morning. Karen watched him charging up the beach after Sebastian, roaring like a tiger with Bella on his shoulders. Thank God he'd bought her story. Now there was just the small matter of what to do next to sort out. She'd secured a foothold on the edifice, but there was a tough climb ahead . . . a tough climb with no safety rope and wearing a blindfold.

Karen unscrewed the thermos flask, glanced at Linda, and the question about more tea she'd just been about to ask froze in her throat. Linda was looking at Tris coming up the beach too, and not just looking, but *looking*. Cheeky madam! How the hell had she not noticed this woman lusting after her husband before? Had Tristan noticed? Did he feel sorry for her or was there more to it? The flask shook in her hand and she shoved it back in the picnic bag. *Hell, Karen, calm down, your head is full of shit after last night.*

'Any cake left?' Tristan said, setting Bella down and flopping out of breath beside Karen on his back. 'Isn't it glorious for this time of year?' He undid his shirt and closed his eyes.

Karen looked for cake in the bag while taking little surreptitious glances at Linda. Bloody hell her eyes were all over him, watching the rise and fall of his chest as his shirt fell open, and then lingering on the crotch of his jeans. Linda caught Karen looking at her and rapidly shifted her gaze.

Putting her hand on Karen's arm she said, 'You are so lucky to have such a handsome and lovely guy for a hubby, Karen, you know?'

Karen nodded and added a watery smile. 'Believe me, I do know.'

Linda turned her eyes on Tristan again. 'Anyone ever told you that you are too good-looking to be a doctor, Tris? Bet the lady patient's heart rate goes up when you do their blood pressure.' Linda giggled.

Karen wanted to retch.

Tristan sat up and grinned, his cheeks pinker than normal. 'Not that I can remember, but thanks for the compliment.'

Karen noticed a twinkle of a flirt in his eye and thrust the cake at him. *Right, that's it. This woman is finding another GP, pronto.*

'Have you thought of going back to work at the bookshop, Linda? You seem *so* much better today.' Karen smiled, shuffling round to block Linda's view of Tris. Tris frowned a 'you joking?' signal sideways at her.

A shadow fell across Linda's face. 'No. Like I said when you picked me up the other day, I'm feeling quite anxious again lately. I guess being here in your family's company helps to lighten my mood a bit. I'm so grateful to you for having me.'

Karen tossed her a tight smile. *Just so long as you don't think my husband is going to 'have' you.* 'No problem. I do think it might help get you back to your old self though. As much as we like seeing you, having a set routine is often the best option.'

Linda sighed and started to pick at the sleeve of her cardigan. 'I'm . . . I'm not sure I'm ready for—'

'No, you're not. Take things one step at a time,' Tristan soothed and shot a frown at Karen again. 'How's the counselling going with Christopher?'

Linda brightened and looked at Tristan with deep soulful eyes. 'Oh, he's helping, thanks. It's just when I come home to the empty house there are so many memories, dreams that never came true.' She looked down and dabbed at her eyes. Tristan moved over to her and took her hand. 'Hey, come on. It will get better, I promise.'

Karen rolled her eyes at the back of his head. *Oh please, can't you see what she's up to?* 'Right,' she said jumping up. 'Who's for rock pooling?'

Sebastian picked up his net and did a happy dance. 'Daddy, are you coming pooling?'

'Of course Daddy is pooling, we all are. Come on let's see who can find the biggest crab!' Karen handed a net to Tristan and a bucket to Bella.

'Come on, Linda, we don't have another net, but I'm sure you can help the little ones,' Tristan said, getting to his feet.

'Oh, no, don't worry. I'll stay here with the picnic stuff if you li—'

'Lovely idea, save us lugging it,' Karen jumped in before Tristan could do his *Oh no you must come* bit. She noted Linda's crestfallen expression but right at that moment couldn't give a damn. 'Come on kids, race ya!'

Two shrimps, a crab and a snail or two later, Tristan said, 'I think it's time we went back to poor Linda. She's still feeling fragile you know.'

Karen closed her eyes, tilted her head up to the sun and captured a lungful of salt air. God, he was really starting to annoy her now. 'Poor Linda volunteered to stay with the stuff, even though you asked her to come pooling.'

'Yeah, but she was only trying to be polite. You didn't really give her much of a chance, did you?'

'Oh for God's sake, Tris,' Karen hissed, mindful of the children a little way off. 'You were saying only the other day how she was taking advantage of our friendship. She's round nearly every week for one reason or another.'

'Yes, I think she is taking advantage, but I'm worried that she's taking more tablets than she should and being with us this afternoon has definitely calmed her. She even laughed a few times earlier.'

'Hmm, well I think she should find another GP. She's obviously struggling. Christopher's counselling doesn't seem to be having much effect either and you're too soft with her to say so.'

Tristan shook his head. 'Oh yes, that would really go down well wouldn't it? By the way Linda, I know you're going through a really tough time but don't come round anymore and find another doctor.'

Karen sighed and tipped a crab back into the pool. 'You wouldn't say it quite like that obviously . . . but you do need to tell her, Tris.'

Tristan watched the crab scuttle for cover and pursed his lips.

'What's the face for, now?'

'You just seem a bit harsh that's all. Has she done anything to upset you?'

Karen shrugged. She didn't want to get into all that now. Bitch was insisting on being dealt with

139

and had elbowed Linda into second place. She told the children to put the sea creatures back in the rock pool as they had to go, and gathered up the nets.

'So has she?'

'Has she what?'

'Done anything to upset you?'

Karen jabbed the nets under her arm, guided the kids down the rocks and shepherded them along the sand.

Tristan slipped his arm around her waist. 'Well?' he murmured in her ear, as he fell in step beside her. 'Spill the beans.'

She looked up at him and then away across the sea. 'Can't you see that she's besotted with you?'

Tristan's eyes nearly popped out of his head. He stopped and put his hands on her shoulders. 'Besotted . . . with me?'

'Yes, Tristan, with you.' Karen shrugged his hands off and hurried after the children. 'Come on, let's get the kids back and Linda gone,' she tossed over her shoulder.

The force of the dishwasher door slamming shut rattled the cutlery into a frenzy. A frenzy of rattling emotions whirled around Karen's head too. She opened the door again, tossed in an eggy spatula, flung the door shut and then kicked an errant onion across the kitchen floor where it slapped into the wall and then rolled back towards her feet. She aimed another kick, but instead picked it up and placed it gently on the chopping board.

Dragging air in through her nose she exhaled softly through her mouth to try and calm her jitters. Chicken stir fry and egg fried rice was on the menu, though if she didn't get a wriggle on it would be nowhere near ready when Tristan and the kids got back from dropping Linda home. *Calm your temper and focus. You've made the decision about Bitch, now forget her.*

Karen grabbed a carving knife, hacked into a chicken breast and thought about the words she'd had with Tristan on their return from the beach. He wouldn't have it that Linda fancied him and had said Karen was overreacting. Perhaps she had been a little, given her state of mind, but her eyes hadn't deceived her when she'd seen Linda drooling over Tris on the beach.

While the kids played in the garden and Linda was in the bathroom, Karen had told Tristan that he should tell her gently over the next week or so that he'd found her another doctor and that it would be best for everyone. 'I don't like the way she is with the kids either, Tris, all gushy and over the top. They don't know what to make of her.'

'Really? I think she just likes being around them that's all . . . given her circumstances I think she's quite controlled.'

A red pepper met its match as Karen sliced the cleaver hard down through the middle of firm succulent flesh. Quite controlled? What planet was

141

he on? She'd told him that of course Linda's circumstances were tragic, but if he allowed her fixation on him to flourish, it could make her even worse in the end.

Tristan had still questioned that Linda fancied him at all, but said he'd pay particular attention to it now that Karen had pointed it out.

'And are you going to tell her to find another doctor?' she'd whispered urgently, as she could hear Linda coming back downstairs.

'Yes, but not today, obviously,' Tris had said with a sigh.

'Not today, what?' Linda had said, breezing in.

You butting into our private conversations, Linda, we don't want that today or any other. 'Er . . . we were just saying that the front garden needs weeding, but we wouldn't do it today.' Karen smiled.

'Oh, well, I love gardening . . . I could come over next week and do it for you?' Linda beamed at Tristan.

'No, really, that's okay,' Tristan said, slipping his arm around Karen. 'We like doing it together, don't we?'

Karen leaned in and planted a firm kiss on her husband's lips. 'We do indeed, and not just gardening.'

Linda had flushed and picked up her bag. 'Oh, no worries, just thought you might need help what with the children and all.'

Peeling the battered onion, Karen felt a bit

sheepish as she remembered Linda's downcast face. The poor woman had gone through a really shit time and all she could do was try and get rid of her. Yes, she fancied her husband, he was gorgeous after all, but that could also just be the effect of Tris being kind and doctorly. Still, that could get more serious and cruel to be kind seemed the best option. She had enough on her plate already. Tomorrow was the start of the first hurdle up the edifice of her problems. Hang on, she was mixing her metaphors? How could there be hurdles on edifices . . . or was it edify? A little squeal of hysteria escaped and she took another slow deep breath. Right, now to ring Jenny before Tris got back.

'Of course I'll have the children! Can't wait, it will be good practice!' Jenny giggled.

'It will only be for about an hour or so. I just feel like I need a good run.'

'Take all day for me, hon. And I hope you'll come to practice on Saturday after the recent Michael bombshell. I had a good talk to him and he's agreed not to do anything else about the competition until he's apologised and talked to you about it all.'

Karen rolled her eyes and took a sip of wine. What with everything else she'd not really given much thought to the choir. 'I'm sure he means well, and it really *is* a great opportunity for the choir . . . just not sure I could face the TV cameras though, Jen.'

The disappointment in Jenny's voice was tangible on the other end of the phone. They both knew that without Karen the choir might not even get picked for the programme, but her words were as positive as ever. 'Right, I can see that. But don't make any decisions yet. We'll have a chat and see what we can come up with.'

Ten minutes later, the car door slammed and the sound of Bella and Sebastian's laughter heralded the return of her little family. 'Mummeee . . . Mummeee, hello!' Bella yelled, toddling up the path and into her mother's arms.

'Hello, my darling.' Karen squeezed her daughter tight and a smacked a big kiss on her cheek. 'Did you remember to get the milk?' she called to Tristan over Bella's head.

Tristan pointed at Sebastian emerging from the other side of the car, a frown of concentration on his face, lips pursed, carrying a carton of milk as if his life depended on it. 'And I thought you could use these too,' Tristan said, leaning back in the car. He pushed something behind his back and then walked up the path. A few feet away he revealed with a flourish a brightly coloured bunch of flowers.

Karen was overtaken by a sudden rush of love that rocked her on her feet. How could she ever live without moments like this, on the surface seemingly quite ordinary, but underneath the most precious in the world? Tears pricked behind her eyes and though she tried to keep them there, they spilled onto her cheeks and rolled down her face.

Bella looked up and poked a teardrop with a pudgy finger. 'Mummy cry?' she said, her own face crumbling in response.

'No, Mummy been peeling onions. I'm happy, honestly!'

Tristan slipped his arms round them both and looked at her concerned. 'The onion trick won't work on me, you okay?'

'Yep, I just love you all so much and sometimes I can't believe how lucky I am.' Karen set Bella down and hugged him tight.

'I'm lucky too. And about Linda, I've already dropped a small hint on the way back about the time she spends here. Don't worry; she seemed to take it all in her stride.'

'Good. And I do feel sorry for her, but—'

'I know, and you're absolutely right about her fancying me.' Tristan laughed kissing her on the forehead. 'She actually squeezed my thigh when she said goodbye and thanks for a lovely day.'

'Told you!' Karen grinned and poked him on the shoulder. 'Well, she can't have you, you're all mine.' She swallowed, blinked away fresh tears, and looked at the floor.

'Hey, what's up?' Tristan put a finger under her chin and tilted her face up to look at him.

'Oh, nothing. I'm just feeling emotional today. I just don't know what on earth I'd do without you . . . without all of you.'

'Huh, like that's ever going to happen . . . I'd never let that happen.' He kissed her gently on the corner of the mouth. 'Come on, there's a delicious smell wafting out of that there kitchen and my stomach's a grumblin'.' Tristan took her hand and led her inside.

As she followed her husband into the kitchen, Karen swore that she would never let that happen either . . . whatever it took.

CHAPTER 20

With the children safely despatched to Jenny and Michael's, the next toehold on the mountain slope was the bank in Kelerston. Mountain, edifice, brick wall, these images were all preferable to the face of Bitch hovering behind Karen's eyes. Hovering, sniggering, waiting for a chance to leap out and scare the living daylights out of her.

Pulling into a space outside the local supermarket, Karen rummaged in her bag for sunglasses. They were hardly the best disguise in the world and Karen didn't really intend to use them as such, but taken together with the jogging outfit and trainers, they might prevent immediate recognition and thus her being roped into conversation by a friendly local. And anyway, somehow she just felt safer behind them. Perhaps she could pretend that someone else instead of her was about to get out of the car, walk to the bank opposite Jackson's butcher's shop and casually withdraw £2,000 out of their savings account.

Stepping through the door into the bank felt like stepping back into childhood. There had been a bank just like this in Karen's village, right down to the Victorian coving, a heavy wooden chair by the side of the shelf bearing the obligatory pen on a chain, and a whiff of pine disinfectant to cover the odour of nervous sweat emanating from years of serious transaction weighing heavy in the wallpaper and on the soul.

The transaction that Karen was about to make was definitely serious. The sound of her heart pounded in her ears as she shoved her sunglasses up on to her head and waited behind the only customer at the teller's window. Preoccupied with the next climb up the mountain, she didn't take much notice of the person in front, apart from the fact it was a man in a green raincoat.

As he turned to leave, her heart left Karen's ears and plummeted to her feet. Harold Jackson's moon face broke into a huge grin as he recognised her.

'Well, fancy seeing you here,' he chortled, patting her shoulder. 'Not seen you for a year near on and then twice in as many weeks, eh?'

God, that's all she needed. Questions, small talk and hyena laughter for no apparent reason. Karen just wanted to get the money and go. She rolled her eyes internally, fat chance of that now. 'Yes, isn't that a coincidence?' Karen smiled briefly, and stepped forward towards the window.

Harold sidestepped her and put a meaty hand on her forearm. 'So, how are you anyway? Still battling that agorapheebria?' He stuck out his bottom lip and folded his arms as if he expected chapter and verse on the state of her health.

Bloody hell, she'd told him when she'd gone into his shop the other week that she was fine now. Had he short-term memory loss or something, or was he just a very annoying person who needed to get a life? Banking on the latter, Karen sighed and said, 'No, as I told you last time, Harold, I'm fine now. And yourself?'

'Oh, aye, I'm always fine.' He threw back his head and barked a few times. 'In fact, you could say I was in rude health . . . least my missus says I'm rude!' Another barrage of kookaburra style cackles echoed around the stately bank and Karen caught sight of the teller looking at her watch and rolling her eyes at her colleague. A sigh from behind alerted Karen to the fact that someone else had now come in and this gave her a way out.

'Well, glad to hear it, but you must excuse me now, Harold; we have a bit of a queue forming.' Karen stepped forward again. But though Harold allowed her past, he still hovered next to her like a bad smell.

'You withdrawing all Doctor Tristan's hard-earned pennies, then?'

Karen nodded tightly. 'Perhaps not all of them.'

'My wife clears me out every so often; she is partial to a bit of shopping in Plymouth once a month, you know.' Harold winked and opened his mouth presumably to release another cackle, but Karen's temper flared through her body like a fever.

'Sorry, Harold, but I really must get on, people

149

are waiting and I have a lot to do this morning.' She stepped closer to the window and turned her back on him. Harold mumbled something about just being friendly and then he stomped off and out.

'Hello, how can I help you today?' the teller said smiling conspiratorially, obviously impressed that Karen had dispatched Harold so effectively.

'Hi, I'd like to withdraw two thousand pounds out of my account please.' Karen tried to keep the tremor out of her voice as she gave her details. She felt like a bank robber even though it was her and Tris's money. 'I'd also like this withdrawal not to appear on our bank statement if possible.' She lowered her voice to a near whisper. 'It's for a surprise for my husband's birthday.'

The young woman frowned and looked uncomfortable. 'I'm sorry, Mrs Ainsworth, we can't do that as it's all done by computer.'

Karen nodded and shrugged. She'd expected as much really, but had to try. Tristan was never the most vigilant at collecting the post and checking the account online anyway. She'd just have to make sure that she was ready with an excuse if he did.

If looks could kill she'd fall dead on the pavement as she stepped out of the bank and met the glare of Harold Jackson through his shop window. There he stood, once more clad in a white, blood-spotted apron, hands planted on hips and an expression on his round visage that would curdle milk. Great, she couldn't afford to make any more enemies.

Lifting a hand she waved cheerily and beamed a smile that she hoped would un-curdle the milk and whisk it into a nice milkshake, probably strawberry, judging from the colour of his cheeks. A curt nod and his back was all she achieved as he 'busied' himself with a string of sausages hanging from a hook. Ah well, couldn't be helped, Karen thought as she hurried in the direction of the church. Harold was the least of her worries.

The church huddled under a bank of black cloud gathering in the west and a keen wind whistled along the driveway. Why was it that each time she came here lately the weather worsened? Half an hour ago it had been another sunny, if briskly crisp, autumn morning. Now the scene before her looked like a set for *The Bride of Dracula*.

Karen zipped her top up to the neck, pulled her hood up, patted her pocket for the umpteenth time and was reassured by the bulk of its contents. It had only been a three-minute walk from the bank, but she'd never carried so much money all at once and she had visions of it rolling out and blowing over the town like confetti. She patted her other pocket too, the contents were smaller, but hopefully just as welcome to the recipient.

Silence poured into the gap left by the church door creaking into place. Karen leaned her back against it and tried to calm her galloping heart and adrenaline fuelled panic. With deep breaths and eyes focused on the candles at the altar, it took a

151

few seconds before she was ready to creep along the pews to the verger's office and vestry beyond.

It was still silent in the church apart from the occasional squeak of her trainers on the wooden tiles. Shit, what if she wasn't there? Karen would have to go through all this again tomorrow. She shook her head and leaned heavily on the back of a pew. No, she couldn't, because Michael would be back from Truro tomorrow. She'd picked today as she knew without a doubt he was visiting his brother this morning. With him floating around the church the whole thing would get too tricky . . . she reigned herself in. Wasn't it too tricky already?

The lovely Christmassy cinnamon smell she'd enjoyed the other day before Bitch found her, now just made Karen's stomach roll as she placed her hand on the door to the little offshoot kitchen. The door opened a crack to reveal an empty kitchen with no discernible sign of human activity. But would everything be open like this if nobody was around? *Of course it would, this is Kelerston not New York.* Karen walked in, sat at the table and rested her chin on interlaced fingers. That was it then, she'd have to think again.

A clatter of metal on wood whipped her head around towards the door at the end of the kitchen. A figure bustled through it carrying a mop and bucket and then stopped open-mouthed when she saw Karen. 'Well, stone me, if it isn't our Melody,' Bitch said, baring a row of yellow teeth in a parody of a smile.

Thank God, now get it over with. Karen stood and folded her arms. 'Right, this is what's going to happen. I give you money today and that's it. We don't have fifteen grand . . . this is all I could get without my husband getting suspicious.' She pulled the roll of notes out of her pocket and placed it on the table. She faced Bitch's glare without flinching, even though every nerve felt as taut as a tightrope and every vile memory of the woman told her to run.

Bitch came over, grabbed the bundle and with a quick but careful eye counted the amount. She gave a snort and looked into Karen's eyes. 'You think I'm simple? Two fucking grand? It will take a darn sight more than this to keep me quiet.' She pocketed the money and snarled, treating Karen to another look at the yellow gravestones lining her gums.

Now she had the dubious benefit of full daylight, close up Bitch looked to Karen even more hideous than she had in the moonlight . . . and so old . . . old beyond her years.

Karen swallowed and slipped her hand into her other pocket. 'I told you that's all the money we have . . . I can get you these on a fairly regular basis though.' She tossed a small cardboard package onto the table.

Bitch frowned, picked them up and peered closer. 'Antidepressants,' she puzzled. 'Anti-crappy-depressants? Why would you bring me these?'

'Because you're an addict and these are strong tablets so—'

'You are *such* a dozy mare!' Bitch chortled and threw the tablets at Karen. 'You think I need these when I can get crack any day of the week?'

Karen walked over to the window and looked out over the gravestones. She'd half expected this reaction, but failed to see what other option she had. The main thing was that she should stand her ground. Isn't that what they said when confronted with a bully in the schoolyard or work-place? Trouble was, she'd met this particular bully before and had always come off worse.

She turned back to look at Bitch, who had perched her scrawny backside on the edge of the table and pulled a packet of cigarettes out of her overall pocket. Karen watched her light up and blow a plume of acrid smoke across the space between them. She had once smoked for about a year during the worst time of her life, but now just the smell of cigarette smoke wafting past her nose in the street made Karen hold her breath.

'Not sure Michael would like you smoking in here.'

'No, he wouldn't, but he's not here is he as you well know.' Bitch took a long drag and blew it forcefully in Karen's direction. 'Bit of all right though, ain't he? Often thought about shagging the arse off him. No chance with that simpering little cow all over him all the time though.'

Karen thought there would be as much chance of Michael looking twice at Bitch even if he was

154

single, as her suddenly growing wings and flying round the kitchen. 'Jenny is not a simpering little cow; she's lovely and a very good friend.'

Bitch coughed out a laugh with another lungful of smoke. 'Very good friends, eh? So you're sleeping with her . . . always wondered if you two were getting it on . . . very touchy-feely together I've noticed.' She leered towards Karen and winked.

A rush of anger and disgust flared up from Karen's feet, replaced her fear and left her itching to punch the other woman's nasty little face in. Instead she put her hands under her armpits and spat, 'You really *are* a vile piece of DNA.'

'Yep, and you really *are* going to be in a shit load of trouble if you don't get me more money and stop messing around with these Smarties.' Bitch gestured to the tablets with her cigarette.

'I've told you, that's all there is!' Karen yelled, dismayed to hear a voice that belonged to a frightened and desperate woman rather than one who was standing her ground, calling the shots.

Bitch said nothing for a few moments and finished her cigarette as if lost in thought. She then threw it to the floor, hopped off the table and crushed it underfoot.

Karen knew how that felt.

'Look, because I'm a nice lady, I'll give you a while longer to sort out some money.' She grinned at Karen and walked closer to her. 'I'll take these tablets because I can sell them and in the meantime you can get me regular supplies of these and let's say . . . methadone. I'm sure hubby has some in his little magic bag.'

'Methadone?' Karen gulped. 'Doctors only have controlled drugs about their person for limited patients. It's very rare to have—'

'Do it! Find a way or that's it!' Bitch spat and jabbed Karen on the shoulder with a bony finger.

Karen saw red and jabbed her back. She couldn't help it. How dare she treat her like this? 'He would notice it had been taken, you stupid bitch!'

Bitch's response was swift and painful. 'Don't you ever call me that or touch me again, do you understand?' she hissed, closing her talons around Karen's throat and pinning her against the sink. For a scrawny woman she had the strength of Hercules. She also had the breath of a dog; in fact that was probably doing dogs a disservice.

Twisting her face away Karen nodded. Bitch released her, picked up her bucket and ran water into it. 'It's because of you that I have to do these menial jobs, snitching on me like you did all those years ago.'

'Look, I don't want to go over all this again,' Karen said, rubbing her neck. 'I'll try to get the methadone, but as I said it won't be easy.'

'Well, you know what will happen if you don't,' Bitch said, setting the bucket down and aiming a squirt of disinfectant into the water.

'Perhaps I'll take my chances. I did nothing wrong, I just thought people might think I had,

156

and my life at the time was so hard . . .' Karen sighed almost to herself. She just couldn't live like this, a threat constantly hanging over her head. And this was obviously just the beginning. Bitch would never be satisfied.

Bitch dipped the mop in the bucket and leaned on it. 'You did nothing wrong? Oh, yeah, sure, sweet and innocent Melody Rafter. The gossip round the town at the time said you deffo did and that you were a nasty little witch. They also said that you deserved what was coming.'

That news slapped fear into Karen's heart. 'They did? Why?'

Bitch raised her eyebrows and tutted. 'Duh, not very bright, are you? Work it out for yourself. And you ought to be punished double really, after what you did to me. I have nobody now. My parents went off to Spain to retire . . . and they disowned me for years before that.' She glared at Karen, her eyes bright with angry passion. 'Even though I was their only child . . . so I buggered off to London, out of the way. And here you are after what *you* did, happy, pretty, lovely family. Yeah, poor Melody, she had *such* a hard life, NOT! While nobody even knows if I'm alive or dead . . . nor cares.' She grinned slyly. 'Just one thing makes me happy . . . if they find out about you, they'll throw away the key.'

Karen shook her head and grabbed the back of the chair for support. Her whole world felt like it was being sucked into the vortex of evil, swirling

157

in Bitch's coal-black eyes. She was clearly delusional and twisting things; Karen wasn't to blame for any of it. 'I didn't do it . . . well, not on purpose. All I did was protect myself . . . you have no idea what it was like, I—'

The sound of whistling along the corridor heralded the arrival of the verger, Mr Proctor. 'Right, shut up and let me sort this, okay?' Bitch whispered, her eyes flashing.

Karen folded her arms and tried to control her shaking limbs as Proctor stepped through the door, a frown on his normally cherubic face and his nose wrinkling in disgust. 'Morning, ladies. Didn't know you were here, Karen,' he said with a question in his voice, 'and there's a horrid smell of cigarette smoke in here.' He fanned a hand in front of his face and flung open a side window.

Bitch quickly tugged her sleeves down over her needle-pricked arms and made a show of wringing the mop out. 'I know, terrible isn't it? I came in just now to find a tramp sat at the table puffing away, large as life and twice as ugly. Drunk as a lord he was and shouting the odds. Good job Karen here popped through to get a drink of water. Wouldn't have fancied tackling him on my own,' she finished, sloshing the mop across the stubbed out cigarette.

Proctor's hand fluttered to his mouth and he knitted his bushy grey eyebrows together. 'My goodness, we'll have to make sure we lock up more carefully. Are you both okay?' He directed this to Karen.

'Er, yes, thanks, Graham. It was a bit of a shock but no real harm done.'

'Right . . . and were you looking for Jenny, because—'

'No, I was hoping to catch Michael. I'd completely forgotten that he was in Truro.' Karen smiled and looked at her watch. 'Well, I'll get going, now. Cheerio, both.'

Bitch looked up from her mopping and flashed Karen a cheesy smile. 'Yes, cheerio, hon, see you soon . . . and remember I'm always here for a chat.'

Karen gave her a brief nod and hurried out.

Making her way through Kelerston's busy streets, Karen could hardly grasp the enormity of her problem. How the hell was she going to get methadone without Tris noticing? The answer blew back at her on a bitter wind – she couldn't. So, the end of her world would either be delivered courtesy of Bitch as a result of not getting her way, or by Tristan noticing the missing drugs and demanding to know why she'd taken them.

If it were the latter, perhaps by some miracle she could make something up. Just what escaped her at the moment, and miracles were thin on the ground. But if it were the former, that would be it – no excuses, do not pass go, do not collect two hundred pounds . . . go straight to jail. Jail had never seriously been on her radar, just bleeping away faintly at the edges. She'd always worried more about Tristan not being able to cope with her deception but what if Bitch had been telling the truth about the gossip all those years ago? What then?

Sitting behind the wheel of her stationary car, Karen stared ahead from unseeing eyes. If her life recently had been a bad dream, the future looked like a nightmare.

CHAPTER 21

Mrs Babcock's piles were absolutely the last thing Tristan wanted to look at on a Monday morning. In fact, on any morning save perhaps for Mr Babcock's weeping groin boil. He'd been treated to that lovely sight the week before and now his wife sat opposite, twenty stone, hairy-chinned and, Tristan's nose told him, definitely unwashed.

The Babcocks were a little eccentric and lived in an old farmhouse on the outskirts of Kelerston's boundary. Mrs Babcock had lived there all her life and had inherited the farm at the age of forty when her father had died. Mr Babcock, a peripatetic farm hand, had met her at the annual bullock show and they had apparently fallen instantly in love. Preferring to keep their own company and that of their animals to other folk, they only ventured in to the village when absolutely necessary.

Mrs Babcock's expression was conveying the absolute necessity of this particular visit. Sitting on one buttock she screwed up her face and rasped heavily through the gap in her front teeth. 'They're playin' up somethin' awful, Doctor. I can hardly sit down and when it comes to passin' . . .' her big face turned puce. '. . . the necessaries, it's pure agony.' She pushed her greasy dark hair back from her eyes and winced again.

'Have you been using the cream and the suppositories I prescribed?'

Mrs Babcock's eyes became round and earnest. 'Oh, yes, Doctor, regular as clockwork, but it's made no difference.' She shuffled in the chair. 'Though I don't see 'ow insertin' 'em in my . . . you know what, would 'elp my bottom problem.'

'Your "you know what"?' Tristan began to have an inkling as to why the treatment wasn't working. *God help us all.* Still, he wouldn't have to look at her arse this morning.

Mrs Babcock looked away and turned ever redder. 'Yes, my front bottom.'

'But why would you insert them there? Your piles are in your back passage.' Tristan took his glasses off and sighed in exasperation.

Her forehead creased. 'We don't have a back passage . . . oh, my bum, you mean? Well, it was too sore to put them up there, so I asked Charlie about the instructions because I didn't really know what insert into anus meant. Charlie reckoned anus was a fancy name for fanny, I mean . . . my, "you know what", and that it was hurting because I was trying to put them in the wrong place.'

'Vagina you mean . . . and anus means your bottom, Mrs Babcock,' Tristan said, biting the inside of his cheek to stop a guffaw bursting out.

'Eh? But it hurts too much—'

'Well, you must try harder. I promise it will get easier after the first few times you use the suppositories. Come back after a week if there's no improvement.'

Once the door had closed behind a baffled Mrs Babcock, Tristan sat in his chair and rocked with laughter. The past few weeks had been so miserable that he'd almost forgotten how it felt to laugh like that. Hiccups in his chest and tears streaming down his face alerted him to the fact that perhaps he was a little too close to hysteria than he felt comfortable with, and so he banished images of Mrs Babcock from his mind and took a few deep breaths to calm himself and to try to get rid of the hiccups.

The source of his misery was the return of Karen's agoraphobia and increased strange behaviour. Around two weeks ago Tristan had been shopping in Kelerston and had popped into the butchers for some sausages. Harold Jackson had been almost indecently eager to tell him about Karen's shortcomings the day before.

'I was wondering if your missus was all right today, Doctor Tristan, because yesterday she was really not her normal self, not her normal self at all,' Harold had said, shaking his jowls. 'She more or less snapped my head off to be honest.'

'Really?' Tristan said feeling uncomfortable and at a loss. Karen was never rude to people. 'Perhaps the children were running her ragged.'

'Children? They weren't with her. She was in the bank making a withdrawal I think.' He looked at Tristan carefully. Tristan kept his eyes blank and nodded. 'And anyway, I stopped on my way out to pass the time of day. She just cut me off and that was that.'

'Oh, well, I'm sure she didn't mean to. I'll ask her what was up if you like. Cheerio, Harold.' Tristan took his sausages and left before Harold could draw another breath.

Walking back to the surgery Tristan had wondered who had looked after Sebastian and Bella while Karen went to the bank and why was she making a withdrawal? Tristan normally looked after the money since the kids were born, as Karen never had a spare minute and most bill payment was done by standing order. If Karen needed money she'd normally just draw it out of the ATM unless she wanted more than three hundred pounds, but why on earth would she want more than that? Tristan shook his head. Bloody Harold Jackson had got him worrying for no reason, stupid old gossip. Karen would have a perfectly reasonable explanation.

But when he'd got home that evening asking Karen about the bank had completely slipped his mind, because he'd walked into the kitchen to find her drunk and in floods of tears. Apparently she'd taken the kids to Jenny's so she could go for a run, she'd done that a few times lately and loved it she said. But that day, the old fears of being outside and away from home had hit her like a freight train once she was out running.

Fleeing home, she'd been so upset that the agoraphobia was back that she'd grabbed a bottle of brandy and took a tot just to calm her nerves. Somehow one tot had led to two, three and four. On an empty stomach, it wasn't long before she'd succumbed.

Tristan made her black coffee and tried to find out what had caused this setback. Karen insisted that she didn't know and that she'd been perfectly happy until that day, but Tristan knew his wife and he could see the way her eyes danced evasively away from his on the end of a carefully placed direct question or two.

Since that day Karen had become more or less a recluse again. Choir practice was written off and she asked Jenny to babysit far too often in Tristan's opinion. He'd also noticed things going missing from his medical store, which was always stashed in the safe when he wasn't using it. At first he'd thought he'd been imagining it, when a packet of antidepressants had gone and he'd assumed he'd miscounted. But when he was another down, he began to worry.

Going apeshit was mild as a description of what Karen had done when he'd asked her about it. Her lovely blue eyes had become cold grey bullets when she'd looked up from her newspaper the previous Sunday morning. 'How the hell should I know where they are?' she'd asked, her voice a low growl.

'Well, you're the only one besides me who knows the combination to the safe, and I doubt the little ones have figured it out,' he replied with a chuckle, attempting to lighten the mood.

'I'm glad you're laughing, Tris, because I fail to see the funny side. I might have the agoraphobia back but I'm not stealing your fucking antidepressants.'

That had shocked him. Karen rarely swore like that. He'd frowned and put his finger to his lips. 'Shh, the kids are only in the playroom. We don't want them picking up *that* kind of language, do we?'

'Oh no, we don't, Tris . . . so perhaps you'll just lay the hell off me and concentrate on counting your stock properly,' she hissed, throwing the newspaper at him.

Tristan had seen a flicker of regret in her eyes and a suggestion of the old Karen momentarily, then the shutters had come down and she'd barely spoken to him since, no matter how much he'd begged her to tell him what was wrong.

She'd even moved into the spare room three nights ago as she said she couldn't sleep for him snoring. That had really hurt. He'd begun to think that perhaps she *had* been seeing someone ever since the night of the storm and he'd been too stupid to see through her stories. That would account for her depression; perhaps the thought of breaking up the family was tearing her apart.

Exhaling, he waited for the next hiccup. Nope . . .

they appeared to have gone, that was something that had gone right at least. A sudden urge to see Karen and have it out with her twisted his gut instead of the hiccups and he leaned forward and nudged the mouse on his desk. Glancing down the list on the computer screen he saw that his last appointment had been Mrs Babcock and the first appointment of the afternoon was 2.15 p.m. He only had one house call before that. Kelerston was uncommonly healthy today. Good, that settled it. He'd do the house call and then go and see his wife. He needed to know the truth and one way or another he'd get it.

As he swung the car into his drive, Tristan saw Kevin the postman dismounting from his trusty cycle. Kevin had been a postman in Kelerston for nearly thirty years; he'd bought the bike new the day before he'd started the job.

'Hi, there, Tristan. Just a couple of letters today. I'm sorry I'm late on my rounds but the bike got a puncture.'

Tristan took the letters and put his hand on Kevin's shoulder. 'You think it's about time you got a new one?' He winked.

'Eh? No fear, she's served me well all these years, plenty of life in her yet . . . just like me.' Kevin laughed and rode away.

Slipping his fingers under the seal along one of the envelopes, Tristan pulled out a bank statement. He flicked it open and pushed on the kitchen door. That's funny. Karen never normally locked the door. He searched in his pocket for the house keys and opened the door while squinting at the statement. Where were his reading glasses?

'Karen, it's me! Thought we could spend an hour together before afternoon surgery!' he shouted, hanging his coat on a peg in the hall and retrieving his glasses. 'Karen, are you upstairs?' No answer. No sound of the kids playing either. All of a sudden he remembered that Karen had told him that the children were going to Jenny's for a few hours . . . again, while she had a bit of 'me time'. Did she ever have anything else lately?

Walking into the kitchen and then further afield, he gave a cursory glance at the statement but was more concerned with the fact that Karen wasn't in the kitchen, playroom, living room, dining room or conservatory. *Calm down Tristan, she's probably upstairs in the bathroom; she wouldn't have gone out in her state, would she?*

Three steps up the stairs he stopped dead and re-read a line about halfway down the page . . . *27 September – K Ainsworth – payment – £2,000.* Two thousand pounds? What the hell? Tristan felt his fingers tightening on the banister as he realised that was the day that Harold Jackson said he saw Karen in the bank and she'd been short with him. She withdrew two thousand bloody pounds without telling him? 'Karen, are you up there?' Racing up the stairs he flung open all the doors along the corridor. No. Karen wasn't up there.

Tristan walked slowly downstairs, the statement scrunched up in his hand, his face set in anger. So, she dumps the kids on Jenny, no, in fact, *actually* gets Jenny who is pregnant and often tired, to collect them, while she – his poor 'agoraphobic' wife – swans off somewhere the moment Jenny drives away. *And where is she swanning to, Tristan, eh?*

'Hi, Jen, it's Tristan. What time are you bringing the kids back?' He gripped the phone so hard his knuckles were white as he paced around the ground floor.

'Um . . . about two Karen said. Why, is there something wrong?'

'And what time did you pick them up?'

'Twelve-thirty. What's up, Tristan?'

Tristan was torn between telling Jenny everything, including the fact that Karen wasn't home, or keeping the whole thing to himself. Karen and Jenny were very close; perhaps Jenny knew things that he didn't. He sighed. 'Nothing, really. I'm just a bit concerned that she's taking advantage, that's all.'

'Oh, I love having them, Tris. They are such a joy and it's good practice . . . besides with Karen like she is . . .'

Tristan stopped pacing. 'Yeah, do you think she's getting worse, Jen?'

'I'm not sure. She certainly isn't getting any better.'

Tristan thought she sounded genuinely concerned,

not cagey or anything. Still, he didn't want to risk it.

'Such a bloody shame when everything seemed to be going well, isn't it?'

Tristan sat down at the kitchen table and ran his fingers through his hair. 'You can say that again. Okay, well let me know if the kids get too much and, Jen, let me know if there's anything about Karen that worries you. I mean more than normal.'

'Yes, of course. And you look after yourself, okay?'

'Yeah, I will. Bye.'

Tristan glanced at the kitchen clock – 1.00 p.m., an hour before Jen brought the kids back. His first appointment was 2.15. Should he just wait and confront Karen? Surely she'd come back at least fifteen minutes before two? His eyes fell on a discarded teddy on the floor by the cooker and he felt a sudden empathy with it. You and me both, eh, Ted?

This marriage was turning into a re-run of his mum and dad's. Dad waiting at home wondering where his 'girl about town' wife was, money going missing from the bank, Tristan and his sister Emma last on the list. Tristan shook himself and blew out a sigh of frustration. No, his marriage wasn't like that at all. His mother had been a first-rate bitch, he didn't think that she'd ever actually loved his dad, or her children come to think of it.

170

Karen on the other hand was a fantastic mother and wife until this illness had grabbed hold of her. But if she was so ill, how could she have gone out? Tristan ran water into the kettle and stared out of the window down the drive and to the fields beyond. Perhaps it wasn't agoraphobia, he surmised. Perhaps it was full-blown depression and she was stealing the tablets from him because she felt ashamed to admit it or something?

Whatever it was, he should damned well stop grizzling and wait it out. No confrontation, no awkward questions. If she was hiding something like an affair it would come out sooner or later anyway. And the money? Who knew, but he resolved to just monitor the whole situation for a while. If he panicked, pushed her over the edge, she might leave and that would be that.

His mother's face surfaced against the low cloud over the field opposite: red lipstick, pencilled on eyebrows, a cloud of peroxide hair, and a wild look in her green eyes. That cow was still making waves from beyond the grave. It was textbook really. Because of her he was so dammed insecure about his looks, his self-worth and now he imagined that Karen was off with someone else, because why in the world would such a beauty want such a poor sap as him for a husband? God, it was all too pathetic really. Tristan knew all the answers, had done a spot of self-psychoanalysis from time to time, so why couldn't he just set the past aside instead of keep letting his mother chuck

171

a spanner in the works? Well, she wouldn't win. The past was the past, but Karen was his future. Tristan just hoped with all his heart that he could keep her in it.

CHAPTER 22

It had to be methadone today, or nothing. Last week when Karen had met the Bitch she had told her that if it was nothing, Bitch would drop the bomb and Karen's life would go up in flames. The flames were already licking around the feet of her marriage. She'd been so horrible to Tristan lately, but over the last few days he'd been even nicer to her than normal and much nicer than she deserved. After that awful show-down about the antidepressants, he'd stopped challenging her about anything, anything at all. And this morning when he'd gone off to work he'd told her that he loved her and if she had any worries, no matter how small, she mustn't be afraid to tell him. If only.

The last two and a half weeks since Bitch had laid down her demands in the church kitchen had been unbearable. Unbearable in general because of what Karen had been tasked with, and, of course, the consequences if she didn't, and unbearable specific-ally because she was at the beck and call of Bitch twenty-four-seven.

This terrible situation had come about because

173

Bitch had taken to posting nasty little notes through her door. Sometimes there were two, sometimes three notes a day. Karen had felt her stomach roll when she realised that Bitch must be watching the house to see if Tris's car was gone and then sneaking up to the letter box. The content of the notes were taunts, threats – obviously just plain bullying for fun.

Of course Karen could have blocked up the letter box, and asked Kevin the postman to ring the bell, deliver to her personally. He would probably just do it without question knowing him, but what would be the point? Bitch would find another way to hound her and at least she hadn't followed through her threat of coming to the house to tell Tris . . . yet.

The study door swung slowly open and Karen stepped through it with a heart as heavy as her footsteps. Moving to the desk, she grasped the handle on the deep drawer, pulled it open and stared at the safe. A shudder rippled through her whole body. What the hell had she become?

She remembered a few weeks ago when Tristan had come back with the kids, a bunch of flowers in his hand, that she'd sworn to herself that she'd sort Bitch out whatever it took. It had taken too much already. Deception, blatant lies, what amounted to theft of their savings, self-loathing to the extent that she felt so unworthy of Tristan's touch that she'd moved out of their room. Supplying antidepressants for sale on the streets . . . and now the *pièce de résistance* – drum roll – the supplying of dangerous drugs with the possibility that if they were used carelessly, they could be fatal.

Karen watched her trembling fingers hover above the tiny number pad on the top of the safe. Yesterday when she'd taken more antidepressants, she'd seen the methadone and couldn't believe her luck. There hadn't been any for the last two weeks. That she had been happy to find controlled drugs in her husband's medical store had made her stomach roll. But what if they weren't there now? What if Tristan had put them in his bag when he went to work that morning? Bitch would wait no longer, she'd made that perfectly clear in her last note.

Karen slipped her hand into her jeans pocket, pulled out the folded paper. *Tomorrow at the lane, same time as usual and if it's not meth, Melody, then face the music. Get it? Melody and music? I should be on the stage. I remember the time when you were. Do you remember when you were a vile, fat and ugly whale? God, we had such fun humiliating the shit out of you. Anyway, seriously, your time is up. I told you last time we met, I'm sick of this charade. Lots of love xx*

Not only was the woman a sadist, she was a stark staring maniac. Lots of love indeed! Karen glanced at her watch and then back at the safe. Jenny would be back with the kids in just over an hour and she needed to get the damned things and go. If they caused Bitch's death . . . then so be it. If it was

175

her, or Karen and her family's happiness, then there was no contest. Bitch was a bad seed, always had been, always would be, no time for sentiment and human decency. Bitch had never afforded any to Karen, had she?

Without giving herself a chance to change her mind, she punched the code into the safe and opened the lid. Yep, they were still there. Relieved, yet repulsed at her action in equal measure, she grabbed the packet and quickly locked the safe. Shoving the drawer shut she turned to find Tristan staring at her from the doorway.

Tristan, open-mouthed, shook his head and leaned against the door. 'What have you taken this time, Karen?' he asked, bewildered.

Karen couldn't speak, a deep flush crept up her neck and she felt sick. What the hell was he doing home? At a loss, she decided to ask him. 'Why are you back? Are you ill?'

'I came back because I forgot my phone and I thought we could have lunch together. Us and the kids,' Tristan said in a low voice, his eyes never leaving hers. 'But as I see, they aren't here . . . again.'

Karen's flush deepened and she swallowed hard. How in God's name was she going to get out of this one? 'Er . . . I could make us lunch. There's some of that nice ham—'

'Ham? I just come in, watch you open the safe, take out some of my medical supplies and you pretend that nothing has happened?' He closed the gap between them in three strides and opened his palm. 'Hand them over, Karen. Now.'

Karen looked desperately up into her husband's cool green eyes and her heart galloped in her chest as she frantically tried to dream up a story for why she had methadone in her hand. But this time she had to admit she was beaten. And in a weird kind of way she was glad – glad that in a few minutes Tristan would know everything. She couldn't live like this anymore, lying and deceiving . . . being vile to him. Even if it meant that she'd lose everything, fourteen years of living a lie was enough. It was time to tell the truth.

She handed the packet over and took his hand and said in a tremulous voice, 'Let's go and sit in the conservatory. It will take a while to explain.'

Tristan glanced at the packet and the colour drained from his face, but he allowed himself to be led to the comfy green leather sofa that they had often sat on, reading a story to the children, or just gazing down over the lovely garden filled with flowers. Karen surreally noted that the lavender bushes needed a trim and then shook her head. Would she ever work in that garden again?

'For God's sake, tell me what's going on? Why do you need these?' Tristan asked, his face ashen, his fingers trembling as he placed the methadone on the cushion between them.

'They aren't for me. They are for someone who has been blackmailing me.'

'Blackmailing you? What? I don't understand.' Tristan shook his head and raked his hand through his hair.

'It's because of something I did when I was sixteen . . . or something my mother did to be exact. I ran away, changed my identity, and never went back.' Karen nodded at the tablets. 'The blackmailer's an addict. She recognised me a few weeks ago and threatened to tell you who I was. What I'd done.'

'But what did you do? Who *is* this woman?' Tristan looked like he was in the middle of a bad dream. His eyes were red, his hair stuck up from the constant raking of his fingers and his voice shook. 'And your mother? She died of cancer when you were in your early twenties you said. Your dad, too.'

Karen felt the bile rise in her throat when she thought of all the crap she'd been forced to tell him. She swallowed hard and exhaled. 'I lied, Tris. I have lied to everyone for the past fourteen years. My dad died of cancer when I was thirteen. My mother . . .' Karen got up and walked to the door. 'Hang on; it will be easier if I bring you something.'

Karen came back a few minutes later carrying a large book under her arm and sat down next to Tristan. She placed a tender kiss on his lips and the book on his lap. 'I have been keeping a journal this last year. It's how I managed to cope; I couldn't tell anyone so I told the journal. It's all in there. Read it. I'm not sure I could say it all without breaking down.'

Tristan looked at the book, gripped the edges and then looked back at his wife. He seemed reluctant to open it. Swallowing hard he said, 'So all this time you never had agoraphobia?'

'No. Well I kind of did these past few weeks because I was scared of bumping into her. But long term, no, I never had it. I put the medication you prescribed me for it in the bin or down the loo. I'm so sorry for deceiving you, but I just made it all up because I was scared to go out and about around here . . .' She tossed her head and gave a hollow laugh. 'I was scared I'd be recognised being so close to home, and I was right.'

'But you're from Swindon?' Tristan frowned.

'Nope. I'm from Penarthry.'

'Penarthry? But that's only about seven miles from here.'

'Yes, that's why I made such a fuss about wanting to stay in Swindon.' Karen wiped a tear from her cheek. 'I ached to return. I love this area as much as you, but of course I didn't dare. But then I saw how much you needed to come back, my love, and I just wanted to make you happy. Like you said, the children would have a much better life here. And in the end I thought it might be safe after so many years. I *have* changed my appearance drastically after all.'

'So you've not been having an affair?' Tristan said almost to himself, his face registering a mixture of relief and bewilderment.

Karen frowned. Where had he got that ludicrous

idea? 'An affair? No, of course not. I'd never do that to you. I love you more than life.'

'Damn it, Karen. If you did, you wouldn't have lied to me!' Tristan snapped. 'Have you any idea how *I've* been feeling lately? The sneaking off in the night, the mood swings, then the drugs went missing.' He picked up the methadone and threw it at the wall. 'Jesus, I have been going out of my mind.' And then seeing the hurt in her eyes whispered, 'For God's sake, just tell me what you ran away from?'

Karen swallowed hard. 'Read the journal, Tris.'

Tristan looked back at the book. He was silent for a while and then he said, 'I'm scared to. I'm scared that when I open this, our whole lives will never be the same.'

Karen nodded, letting more tears that she'd been holding back flood down her face. 'So am I, my darling. So am I.'

CHAPTER 23

Tristan slipped his finger under the front cover of the journal. Just before he turned to the first page Karen said, 'The last journal entry will explain everything, but you have to read it all to understand.'

He nodded, flipped to the first page and read; *I folded my clothes neatly and placed them with the precision of a drill-sergeant on a flat rock by the shore. I positioned the letter in its blue envelope carefully on top and weighted it down with a round white pebble. Standing before the moonlit water, I felt the caress of the breeze like salt kisses over my naked skin.*

Five minutes later at the end of the second entry, he dashed moisture from his eyes and drew Karen roughly into his arms. 'Oh, my poor, poor baby, what must you have been going through to try and take your own life?'

Karen hugged him back and then passed him a tissue and blew her nose. 'Read on, I'll get us a cup of tea.'

Tristan shook his head. 'Make it a brandy.'

★   ★   ★

Two brandies later and all but the last entry left to read, Tristan, emotionally drained, laid his head on the back of the sofa, closed his eyes and said thickly, 'Jesus, Karen. What a fucking awful life you had. I thought my mother was a grade A bitch, but yours, yours was a . . . a demon!' He suddenly sat upright and looked at her. 'And the girl who bullied you in school, this Andrea, is she the one who's blackmailing you?'

Karen gave him a sad little smile. 'You are clever. Yes, got it in one. When I first saw her I couldn't believe it was her, Andrea Stanton. She had been really stunning at school, long dark shiny hair, pearl white teeth and bright sparkling eyes. Now she looks at least fifty, grey hair . . . and can you believe that *she* blames *me* for getting her chucked out of school and she reckons I ruined her life?' Karen stood up and opened the conservatory door to get some air.

'She was the one who orchestrated my humiliation at the World War II memorial concert and Mrs Goodhale led an investigation and found her out. Old Goodhale was beside herself with fury and was determined to catch those to blame. I told her that I thought I recognised Andrea's voice when the order came to pour water on me from above. Mrs Goodhale questioned her and her mob, and scared that they would get in serious trouble, they dobbed Andrea in. She was permanently excluded as she had a string of bullying offences against lots of other kids besides me. The night of the concert was the last nail in her coffin.'

'But it was all *her* fault. Is the stupid cow delusional or something?'

'Yes, Tris, I seriously think she might be.' Karen turned to look at him. 'She said she became a bum and got into drugs and prostitution, her parents disowned her – and she blames me for all of it. I think she needs serious help with the drugs and everything else judging by her behaviour. Her nasty notes have been awful this past week.'

'She's been sending you notes?' Tristan said aghast.

Karen nodded. 'Yes. She must have been watching the house to make sure you weren't here, evil cow.'

'Bloody hell. Beats me how Jenny and Michael allowed her to work for them, her being so unstable and obviously an addict.'

'Oh, I don't think they know. She's a cunning one is Andrea. When Graham Proctor came and caught us the other day, she hid the needle marks and lied her head off very convincingly. Scared me how good she was at . . .' Karen's voice trailed off. She was a fine one to talk about lying, wasn't she?

'What were you doing – for Graham to catch you, I mean?'

Karen looked away. She'd forgotten that Tristan didn't know about the missing money. She'd looked for the bank statement every morning but for some reason it was overdue. She would feel better telling him all about that when he'd read the last journal entry. Then he'd see that she'd no option but to go behind his back with the money, with everything. 'I'll tell you more when you've read the last entry. Please read it, Tris; just let's get it over with.' She came back to sit beside him and placed her hand on his arm.

Tristan nodded, took a deep breath and looked back down at the journal on his lap.

When my mother found out about what had happened to me at the concert, she'd laughed until she'd cried. She said this was nearly as good as the naked photos incident and she'd wished she'd been there to see it. Mother, of course, hadn't known about the concert because I hadn't told her. But she'd found out what had happened and now she taunted me with it every day for the last two weeks that I lived in Penarthry. 'Here comes the Singing Whale!' She'd say, or 'There she blows!' every time I walked in the door. I didn't let her see that it bothered me, just ignored her and carried on, but it did bother me. After all she'd done to me, I shouldn't have been surprised, but I was. It really hurt to be honest. She was my mother, for God's sake, my mother, but just so unbelievably cruel.

Nothing seemed to work anymore. I had tried to turn my life around and get fit and then the photo incident happened. Then I galvanised my resolve again and I tried to boost my confidence, show off my singing voice and please Mrs Goodhale, and was just humiliated in return. I started to think I would be better off dead. At least all the shit would end and I might see Dad again, if I was lucky.

Mother's temper seemed to be getting worse, too, and so did her alcohol abuse. The men she brought home lasted a couple of weeks and then they'd bugger off, fed up with her moods. But they were hardly step-dad of the year material anyway, mostly drunks like her and just after an easy lay and a laugh. Trouble was, Mother stopped being a laugh early on in her relationships and the whole thing usually ended in a showdown, sometimes spilling out into the street with the bloke getting a torrent of abuse and a shoe smacked around the head. Once I'd seen her set about a man with a frying pan. She was starting to lose her looks too. The cigarettes and alcohol did nothing for her skin and at forty-two she looked more like fifty-two.

The afternoon before the night that I went down to the sea to end it all, she'd come in from the shops and had the usual go at me for being too fat, not tidying up or just breathing too loud. I can't actually remember what it was about now. I was sorting through the remaining few records left in Dad's collection and just let her crap wash over my head.

All of a sudden I felt material tightening around my neck and the stench of her gin-soaked breath in my nostrils. 'Pay attention to me, you fat whore!' she shrieked in my ear and drove her knee into my back as I tugged at the brightly coloured scarf that she was trying to strangle me with.

185

As I struggled, I felt the fury surging up from my depths because that scarf had been a birthday present to me from Dad, the last thing he'd ever bought me. Perhaps that's why she used it, perhaps she didn't even remember, who knew? But it felt like she'd defiled his memory and something snapped inside me. I pushed back with all my strength and with my weight behind it I soon sent her flying with me on top of her.

Mother yelled like a mad woman and hurled all sorts of obscenities at me, mostly she screamed to be let up, but I was having none of it. I turned around and pinned her to the ground as you would a nasty flailing poisonous bug, and put my face an inch from hers. 'I hate you and wish you were dead!' I bellowed, spraying my spit all over her horrified face. 'You are a sorry excuse for a mother, and you're the whore, a filthy alcoholic WHORE.'

She wriggled under me but to no avail. 'How dare you talk to me like this! I'll kick you out, you fat cow!' Her red lipstick had smudged across her nose, one of her earrings had broken and her hair was all over her face. And then I saw real fear in her eyes for the first time ever. Shit, she was scared of me . . . that felt good, really good.

I laughed in her face and spat, 'Now I've finished my exams I'm getting a job and will be leaving anyway, so I'll kick myself out. I never want to see your evil face again!' I moved to the side and let her up.

She pulled herself shakily to her feet with the back

of a dining room chair and turned to face me, her eyes bright with fury. 'You just made one fucking ginormous mistake you rancid heap of blubber.' She pointed a black nail-polished finger at me. 'You'll be sorry you crossed me . . . oh, yes, very sorry.'

I stared back and smiled as if I didn't care, though my heart was hammering and I felt like I was going to faint. She stomped out and a few minutes later I heard the back door slam. I assumed she'd gone to the pub, that's what she always did when she was angry, or anytime really. As I heard her high heels click-clack past the window, the smile slid off my face like butter from hot toast. She meant what she said. She would get her revenge and now it was my turn to be scared.

Mother made good her threat much quicker than I could have imagined. I thought she'd wait a while as she favoured the saying 'revenge is best served cold', but it turned out she wanted hers boiling hot that night.

I'd gone to bed around ten and because of what had happened I tossed and turned anxiously for a few hours. The last time I looked at the clock it was midnight and Mother still wasn't home. I hoped she'd met some new wino and wouldn't come back at all.

Unlucky for me though she did come back, and the first I knew about it was when I heard her shrieking with laughter in her bedroom along the corridor and a man's rough voice telling her to get her clothes off. He sounded foreign, a Greek or

Italian sailor I guessed. She'd had a few of those. Then I heard the slap of a hand on flesh and my mother yelling at him to spank her harder. I shuddered and put my pillow around my head but couldn't drown them out completely, so I grabbed the pillow and blanket and snuck downstairs to sleep on the settee.

I eventually drifted off, only to be woken a few hours later by sharp cold steel pressed against my windpipe. The sitting room curtains were open and the moon's silver beam lit up Mother's manic face and a kitchen knife. 'Don't move. I've had a drink and my hands are shaking,' she snarled. But at that moment, her voice sounded sober, no trace of a slur. She sat on the side of the settee and leaned over me.

I stared wide-eyed at her, but tried to swallow my panic, and in doing so the knife pressed harder against my throat. I felt a warm trickle of liquid slide down my neck into the pillow. I couldn't believe it. My God, she'd actually drawn blood! My instinct was to grab the knife and shove her off, but I thought I might not be able to do it in time. The pressure she was putting on the knife . . . one more push and my throat would be pierced through. 'Why are you doing this?' I managed, now unable to hide my terror.

She snorted and shook her head. 'Because of what you did earlier, you dumb mare. I told you you'd be sorry and I think you are . . . aren't you?' She increased the pressure slightly and I felt more blood ooze down my neck.

'Yes, I'm sorry, please . . . please stop, Mum!'

A flicker of hesitation passed across her murderous eyes and then she shook her head again. 'No, I've had enough of you, always hated you really since the day you were born. I gave you life and now . . . now I'm going to take it away,' she said in a faraway voice, as if she were reciting a line from a play. Her lips curled back from her teeth, hate shone from her eyes in the moonlight and snarling like a rabid dog she pushed the knife again.

I grabbed her hand in both of mine, sat up and pushed her away with all my strength, which even at that angle was quite considerable with my weight behind it. I felt a slight resistance under my hand, heard a sharp intake of breath and then a dull thump as my mother fell to the floor at the side of the settee.

I jumped up and knelt by her. The knife was buried up to its hilt in her chest and her breathing was laboured and ragged. With a shaking hand I flicked on the table lamp and in the yellow pool of light cast across her body, I could see a crimson pool spreading along the yellow and blue patchwork rug like some macabre sunset.

'Mother . . . Mum!' I yelled, my fingers fluttering above the knife that she still clasped tightly in her hand. Something told me not to touch it and instead I touched her face, her ashen face contorted in pain. 'Mum. Please, God, I didn't mean it . . . but you were hurting me so bad . . . Mum!' Her eyes opened and held mine for a few seconds as her life seeped away. I saw no remorse or regret, just hatred and defiance.

★   ★   ★

189

After that, I just felt like I was acting on some weird orders from within, like I was on autopilot. I went back up to my room, got dressed, wrote a note about how I was worthless, and that I couldn't cope anymore and then I left the house for the last time and went to the beach. I went to the arms of the ocean and hoped to wake up somewhere beyond the sea, like the old song my Dad used to love. I hoped he'd be waiting for me there, too. But, of course, it turned out that life had other plans for me.

And now every day I thank God for my precious husband and children. The happiness they bring me sometimes swells my heart so full that I think it might burst. I am luckier than I have any right to be, but one day I fear it will all end. I worry more now that I have come back to Cornwall. But I ached to come home, and so did Tris. How could I deprive him and the children of living in such a beautiful place? My heart and soul is here, my dad's spirit is here. I feel him down by the shore; hear his laughter on the wind.

And I look so different now. I keep telling myself that nobody from the past would recognise me. But mostly it's no good. There's always a nagging voice that makes me look over my shoulder, makes me lie to my lovely Tris. Makes me pretend to have a debilitating condition that I wouldn't wish on my worst enemy, well, I would wish it on Andrea, of course. I wonder where she is now? Somewhere hot and unlikely to freeze over I hope.

My children have suffered too. They have missed

out on so much since the move because Mummy doesn't like to leave the house. But now these past weeks, getting to sing again with the choir and meeting lovely Jenny, my life feels like it might just be turning a corner. Perhaps I can live a normal life . . . if I'm careful. I so wish I could tell Tristan, take him into my confidence, but that is impossible. I couldn't risk losing him and my babies. I couldn't BEAR it if it ended. I love them all more than life itself.

One thing is for damned sure, if it does all end, my mother will be laughing up a storm in her fiery hell.

Tristan, tears streaming down his cheeks, let the journal slip from his fingers onto the floor and folded Karen into his arms. Holding each other tight they rocked back and forth, sobbing like children. Tristan, the first to regain some composure, whispered into her ear, 'My poor, poor love. You were carrying a burden like this for so long . . . and all by yourself.' He placed his hands on her shoulders and looked into her eyes. 'You will never be alone again, do you hear me? We'll sort all this out somehow . . . some way, okay?'

Karen couldn't believe what she was hearing. 'So, you don't hate me for what I did, and for lying and deceiving you all these years?' she asked, wiping her face and trying to quell the shuddering sobs wracking her body.

'Hate you? I think you've experienced enough

hate in your early years to last a lifetime. You only defended yourself; anyone would have done the same. You were bullied at home *and* school, you tried to kill yourself . . . the only real love you ever had was from your dad, and that ended too soon, and I guess, Bob and Maureen.' He shook his head in disbelief. 'I just feel so sorry that I couldn't have been there for you. Sorry you felt you couldn't come to me.' Tristan swallowed hard and wiped fresh tears from her cheeks.

Karen sighed and looked away. 'You are so kind, Tris, so kind. I don't deserve you . . . and I'm a thief too. I took the drugs and money from our account and—'

'Oh, I know about that. It really isn't important anymore. Nothing is important in the light of what I've just read, apart from us coming up with a plan to sort out Andrea,' Tristan said, jumping up and patting his pockets.

'You knew about the money? But how?'

'Statement came last week,' he said absently. 'Have you seen my phone? I need to phone the surgery, tell them I've come down with a tummy bug or something. What time do you have to meet Andrea?'

Karen felt like she was in a dream, everything seemed foggy, unreal, slowed down. She looked at the clock. 'Um, in ten minutes . . . then Jenny will be back soon with Sebastian and Bella.' She put a hand to her mouth when she realised they were fast running out of time.

'Right, I'll ring the surgery and then I'll ring Jenny, ask her if she'd mind hanging on to them for a while as you are really down this afternoon and I'm here to talk you through it. Then we'll go and meet this Andrea and sort her out,' Tristan said, spying his phone on the arm of the chair opposite.

Karen noted that he'd assumed control, a spark of determination glowing bright in his green eyes. She felt so much safer and relieved beyond measure that he'd taken the truth in the way he had. It was beyond her wildest dreams that he'd accepted her grisly past and loved her just the same as always.

Karen was in no doubt that there would be many more questions later, but for now, incredibly, her darling Tristan was on board her sinking ship and taking control of the wheel. For the first time in weeks she dared to hope that her battered sails would once more be filled with a gentle breeze and she'd be blown to a safe harbour.

CHAPTER 24

In the bathroom Karen splashed cold water on her red puffy eyes, and worried about how Bitch, no . . . how Andrea would take the news. She could allow the name Andrea now, because she had lost some of her terror as soon as Tris knew. Tristan's plan to meet her head on and call her bluff sounded plausible, but she still worried that Andrea would just go to the police if she couldn't blackmail anything more from them. Tristan, however, seemed convinced that she'd just back down when faced with the fact that he knew everything about the past.

He reckoned that they'd tell her to do her worst or leave them alone. He also suggested that they say they'd tell Jenny and Michael about her drug habit, that she'd tried to get Karen to help her get drugs and that she was a pusher, too. Andrea would then lose her job and thereby her livelihood. But Karen wondered if Andrea really cared about her job, she *had* seemed to become more and more unstable, even in the short time she had known her.

Downstairs again, Karen found Tristan in the kitchen with his eyes closed drinking orange juice from the carton. She normally told him off for this, but of course she didn't now. In fact right there and then she promised herself that she'd never pick him up for petty things ever again. After the way he'd stuck by her, he could do whatever he liked. While he still looked strong and resolute, she did notice tension and worry in his handsome face.

He opened his eyes and saw her watching him. He wiped his mouth on the back of his hand and pointed to the carton. 'Want a quick drink?' Karen shook her head. 'We'd better get off, pronto,' he said, putting the juice back in the fridge.

'Tris, what if she goes to the police? What if they say that they think I killed my mother, just like Andrea said . . . not in self-defence, but in anger . . . and then, because I was guilty, I tried to kill myself?'

He turned from the fridge and looked at her, his eyes calm and steady. 'As I said, I doubt that she will, but if she does, then you just tell them what happened. They would have a hard time proving it after all these years. Your prints would be on the knife anyway – it was a kitchen knife in everyday use.' He smiled at her, picked up his car keys and slipped his arm around her shoulders. 'I know you said you didn't tell the teachers, but did anyone else know about the years of abuse from your mother?'

Karen shook her head. 'No. I kept it all to myself. Why?'

'I guess that's a good thing in these circumstances. If it was known that your mother systematically abused you, it could look like you had eventually snapped and murdered her.'

'Hmm, but what about me running away, changing my identity, that looks bad doesn't it? Bob and Maureen got me false birth certificates and stuff; I could be done for that, couldn't I?' Karen shuddered at the thought of evidence piling up against her.

Tristan frowned and hugged her. 'What happened to them?'

'They went to visit their eldest son in Australia a few years ago, after I left them. They loved it so much they emigrated there.'

Tristan sighed into her hair. 'Look, you were a child; they're the ones who would get done. Don't get in a pickle; let's just take one step at a time.'

Just as they reached the front door, the doorbell rang. Karen nearly went into orbit her nerves being stretched to breaking point. She looked wild-eyed at Tristan. 'What if it's her?' she hissed.

Tristan looked back and set his jaw. 'Go back into the kitchen and wait,' he whispered.

In the kitchen Karen pushed the door closed behind her, but left it open just a crack. Peeping through it, she saw Tristan open the front door and her heart lifted a little upon seeing that it wasn't Andrea on the doorstep, but sank a little when she realised that it would take a while to get rid of this very unwelcome visitor. She glanced at the kitchen clock, shit they should be there by now!

'Linda, you okay?' Tristan asked, strain evident in his voice.

'Yeah, I'm feeling a bit better this week. Just passing and thought I'd pop in and see Karen. I didn't realise you'd be home. You should be at the surgery, shouldn't you?'

Behind the door Karen rolled her eyes. *Oh, please. Tristan's car is parked in the drive; you obviously knew he must be in, Linda.*

'I should be, but Karen's a bit down this afternoon. I'm staying home so we can have a chat . . . so it's not really a good time, Linda.' Tristan smiled, starting to close the door.

'Oh, sorry to hear that. I could look after the children if you like, I'm not doing anything.'

For goodness sake, take the hint. Karen blew heavily down her nose. They had to get going!

'No, they are with Jenny at the mo. I just phoned and asked her to keep them for the rest of the afternoon, so we're sorted, but thanks for asking. See you later.' Tristan started to close the door again.

'Okay, I'll hold you to that.' Linda grinned and turned away.

Karen dashed out of the kitchen as soon as the door was shut behind Linda. 'Damn woman, we are going to be so late now. And we can't just rush out in case she sees us!'

Tristan put his hands on her shoulders. 'Calm down. We'll give Linda a few minutes and then go. She'll be long gone by then, stop worrying.'

Linda crept along the path by the side of the house, looking furtively over her shoulder. Tristan had looked happy to see her but decidedly shifty, and she was damned sure she was going to find out why. Perhaps he and Karen had had a blazing row; perhaps their relationship was on the rocks. Linda certainly hoped it was. She'd seen how Karen bossed poor Tris about. Her heart gave a back flip; she'd also seen how he'd given her the eye, particularly on that day she'd spent with all of them on the beach a few weeks ago.

Then everything had gone tits up. Tristan said they were seeing too much of her and that she might be better with another doctor. Linda guessed that madam had put her foot down and become 'ill' again. She looked about as ill as a butcher's dog to her. And Karen had definitely become stand-offish after they'd got back from the beach. Perhaps she'd noticed that Tristan was attracted to her.

Part of Linda felt guilty for having these feelings about another woman's husband. After all, hadn't another woman done the dirty on her recently? Another woman had cast her evil net over Luke and carried him away. And Karen had saved her bloody life too. There was no way she should be even contemplating trying to take Tristan. But then, she couldn't help her feelings, could she?

At first Linda had assumed the attraction between them was all bound up in the fact that Tristan was her doctor and their feelings were just misplaced, that maybe he cared, but just in a paternal, doctorly way. But as time went on, she knew it was more than that. He'd admit it too, soon, she could feel it. The way he'd just smiled at her and said 'see you later' spoke volumes.

Linda flattened her back to the wall and peeped around the corner of the house. She could see the conservatory. It looked empty. They had often sat in there when Linda had visited, but perhaps they were chatting in the kitchen. How she'd love to hear them at each other's throats.

Crouching low she scuttled commando-style around the conservatory and peered quickly in at the side of the kitchen window. Nope that was empty too. Damn, that meant they were probably in the living room at the other side of the house. She wouldn't be able to eavesdrop there, as they'd be able to see her coming from beyond the patio doors.

Linda's head whipped round. Were her ears deceiving her? Scurrying back the way she'd come, she peered round the house to the front driveway and yes, sure enough, it was a car engine she'd heard start up. Tristan's car. The front door slammed and she saw Karen run to the car, get in and peck Tristan on the cheek. Tristan then drove the car at some speed out of the gates and away down the lane.

A hundred thoughts tumbled around Linda's head. If Karen was ill, how the hell could she go out in the car? Tristan had told her the other day how his wife was now practically a recluse. Yeah, looks like it! And why had they farmed the kids out to Jenny again? Andrea Stanton had told Linda the other day that they were always round at the vicarage.

Also, if Tristan had had to abandon his poor patients and have the afternoon off to talk to his poor wife, why did she look like she was on some important mission or other, dashing like a bat out of hell from the house? And why did he then drive off as if the dogs were after them?

Linda turned the enigma over in her mind on a loop until she reached the lane. Then she stood still and felt the heat of humiliation flare up her body. She had no answer for why Karen, apparently now back in the grip of agoraphobia, had sprinted out of her house without so much as a backward glance just now, but she did have an answer for why Tristan hadn't allowed Linda in.

Now she thought about it properly, it suddenly hit her that she'd been kidding herself. Why hadn't she seen it before? The look he'd given her when he'd opened the door wasn't one of pleasant surprise but one of irritation, annoyance even. He wasn't attracted to her at all; he just clearly wanted to be rid of her so that he could take madam out somewhere. He'd told her a barefaced lie . . . her lovely caring Tris obviously didn't care one jot, and he felt less lovely with every passing second.

Linda kicked a stone along the lane and felt humiliation tip over into anger. She'd stood there like a stupid idiot and grinned at him like a lovesick fool, even offered to look after the kids, while he just clearly wanted her to leave. Linda swallowed angry tears and shook her head at her own stupidity. It must be the drugs she was on doing funny things to her head. But she could have sworn that he liked her . . . no, more than liked.

So, here she was, dumped again, first by Luke, now by Dr High and Bloody Mighty Tristan Ainsworth. Well, this time she'd not take it lying down. This time she had an idea that if it worked would make him suffer, him *and* his madam of a wife. It was long overdue that somebody else had a nightmare of a life – Linda was so sick of it always being her, to be honest. She kicked the stone again and set off down the lane.

CHAPTER 25

'That's right, yeah, just at the bend . . . Karen?'

The urgency in Tristan's voice eventually shook her out of her stupor. Karen had been lost in the memory of that night fourteen years ago when she'd woken to find a knife at her throat. Minutes later her mother had lain dead and Karen's life had changed forever. If only she had reacted differently. This 'if only' had played on her mind for years, but what else could she have done when her mother had a knife pressed against her throat?

There was no answer to that. Never had been, and never would be. There had only been one alternative that moonlit night when she'd been sixteen, and that had been to do nothing. But if she'd done nothing she wouldn't be sitting here in the car next to her husband whizzing down a Cornish back road. She wouldn't be sitting anywhere because she was one hundred per cent sure she would have been dead. The pressure of the knife on her throat and the look in her mother's eye told her that.

But afterwards she could have stayed and hedged her bets . . . told the police what had happened, couldn't she? But no, she'd run off to kill herself instead. In fact, why had she fought to protect herself against her mother in the first place? She could have let her kill her quickly and keenly – saved herself the bother. It was just instinct, she guessed, self-preservation was a powerful force. Nevertheless, that force had abandoned her an hour or so later when she'd stood on the shore watching the surf tickle her toes, encouraging her further.

Now, drawn back to the future and realising that Tristan was looking at her in exasperation she said, 'Sorry, Tris. I was miles away. What did you ask?'

'I said that when we get to the bend in this track there's a lay-by where she waits for your car, right?'

'Yeah, that's right. She sits in her car with the window down and waits for me to drive past. I check to see that nothing is behind me, stop beside her car, wind down my window and pass the drugs through her window, then I drive on. I just hope she's still there.' Karen looked at her watch anxiously. 'It's fifteen minutes over the time, Tris. I'm so worried that she's already left . . . perhaps even gone to the police.'

Tristan shook his head. 'There's no way she would have gone to the police, even if she's not there. She'd come to me first, see what else she could milk us for.'

As they approached the bend along the narrow

country track, the bramble Cornish hedges almost met in an arc above them and one or two thorny patches screeched along the side of the car as Tristan drove too close to the edge. In Karen's distressed state the screeches sounded like banshees from hell, out to tear them limb from limb. Perhaps her beloved mother had sent them from beyond the grave. She dug the nails of her left hand into the palm of her right. *Come on . . . stop all this weird shit and concentrate, Karen.*

A sigh of relief escaped her lungs as the car rounded the bend and she saw the battered old Fiesta belonging to Andrea parked in the lay-by. 'Thank God. Pull in behind her Tristan.'

Tristan switched off the engine and glanced at Karen. 'Okay, just let me do all the talking. Don't speak unless it can't be avoided. You'll just get upset if—'

'I'll *get* upset? That's the understatement of the millennium,' Karen snapped. She saw the hurt in Tris's eyes and gave herself a metaphorical slap. She'd snapped his head off again just after he'd been the modern day equivalent of a knight in shining armour, and just after she'd promised herself that she'd be nicer to him. When would she ever learn? She grabbed his hand and kissed the palm. 'I'm so sorry, Tris. I don't deserve you.'

'Hey, of course you do. It's no wonder you snapped, given the circumstances. Come on, let's get it over with.'

Karen took a deep breath and got out of the car.

Tristan was already walking over to the Fiesta, his hands shoved into his trouser pockets. He stopped by the driver's window and looked back at Karen still rooted to the spot and then dipped his head down to look in the window. He then stood up again and looked back at Karen, a deep furrow on his brow, raised his hands palm upwards and shrugged at her.

Karen forced her feet to move and joined him by the car, 'What, she's not there?' she whispered, inclining her head to the window. Tristan shook his head, no. 'But where on earth is she?' Karen stepped back and walked around the car looking up and down the country lane. There was neither sign nor sound of her, or anyone save them.

'Keys are in the ignition,' Tristan said.

Karen sighed. 'She can't be far then. Perhaps she was dying for a pee or something.'

Tristan turned in a circle and pointed to a copse halfway along a nearby field. 'I guess she could have gone over there. Not many other private places along here she could go, to be honest.'

Karen looked at the copse and slipped her hand into her back pocket. A shiver ran down her spine when her fingers touched the last hateful note she'd shoved in there. Stupid Andrea might be wandering the fields as high as a kite. No telling what she'd be like when she came back. She looked at Tristan. 'Well, sod her, let's go. We can't stay waiting around here or go off to the bloody copse on a wild goose chase.'

'Okay,' Tristan said taking her hand and walking back to their car. 'It can't be helped. I expect she'll come round to the house next.' He laughed humourlessly. 'It will be a nice surprise for her when she finds that I know everything.'

Out of the front windscreen the world looked wonderfully normal. A few grey-edged clouds shared the soft blue sky with a hazy sunshine and a picture postcard Cornish country road, flanked on both sides by bramble hedges and dry stone walls that framed the fields beyond. In the distance, a regiment of trees marched down and across the gentle slopes and sheep dotted the landscape here and there. The stillness of the autumn afternoon was broken only by the far away cry of a rook. Karen hugged herself. It was all far from normal though; she was being blackmailed by an evil witch. But at least now she had Tris on side and that gave her great comfort.

She pulled out the note and sighed. Tristan jumped into the car beside her and held out his hand. 'Is that one of the notes? Let's have a quick squiz.'

Karen watched her husband take the note and then she snatched it back and ripped it up. She didn't want Andrea's poisoned words to be read by such a man as Tristan. He was too good, too pure to be sullied by her vileness. 'What good would it do for you to be more upset than you need be?'

Tristan nodded and turned the key in the ignition. 'I caught sight of a name, I think, but didn't have time to make it all out before you took it back.'

Karen swallowed 'Come on, Tris. Let's just go.' As Tris sped away she felt a tidal wave of emotion wash over her.

'I think it said Melanie,' Tris said, sounding sad. 'I didn't even think about your real name earlier . . . I can't imagine you being called anything else but Karen. Was it Melanie?'

She shook her head. 'No. It was Melody. My dad picked it because of his love of music. Karen's one of my middle names.' Karen's voice caught in her throat, it had been a long time since she'd spoken that name out loud. And though she tried to stem them, tears brimmed and then spilled silently down her face.

Once home they had a cup of hot sweet tea, more on Tristan's insistence than anything, as Karen couldn't normally stomach it. He said that when a person was in shock their blood sugar drops, and he thought it would do her good. It did help, actually, and her brain started to make more sense. 'I don't get why you say I'm in shock though, love. If anyone should be in shock it's you. I mean, I *have* known about all this for fourteen years.'

'You're in shock because of all the trauma of the last few weeks with Andrea and then telling me the truth allowed the release of years of pent-up misery, sweetheart. You just sit quietly and gather your thoughts, okay?'

Karen nodded and looked into his eyes full of love and worry for her and wanted to melt into him, become physically part of him so she could take on his strength and courage. She couldn't, of course, but she knew that she'd never doubt his loyalty ever again. All these years worrying that he'd leave her if he knew the truth had been for nothing. He loved her unconditionally and that knowledge made her heart thump with joy and gratitude.

As Tristan busied himself with more tea she closed her eyes, took a few deep calming breaths and told herself that things would be okay now. Yes, they still had to deal with Andrea, but she was beginning to think that Tristan was right about her. Once bullies are stood up to they often back down, isn't that what they say?

But then her eyes fell on her bag and a note stuck out of the side compartment where she'd hidden most of them. Why she'd hidden them instead of ripping them up she didn't know. There had been a half-baked plan at the back of her mind to use them in evidence against Andrea. Ridiculous. She picked the bag up from the table and flicked through the hateful messages she'd been sent over the past weeks. The vehemence and hatred in them set her calm pulse racing again and a prickle of panic twisted her stomach. *God, no. It wouldn't be all right. Andrea wouldn't give up, would she? She wasn't your ordinary everyday type of bully, she was a demon from hell.*

Tristan came in, placed the tea down and then noticing her hopeless expression knelt beside her. He took the notes from her. 'Hey, what are you looking at those for?' He balled them up and tossed them into the fire.

'She said such horrible things, Tris,' Karen said quietly, her voice trembling.

'Yes, well she won't anymore. Not when I've had a strong word or two with her.' He stroked Karen's hair and kissed her forehead. 'And now I'm going to get changed out of my work clothes before I go and get the sprogs.'

While she waited for him to come down again, Karen made a few important decisions. Now she was thinking more rationally, she felt like a weight had been lifted. She would go with Tris to collect Sebastian and Bella from the vicarage. It had been horrible skulking indoors because she'd been scared of bumping into Andrea, she'd felt like a prisoner in her own home again. It would be so nice to walk out unafraid in the fresh air with her husband.

It would also be nice to have a chat with Jenny. Jen had been a friend above and beyond lately and she hated lying to her. Karen couldn't tell her the truth even now, but she hoped that soon their relationship could return to a more even keel, and when the baby came, Karen would do whatever she could to help her.

The choir would have to go, of course, if Michael insisted on getting them on telly, but she doubted anyone else would recognise her from the past just going about her daily business in Kelerston. She had changed so drastically it would be really bad luck if they did. She could even put the damned contact lenses back in to be on the safe side.

Yep, enough was enough. This afternoon when they collected the kids they'd tell Jenny that fears of being on telly had triggered another agoraphobic attack, even though Michael had said he'd wait to talk to her before he made a decision. They'd say that Karen hadn't been able to cope with the idea of lots of people looking at her on TV. Even though she wouldn't be able to see them, it still felt too scary. It wouldn't be fair on the others if they withdrew from the competition because of her, and so she'd decided to give up the choir. With her story straight, she felt much better. And anyway, she *had* more-or-less decided to leave the day that Michael had announced the *Voices of Angels* competition. Of course she would obviously love to be in the choir because of the way singing made her feel. But it was impossible. It was a wrench, but it had to be done.

Tristan wasn't as keen on her going with him and explaining as Karen had imagined he would be, when he came down a few minutes later. 'Look, Karen, you're an emotional wreck after telling me the truth about everything. Just let me get the terrible twosome and you stay here. There will be plenty of time to make these decisions later.'

Karen walked over and took his hand. 'But I really want to come with you and get our children, you know, like a normal family? I *need* to feel normal again instead of some crazy freak who always has the chains of the past dragging her back. Please, Tris. Coming with you this afternoon is only a small thing, but it will feel like a huge step forward for me. And we have to have some story ready for why I'm able to leave the house all of a sudden, don't we?'

Tristan sighed, pulled her towards him and kissed her softly. 'Okay, you win.'

With every step up the long gravel drive towards the vicarage, Karen felt her heart grow lighter. She took a deep breath of smoky autumn air with an undertone of ozone and smiled. Here she was, arm in arm with her husband, off to collect their children from a friend's house. Normal, ordinary, wonderful. Tristan had even agreed that they went on the beach for an hour afterwards. He was a bit concerned that his tummy bug fib might be blown, but he said he'd get round that if someone from the surgery spotted him.

Karen knew a walk on the beach as a family seemed a bit of an odd thing to do considering the hellish day they'd had, and that they should be at home comforting each other, but in her heart she felt that this was totally the right thing to do. She had spent too many days hiding from her past. Some fresh sea air, feeling the sand between her toes and hearing her children's laughter was just what she needed.

Tristan knocked on the door and smiled at Karen. 'You okay?'

'I'm fine. Stop fussing.'

Jenny opened the door, her face full of surprise when she saw Karen. 'Hey there . . . wow. I didn't expect to see you out and about!' Jenny stepped forward and enveloped Karen in a warm embrace. 'Come in, come in!'

Once inside, Jenny led them into the living room.

'I can't believe how much I have missed seeing this lovely room, Jen,' Karen said, looking out of the huge picture window to the sea beyond.

'I can't believe how much I have missed seeing you in it!' Jenny laughed. 'Now, can I get you both a cuppa? Sit down, for goodness sake, you know we don't stand on ceremony in this house.'

'No thanks, Jen,' Karen said, sitting down. 'I just want to tell you why I had my attack and what I've decided, before I lose my nerve.'

A small frown creased Jenny's brow and she sat by Karen and listened without interruption. Afterwards she heaved a sigh and said, 'I'm so sorry, love. Michael has a lot to answer for. He's just such a big kid, likes to surprise people, make them happy. It normally works but sometimes it can have the opposite effect.' Jenny folded her arms and looked earnestly at them both. 'I could get him to take the choir out of the running?'

Karen shook her head. 'No way! As I said before,

that wouldn't be fair on everyone else. No, I'm quite resigned to it. And who knows, I might rejoin the choir after they've been on telly!'

'It's doubtful they will make it on the show if you're not singing, but don't you worry about that. Your state of mind is the most important thing.' Jenny clasped both of Karen's hands in hers and her eyes shone bright with tears.

Karen welled up in return and she thanked her lucky stars for such a caring friend.

'Right, I'll get the children shall I, while you two have a quick chat? Are they with Michael in the garden?' Tris asked, looking out of the window.

Jenny nodded and laughed. 'Last time I saw them they had a bit of string round his neck leading him around and he was pretending to be a dog.'

'He'll be a great dad, Jen,' Karen said with a smile, as Tristan went to find them.

The children were having such a good time that Karen and Tristan agreed to stay for supper. Jenny's curries were legendary and Karen's mouth was already watering at the piquant aromas wafting from the kitchen.

'This is more like it, eh?' Tristan whispered in her ear, as they snuggled cosily on the sofa.

'Um, I think you could safely say that, hon.' She kissed him lovingly on the lips.

'Ooh, get a room, you two,' Michael said, with a laugh. Then the doorbell rang and he went to answer it.

A few minutes later the atmosphere changed as a serious looking man in a suit and a young policewoman followed Michael back into the room.

Michael looked shaken and guided his wife to a chair. 'I think you'd better sit down, Jen.'

Karen caught his eye and clutched Tristan's arm. What had the police told him?

Michael took a deep breath. 'Bad news, I'm afraid. Andrea Stanton, the woman who helps out round our church was found dead in a farmer's field earlier today. It seems that she was a heroin addict,' he finished, bewildered.

'Oh my God!' Jenny cried, the colour draining from her face. 'That is just terrible.'

Karen's rationality went into free fall and every instinct told her to run. She jumped up, but restricted by panic, her lungs refused to take in enough air and the floor moved under her feet. She sat back down again with a thud. Tristan pulled her to him and clasped his arm reassuringly around her shoulders.

The man in the suit stepped forward and held up a badge. He was in his mid-thirties, tall, dark brown closely cropped hair, sympathetic grey eyes, his tone kind, but professional. 'DCI Buchanan, sorry to bring such shocking news to you all, but does anyone here have any information that might be helpful concerning Ms Stanton?'

Karen shook her head and then looked away focusing on a red truck that Sebastian was pushing round the rug, while her heart thumped in her ears and the words *OhmyGodohmyGod* ran around her head on a continuous loop. She felt totally removed from herself. Actors droned on around her as if she was watching some macabre drawing room scene from a play. Michael asked Jenny if she'd had any idea that Stanton was into drugs and Jenny shook her head, tearfully explaining that once or twice Andrea had been very moody but that she'd never suspected drugs.

Buchanan explained that there were no suspicious circumstances apparently. Andrea had been found by a farmer driving along his field in his tractor. Then the policewoman asked a few more questions, and afterwards DCI Buchanan suggested that she make everyone tea. Tea? If it weren't so tragic Karen would have laughed out loud. In fact little bubbles of hysteria kept rising up just under the surface and it was taking all her efforts to keep them there.

Thankfully nobody wanted tea and the police left. The Ainsworth family followed them as soon as was polite after supper. God knew how Karen and Tristan managed to get through it, pretending they knew nothing about anything. Apparently Buchanan had told Michael that Andrea's arm was like a pincushion due to years of abuse. Karen had feigned shock and surprise, all the while dabbing at Sebastian's mouth or helping Bella with her drink. She couldn't look Tris in the eye. The curry tasted like cotton wool in Karen's mouth and wasn't easy to force past the guilt blocking

215

her throat. Of course she wanted to see the back of Andrea, but not like this. *Please not like this.*

Later at home, Tristan looked at his wife's face in the lamplight, eyes closed, mouth set, pale and still as a statue as she sat on the end of the sofa in the living room. Her whole body seemed to be on alert waiting for something . . . his poor love, his poor wife. Wife? Of course she was obviously still his wife, but earlier that day he'd found out that his Karen had started out as somebody else, a Melody somebody. She hadn't yet told him her previous surname . . . did he really know her at all?

Yes, of course he loved her, perhaps more than ever after learning the horrors she'd suffered, but in a way it was like looking at a stranger across the room from where he stood in the doorway. Hot chocolate steamed from two cups in his hands but he just stood there wondering if he would ever be able to look at her in the same way . . . did he really know this woman? Had his old Karen gone forever?

Tristan had told her earlier, after he'd read the last diary entry, that he wasn't angry and that he loved her just the same. And that was true. But he had, and did, feel hurt. Deeply hurt. She'd lied and deceived him, especially this last year. The whole time he'd been worrying about her agoraphobia she'd not had it at all. Karen must have gone to the lengths of researching symptoms, pretending to take medication and boy had she played a convincing part. Shit she should get an Oscar.

But then he reminded himself that she'd had something actually far worse than agoraphobia. Karen had suffered the untimely death of the only person who had truly cared for her as a child, the terrible mental and physical abuse from her mother, and then the weight of fourteen years of guilt about what she'd done, all threatened to flatten her – and now blackmail. *Yeah. But why didn't she come to you, Tris, eh? You would have gone to her in her shoes, wouldn't you? She obviously didn't love you enough – trust you enough.*

Then he shook himself. For goodness sake, of course she did. And if truth be known, he might have acted exactly the same if it had been him. Tristan would do anything to keep his family intact, any right thinking person would, and that's what his wife had done. Getting introspective and maudlin was the last thing either of them needed at this point. The main thing was to try to be strong for her and to get through this hellish chapter in their lives.

He stepped into the room and set the cups down on the coffee table. Karen's eyes shot open. 'I keep thinking it's all been some terrible dream and the phone will ring or the doorbell will sound and it will be Andrea come to spill the beans.'

'No, unfortunately it's all real, my love. Let's just hope there aren't any more notes to you at Andrea's house for the cops to find.'

'Oh my God! I never thought of that!'

Damn, why did he let his mouth run away with him? She was already distraught. But then so was he, it had been a hell of a day. He handed her a mug and sat beside her. 'Um, I don't see why there should be. And if there are, they will have your old name on them . . . don't worry.'

Karen's hand shook so much that the liquid spilled over the rim of the mug and he took it from her and placed it on the table.

'Hey come on now, babe,' he said, looking into her eyes – two deep blue pools of pain and bewilderment in a milk-white face. 'We'll get through this. You'll feel better after a good night's sleep.'

Karen shook her head and heaved a heartfelt sigh. 'Andrea is getting a good sleep isn't she? A permanent sleep, just like my mother, courtesy of yours truly.'

Tristan couldn't believe what he was hearing. He placed his hands either side of her face, made her look into his eyes. 'Now listen. None of that is your fault, neither Andrea nor your mother's death, okay?'

'But if we had looked for Andrea today, we might have found her before she stuck a needle in her arm. She'd have driven off after we'd talked to her and—'

Tristan put his finger on her lips. 'And gone off home and stuck a needle in her arm. She was an addict, Karen, and a very unstable one by your account. It would have happened sooner or later.

And where your mother was concerned, you had no choice, did you?'

'I . . . guess not . . . no.'

The anguish in her eyes sent a kick to his kidneys. God, how he loved her. She looked just like a child; scared, vulnerable, desperate. She was actually feeling guilty about the death of the woman who was vicious and cruel to her at school and had recently blackmailed her. Poor Karen. Most of the time since he'd known her, she seemed outwardly confident and strong, but just under the surface it was obvious that her mother had done serious damage to her self-esteem and he hated her for that.

Tristan ran his fingers over her cheek and traced the curve of her chin. He wanted to wave a magic wand, make everything all right, wanted to scoop her up and keep her safe, protected. He didn't have a wand, but he did have a love as wide as the sky and he had the warmth of his arms. Tristan stood, extending his hand. Karen looked up and took it, a question in her eyes. 'Come on, let's go to bed,' he said.

CHAPTER 26

Each little figure looked almost alive. The farmer's wife bent to feed the chickens, her red scarf tugged by the wind. The farmer, round headed and ruddy faced, striding across the cobbled yard in his green wellington boots, and the animals from sheep, to cows, to hens, to the black and white sheepdog barking at a fat cat on the wall, all seemed to glow from within with a life of their own. Incredibly, somebody had fashioned these from wood, handmade in Truro a sign said, proudly positioned next to the duck pond. This was *real* craftsmanship, none of your plastic mass-produced tat that packed the shelves of soulless chain stores.

Tristan wiped his nose with the back of his hand and noted that he could see his breath in the early November evening air. Looking back at the brightly lit farm scene in Manley's Toyshop window, he decided to go in and buy it for Sebastian whose birthday was only a few weeks off. Karen had suggested they bought a bike, but he wouldn't get much use out of it until the spring and he could have a bike anytime. Something about the farm called to Tristan. Perhaps it was because he'd had one just like it as a kid.

The bell jingled above the door as Tristan stepped through into the warmth of the old-fashioned interior of the shop. Shelves were packed with wooden toys of all description: spinning tops, building blocks, toolsets, train sets packed into boxes depicting fierce red steam engines roaring across the countryside and through tunnels, all manner of things apart from computer games and overpriced plastic figures from various TV shows.

Edwin Manley made it his business to stick to the old traditional toys and he seemed to do quite well in Kelerston. Children obviously still did appreciate his wares and, although expensive, Kelerston's parents and grandparents clearly were in the same mind as Tristan – you paid that bit extra for craftsmanship, even if you had to save up for it. Tristan furrowed his brow, goodness that sounded so stuffy. Was he getting stuffy?

'Doctor Ainsworth, what can I get you?' Edwin appeared from behind a navy velvet curtain at the side of the shop.

Tristan had to suppress a smirk because he was reminded of the shopkeeper in the old *Mr Benn* animated series he'd watched as a child. As far as he remembered the shopkeeper had appeared 'as if by magic' almost like from behind a curtain and Edwin was a dead ringer for him too. He always wore a bow tie and round spectacles, though the fez was absent.

'Evening, Edwin. I would like the farm in the window please. I hope you have one in stock?'

Edwin pressed his lips together and ran his hand through his thinning brown hair. 'I'm not sure if I do. There were three, one's in the window, but I have a feeling that I sold the other two.'

Tristan's face fell. 'Oh, it was for Sebastian's birthday. Such a shame, I had my heart set on it.'

Edwin held up a finger. 'Wait a second, I'll check in the back, and if not, we'll come to an arrangement over the one in the window if you like. I'll knock a couple of quid off.'

Fifteen minutes later Tristan handed over ninety pounds to Edwin and picked up the boxed farm. Edwin wanted to charge him eighty-five because it had been on display in the window for a few weeks, but Tristan wouldn't hear of it.

'I hope Sebastian loves it as much as his dad does,' Edwin said with a chuckle, as he pushed the till closed.

Tristan nodded. 'I'm sure he will, Edwin, and Bella too. Thanks for dismantling your shop window for me!'

'No problem, and before you go, is there any chance that we'll see your Karen back at the choir soon? As you know my Jacqueline is a member and she says it's not the same without her.'

'Funny you should mention that because Karen was only saying the other day that she would like to come back in a while – now that the choir probably isn't going to be in the competition.'

'By gum that was a rum do wasn't it?' Edwin took his spectacles off and folded his arms. 'Karen having another attack just thinking about being on the TV? Daft really, when you think about it, her being such a lovely lady. So is she fine now . . . or might she have another wobbly, do you think?' His eyes held a flicker of mockery.

It was obvious to Tristan that Edwin was after some gossip and right now he reminded him more of Harold Jackson the butcher than Mr Benn's shopkeeper. 'I hope not, Edwin. But mental illness can happen to any of us. Remember, it doesn't discriminate between nice and nasty folk.'

'Oh no, of course not . . . it's such a shame, isn't it?' Edwin painted on a suitably abashed expression and held the door open for Tristan.

As he walked to his car, Tristan wondered what expression Edwin would wear if he knew the whole story about Karen. He and Harold would probably collapse on the floor from heart failure. The trouble was that Karen had recently been talking about doing just that, revealing all to everyone.

Three days after Andrea's death, Karen had stunned him with the revelation – as if he'd not had enough of those from her recently – that she felt that she had to tell the whole truth and nothing but the truth about her past. She believed that Andrea's blackmailing and subsequent death had been punishment for hiding her secrets all these years and a sign that it was time to come clean and be true to who she was. She wanted to wait until after Sebastian's birthday, then she'd like to go for it.

Tristan thought that it was just the aftermath of the considerable trauma she'd recently endured and that perhaps leaving sleeping dogs to lie would be the best option. After all, now that Andrea, clearly her biggest threat, was dead and he himself now knew everything, there was no *need* to tell anyone else.

Michael had laid Andrea to rest a week ago, a lonely little affair, with just Michael, Jenny and Graham Proctor to see it. The police had contacted her parents in Spain, but her dad was in poor health and they had decided that travelling would be too much for him. The mother had apparently told Michael on the phone that their daughter had been dead to them for years.

There was also an aunt in Scotland, her dad's sister, but she thought that the journey was too far. They'd lost touch years ago, but she did send flowers, a small bunch of yellow lilies Jenny had told them. Andrea had apparently liked them as a child.

So Andrea was gone, but his problem wasn't. Even though at first he had allayed Karen's fears when he'd learned how her mother had died, because she'd been the one fretting about perhaps being sent to prison, Tristan's biggest worry now he'd had time to think more clearly was that once the police were involved, as involved they obviously would be, they *could* bring a case against Karen. Self-defence or not, she might well end up behind bars, and then where would they all be?

Karen had been doubtful about that idea. She said that at first she'd been terrified because of the poison Andrea had put into her head about the police chucking the key away. But now she thought that Andrea had made it all up. It *was* self-defence after all and everyone who had known her mother would believe that, wouldn't they? His wife just seemed set on a quest to do the right thing.

Tristan would normally be cheering that sentiment on, but what if the right thing was at the expense of Karen, the children and himself? What if the right thing meant that Sebastian and Bella lost their mother, he lost his wife, and Karen lost her family and freedom, just for the sake of coming clean? He'd told her that he'd been sadly naïve to think that the police would just accept it and they should keep quiet. But was it immoral to keep her dark secret, given the way that her mother had tormented her? He didn't think so.

Tristan got behind the wheel and blew into his hands. The cold damp November air seemed to have permeated into his bones and the idea of Karen's wish to confess had permeated a chill of fear into his heart. How could he sit back and let it happen, watch his whole world fall apart? Catching a glimpse of his haunted eyes in the rear-view mirror he promised himself that he couldn't.

Most of the day, as he'd tended patients, his mind had been elsewhere. Weighing up the pros and cons of getting a third party involved and wondering if he could trust that person a hundred per cent. Turning the key in the ignition, he finally made up his mind that he could. Besides, Karen had to have the facts and there wasn't a lot of choice as far as he could see. And, furthermore, he resolved to tell Karen exactly what he intended to do as soon as he got home that evening.

The delicious aroma of stew and dumplings whooshed into his nostrils as he stepped through the door. Yesss! He'd forgotten they were having that for supper. His mouth began to water, just what he needed after a busy day, and on such a cold evening. Setting the box containing the farm on the bottom of the stairs, he shrugged out of his coat and wondered if he should broach his idea with Karen before or after his belly was full of stew?

He sighed and pulled his tie off. If he talked to her before he could enjoy the food without the problem hanging over his head. If he did it after, he wouldn't enjoy it as much, but then again if he told her before and the whole thing turned into an argument they wouldn't enjoy it anyhow. Tristan smoothed his hair down and glanced at his reflection in the mirror. Steady green eyes looked back. What did the enjoyment of a bowl of stew matter when the security of his family was at stake?

Shoving the box to one side he sat down on the step and undid the laces of his shoes. Stew was just a red herring. He laughed softly at the unintended pun and wondered briefly what red herring stew would taste like. There you did it again, Tristan, procrastination of the thought. Filling your mind with largely irrelevant problems so that you don't have to deal with the enormously relevant one.

Shoes off and neatly placed in the shoe basket, he wiggled his socks on the cool wooden floor. Perhaps he should wait until they were in bed and casually start the conversation after they had made love. A niggle at the back of his head came to the fore again. Damn, he needed to organise that romantic break away soon. Because of everything that had happened it had gone right out of his mind, but some relaxing time together was needed even more now.

They tended to make love a lot lately, mostly instigated by Karen. Perhaps in her head she was making up for the fact that she'd kept things hidden from him. He knew she felt guilty about that and had told her that he'd have done the same thing in her position. But she hadn't listened and seemingly preferred to sooth her conscience by finding new and inventive ways to please him in the bedroom.

Tristan wasn't complaining and wondered if she might wear that new sexy red sheer underwear set she bought last week again. He swallowed hard and felt his excitement grow as he remembered the way that Karen had just walked into his study last Sunday afternoon, let her silky dressing gown slip to the floor revealing the new bra and skimpy knickers, brushed the papers he was working on off the desk and straddled him as he sat on his chair.

She had whispered in his ear that they had to be quick as the kids were only having a nap, which was lucky as his libido shot sky high. And in his mind's eye now as he sat on the stairs, he could see her hard nipples pressing against the sheer material as her breasts bounced in front of his eyes, could feel the lace elastic in his hand roll over her smooth cool thighs as he pulled her knickers off and thrust hard into her, and though he didn't last long, he could still remember his ecstatic release and her shudders of pleasure running through him.

Tristan stood up and looked down at the bulge in his trousers that memory had caused. He'd neatly sidestepped the problem at hand yet again, hadn't he? He sighed. If he waited to talk to Karen until after they'd made love he probably wouldn't be able to perform for worrying about what to say afterwards. The aroma of stew tickled his tummy again. Right, he'd eat and then say what he had to, final answer, no ask the audience, just go for it. He picked up the box and walked into the kitchen.

'Hello sexy, what's that?' Karen asked, nodding in the general direction of his waist. Tristan looked down at his trousers. Was the telltale sign of his excitement still there? Nope, not too obviously anyway.

'Er . . . what?'

'That big box clasped to your hip, silly,' Karen said, flapping a tea towel at the smoke alarm that was making threatening beeps at the open oven door.

Tristan chuckled. 'Oh, it's a farm for Sebastian's birthday. Just wait 'til you see it. Real handmade figures, not your plastic crap from—'

'Soulless chain stores. Yes, Tris. But go and hide it somewhere. We don't want Sebastian, or Bella for that matter, seeing it.'

'Aren't they in bed?' This was Tristan's late night and he'd shopped for Sebastian's present tonight to avoid little eyes spying surprises.

'No, they are in my pocket.' She shot him a withering look. 'Of course they are in bed, but I'm just about to serve dinner and knowing you it will be left lying around until morning.'

'So you're not mad that I didn't get a bike?'

'Nope. After everything that's happened I have made a new resolution never to get mad or even tetchy anymore without a good reason. Sebastian will love the farm I'm sure. Now hurry up, this stew is hot . . . just like my husband,' she added, and blew him a kiss.

Considering Tristan had a lot on his mind, the stew did the quickest disappearing act he'd seen for a while and he found himself nodding when Karen asked if he wanted more. Perhaps this was a new form of procrastination. Eat so much that your gut explodes rendering you incapable of further speech; the downside would be a long stay in intensive care.

Swallowing his nerves with the last bit of dumpling, he looked at Karen and said, 'I know you're set on telling everyone who you really are, love, but I don't think you've thought it through regarding the repercussions.' He closed his hand over hers across the table. 'You could end up in prison.'

Locking her freckled blue eyes on to his green ones, Karen shook her head. 'Really? Even when they know what my mother was like and everything?'

'Jeez, I don't know. But why do you need to test it? Why is it so important to you?'

She pulled her hand free and leaned back in her chair, the warmth in her eyes fading to grey. 'Because I want to be me again. For years I've been looking over my shoulder wondering if someone will recognise me, lying to you, to everyone I care about. I just want a normal life.'

Tristan realised she was getting upset but he couldn't let it drop now, as much as he wanted to. 'I understand, of course, but you might risk everything if—'

Karen sighed and reached for his hand again. 'So what's your answer, love? Do I keep on living a lie, staying hidden in this house, unable to do the things I love best like singing in the choir . . . move away from Cornwall? Because we'd have to if we were to have a fighting chance of keeping my identity hidden.' She poured a glass of wine, took a gulp and blinked at him. 'Is that what you want?'

Tristan thought for a few moments. 'Yes, if it means we'll keep this family safe.'

Karen said nothing for a while, stood and paced up and down lost in thought. Eventually she shook her head and came to sit back at the table, a sad little smile on her face. 'You know as well as I do that moving from here would be no guarantee. It would lower the odds, but we would still always wonder, always have to look over our shoulders, guard what we say to people. And we're so happy here. Don't you remember how much you wanted to come back to this part of the world?'

'Of course I do, but we could find somewhere else, perhaps by the sea. Wales is nice,' he said without much conviction.

She laughed. 'Yes, it's beautiful, but you sound as much like you want to move to Wales as fly to the moon. This is your home, Tris. You feel like you belong here. So do I and I just want to feel like me again.'

Tristan looked at her wistful little face and his heart went out to her. But then an idea occurred to him. 'What about if I call you Melody at home. Would that help?'

'It's not about my name,' she said, and then paused, tracing her fingers along the stem of her glass. 'Having said that, I guess I would like to return to Melody if you can hack it. My dad gave me the name after all.' She looked into his eyes. 'But it's more about knowing who I am, who you and the kids think I am and about being honest. I want our children to know about my past when they're older without me having to censor everything and being worried about a slip up. I have nothing to be ashamed of. It was self-defence, Tris, and it's time for me to stop running.'

She put her head on one side and poked his arm. 'And do you think it's morally right, as a fine pillar of Kelerston, to keep all that hidden?' She gave him a mischievous smile on her last words, but he could tell she meant every word.

Tristan leaned forward and rested his elbows on the table. 'Hm, I'm a fine pillar, eh? You make me sound like a mausoleum.' A thought suddenly occurred to him. 'Tell me, sweetheart, what exactly did your suicide note say?'

Karen sighed. 'The note was short and to the point. It just said that I had nothing to live for. I felt unloved, was ugly and because of my size I felt like a monster. My dad was dead and now my mother was too. I wanted to end it.'

'So you didn't say you'd fought with her and stabbed her?'

'No.'

'And what did the news reports say at the time?'

'That I had disappeared, left a suicide note, presumed drowned. That my mother had been found dead in suspicious circumstances. That the two things may or may not be connected. Stuff like that.'

He reached across for her hand and brought her fingers to his lips kissing the tips tenderly. Karen's lovely face was pinched and dark circles shadowed her eyes. In that moment Tristan understood that to resume her true identity was more than a whim, a desire, but a real need. One of the things that he loved about her was that she had a strong moral compass, and he had to admit, so did he.

The ticking of the clock filled the silence between them and he realised he was coming round to her way of thinking. And in the light of what she'd just said, the situation might be better than he'd first thought. Karen hadn't actually admitted in writing to killing her mother. The evidence must be pretty circumstantial. He shot her a warm smile. Perhaps it was time to bring up his idea.

'Being the stubborn mule that you are, I guessed you might say all that. But I had to try again to get you to go for the safest option, if not the ethical one. The best news I've heard for a while though is that you didn't write that you'd killed your mother and the news headlines didn't scream that you had either. Anyway, I have been thinking of another plan. It might help, it might not.'

Karen wound a strand of hair around her finger and chewed her bottom lip. 'Another plan? Let's hear it then.'

'I think it's best that we got some advice from someone who knows the law. I think the only person we can trust a hundred per cent is my sister.'

'Emma? You mean tell her everything?'

'Yes, and also tell her that you want to blab to the police.'

'God, Tris, I don't know. You know she's never really liked me. And blab to the police . . . You make it sound like a confession . . .' Karen's voice tailed off.

'I think she's just been protective of me that's all, rather than not liking you, love.' He smiled. Though he did acknowledge silently that he suspected Karen was right about his sister's feelings. 'But I think Emma will be able to advise us which way to go.'

'I don't see that there are different ways to go. Either I stay as I am, or come clean.' Karen gave him a weak smile.

'That's why I said it might not help if I tell her, but we have to try to see if there's some way you can become Melody again without ending up in prison. What do you think?' Tristan looked at her hopefully.

'What if she thinks I'm guilty?'

234

'Don't be daft. I'll just tell it to her like it is.'

Karen sighed, leaned forward and kissed his cheek. 'Then I guess you'd better go and see your sister. And Tris . . .' She heaved a huge sigh as if she'd released an age of pent-up tension. 'I'll go with what you decide. I owe you that much.'

CHAPTER 27

Tristan stepped from the train at Exeter station, turned the collar of his coat up against the driving rain and ran to the rank of taxis waiting forlornly in the grey morning.

Despite it being a Saturday, Emma had some work to do and had suggested that he came up to meet her at her chambers and then they'd go to lunch. It was only a five-minute walk from the station, but Tristan decided to take a taxi as the rain had drenched him through once already.

At the end of the short journey, digging in his inside pocket for some cash to pay the driver, Tristan glanced out of the half-fogged window at the grand old red and white brick Victorian building where Emma was based. He was struck by the way he and his sister had both landed successful careers despite the odds being stacked against them.

Pride grew in his heart when he thought of how they had fought and won against the psychological barriers the past had heaped in their way. Another thought struck him as he left the taxi and hurried up the steps to the grand double doors: he ought to pay Aunt Helen a visit soon. If it hadn't been for Dad's sister taking them in after their parents had died he very much doubted that they would have been as successful. There never seemed enough time lately, but he'd have to make some.

'Yay! Great to see you, big brother!' Emma's pretty face broke into a huge grin and she hurried to hug him, her high heels tapping across the office. 'Ugh,' she said, changing her mind about the hug. 'Take your coat off, you're soaked.' She held the coat at arm's length and hung it on an old-fashioned coat rack. 'And it's been too long, four months.' She pursed her lips and narrowed her hazel eyes. 'No, it's more like five. What the heck's kept you so busy? The kids won't know me. I was saying to Aunt Helen only the other day . . .'

Her chatter tumbled abruptly to a halt when she noticed Tristan chuckling and shaking his head. 'What?' she said, self-consciously tucking her short chestnut bob behind both ears.

'You don't change, do you? Rattling along like a machine gun asking questions and not giving me a chance to get a word in edgewise.' Tristan felt a lump in his throat unexpectedly. 'You were just the same when you were little.'

Emma smiled, walked over and hugged him at last. 'And you were always the one who listened.' She stepped back and put her hands on his shoulders. 'You aren't happy are you, Tris? What's up?

You sounded cagey on the phone and way too serious.'

Tristan looked away from her searching eyes and at his watch. 'Look, it's almost noon. Let's grab some lunch and I'll tell you all about it.'

She nodded, slipped on her black suit-jacket over her white shirt and grabbed an umbrella.

'Well, that is if you can actually walk in those stilettos, of course,' he added, receiving a baleful stare in response.

The Jolly Sailor, five minute's walk away, was a well-attended, yet relaxed pub with a cracking lunch menu and real ales. The old-fashioned interior – whitewashed walls hung with horse brasses, dark oak furniture and a roaring fire – was just the ticket for such a damp and dreary afternoon. Even stepping through the door made Tristan feel a bit more cheerful.

Ordering a couple of pints, Tristan handed the menu to Emma as they rested their elbows against the bar. 'Ooo, steak and ale pie for me, I think.' Emma smacked her lips and took a sip of beer.

'Do you know, I fancy that too . . . and a heap of chips. Don't suppose you'll have them though?' Tristan looked at his sister with his best 'I dare you' expression.

'Then you suppose wrong. I skipped breakfast so I can indulge myself without too much guilt.' She poked him on the shoulder. 'Let's sit over there at that corner table where it's quiet so we can have a chat.'

Once seated, Tristan didn't know where to start and so talked about the weather and how nice the fire was and the beer, but Emma wasn't having it.

She folded her arms and fixed him with her best hard stare. 'Okay, cut to the chase. What was the point of law you mentioned you wanted to talk to me about on the phone?'

Tristan sighed and took a sip of beer. 'It's a bit complicated and it will take a while . . . also I struggled with the idea of involving you at all. You're a solicitor and I know a very moral one at that. I'm worried that if I tell you something in confidence you'll feel compromised between your professional duties and your emotional tie to me.'

Emma furrowed her brow. 'Bloody hell, Tris. What have you done?' she said quietly.

'It's not what I've done . . . it's Karen.' Now that he'd said it he felt that he couldn't go any further. It was as if an invisible man had leapt up and squirted super glue in his mouth, the words stuck fast in his throat.

'Take your time, Tris, it's okay, and short of murder, I can't see what I'd be compromised about.' Emma grinned nervously and fiddled with her napkin.

Tristan looked at her stony-faced.

She stopped fiddling. 'Hell on wheels . . . she didn't . . . did she?'

Tristan was prevented from answering by the

239

arrival of their steak and ale pies. The waitress set them down and another brought a huge bowl of chips and condiments. 'Anything else we can get you?' the girl asked, flashing a bright smile.

Tristan wondered if she'd got a solution to the whole mess behind the bar, he'd quite like one of those, but he just smiled weakly.

Emma shook her head and said everything looked wonderful.

Handing him cutlery, Emma raised her eyebrows. 'Well?'

Tristan sighed and looked at her forlornly. Where to start? But after a forkful of pie and a sip of beer miraculously the glue in his throat loosened and the words he dreaded speaking tumbled out freely for the next ten minutes.

Emma didn't say anything after an initial few gasps of shock early on, and an outpouring of sympathy for Karen. Then she encouraged him to keep going while she just ate her food and listened. When he'd finished however she had plenty to say.

'So, let me get this right.' She pushed her plate away and steepled her fingers. 'If Karen hadn't fought her mother off, she would have been killed . . . no question?'

Tristan nodded and stuffed a chip into his mouth. He felt strangely hungry; perhaps it was the relief after he'd unburdened himself. 'Yes, and that's what she's pinning her hopes on at the moment. She says it was a straightforward case of self-defence, and everyone will see that.' Tristan

240

blinked his eyes. 'I think it's more complicated, don't you?'

Emma nodded gravely. 'I do. It was the whole thing of her trying to commit suicide immediately afterwards . . . then later running away and changing her identity. That would suggest guilt in a jury's eyes.'

The word 'jury' wrapped itself around a half-eaten chip and stuck to the side of Tristan's throat. Jury – that sounded so serious. He took a swallow of beer to dislodge the chip and his appetite went down with it. 'So you think it would come to court and she'd go to prison, even though it's a "cold case" and the evidence is probably non-existent?'

Emma pressed her lips together and tucked her hair behind her ears again. 'I think there's a chance, Tris. You see, as well as absconding, the fact that she was systematically abused wouldn't necessarily be a plus in her favour. It could add to the prosecution's case. They could say that she eventually flipped after years of torment and killed her mother outright. It would therefore become murder, not manslaughter.'

'But that's *not* what happened.' Tristan sighed, pushing his plate away, too. He drained his glass and immediately wanted another pint. 'God, it's so unfair. All Karen wants to do is set the record straight and be herself again.'

Emma put her hand on his arm. 'Please, Tris. I know you love her, but are you really sure that she's telling it like it was? Can you trust her completely?'

Tristan's face flushed, he jumped up and grabbed his glass. How dare she suggest Karen was a liar? 'Want another?'

'Yes, several . . . and don't be angry. You would have asked the same in my shoes,' Emma muttered folding her arms.

Tristan's anger calmed and he put his hand reassuringly on her shoulder. Hadn't he thought along similar lines the day he'd found out about Karen's past?

Unconsciously mirroring each other exactly, the brother and sister sat opposite each other sipping their drinks in thoughtful silence.

Emma wiped froth from her top lip.

'Missed a bit,' Tristan smirked.

Emma smiled, but there was little humour behind her eyes. 'So Karen's hell-bent on doing the right thing, even though she's not sure of the consequences?'

'Not hell-bent. She said that she'd go with what I thought in the end and she'd be open to advice. That's why I am here today.'

Emma put her head on one side. 'What made her suddenly decide to tell you anyway?'

Tristan forced himself to meet her eyes. No need to mention Andrea, was there? She might blow a gasket at even more drama. But still, he may as well tell her, she knew about everything else after all. It might make her empathise with Karen more too. He gulped another mouthful of beer and told her.

Emma didn't blow a gasket, she just sat there, stunned.

'So there you have it. It was lots of things,' he said in measured tones. 'Overall she felt like she was being punished. And then the strain of moving from Swindon to Kelerston . . . she couldn't keep the pretence of agoraphobia up forever . . . and of course there was the choir thing with the TV programme.'

'Well, my goodness.' Emma blew out her cheeks. 'You have been right through the sodding wringer, haven't you?' She took a moment rubbing her forehead as if to smooth away jumbled thoughts. 'Right, I see. Hm . . . I can understand her not wanting to have to look over her shoulder, as she puts it. But really, Tris, I think it would be best if she kept quiet. Then there's the whole fraud thing too, using false names on official documents.'

'But won't that be down to Bob and Maureen?'

'Yes, I think so, and of course they'd have to prove intent to defraud on Karen's part. What exactly has she changed about her name? You said that Karen is one of her middle names?'

'Yes. Her real name before we were married was Melody Hermione Karen Isabelle Rafter.'

'Bloody hell, that was a mouthful . . . but you knew her as just Karen Rafter. She kept her real surname?'

'Yep.' Tristan nodded. 'Bob said that anyone trying to trace her for any reason wouldn't expect that.'

Emma heaved a sigh and gave a fleeting smile.

243

'I'm glad it is her real surname, Tris, because when you first told me, I immediately thought that you aren't legally married. I don't know for certain without checking the middle name thing, but I think you are okay. Karen is one of her real names after all.' Emma looked hopeful but he knew she was more uncertain than she was letting on.

Tristan couldn't believe the humongous heap of crap rising up around him. If things weren't bad enough, now there was a possibility that Karen wasn't his wife at all! That had never occurred to him what with the more serious issue hanging over them. He sighed and took a huge swallow of beer. 'It never rains, eh? So you think there's no way round it, Emma? No solution to her becoming Melody again and still keeping out of trouble?'

Emma looked into the fire for a few moments, lost in thought. 'I did wonder about one thing,' she said presently. 'But it would involve another lie and you say she wants to get away from those.'

Tristan leaned forward; any straw would be worth clutching at. 'What . . . what is it?'

'Well, the fact that Karen said in her note that her dad was dead and now her mother was, she felt like she wanted it all to end. She didn't actually *say* she had killed her mother, did she?'

Tristan felt his hopes rising. His sister had latched onto the same point that he had the other evening when he'd spoken to Karen. 'No, she didn't, Ems. I think that's a good thing in her favour, maybe *the* best thing. And the newspapers were pretty benign. Well, as much as they could be.' Though he knew the situation was still a mess he couldn't keep the enthusiasm out of his voice.

Emma nodded. 'And the guy Karen's mother was having sex with that night. What happened to him?'

Tristan shrugged. 'Karen said there was no trace of him. He must have left before her mother came in and attacked her. Why?'

A deep sigh escaped Emma's mouth, as if she were wrestling with her conscience. 'I can't believe I'm coming up with this, and you mustn't blame me if Karen goes for it and it doesn't work.' She looked at Tristan sharply. 'And you mustn't *ever* say that I came up with it to anyone else but Karen. It's against the law for me to suggest a different scenario and if it got out my career is over – permanently.'

'Of course not. Tell me what you're thinking. Anything you say will be just advice or ideas.'

Emma went to tuck her hair behind her ears and then realised it was already tucked. She instead examined her nails and took a deep breath. 'I wouldn't do this for anyone else, Tris. Not anyone.'

He nodded encouragement.

'Well . . . Karen could tell a partial truth. That she woke to hear her mother having sex with a man and tried to drown it out with a pillow. She fell asleep and then in the early hours got up to get a drink . . . she found her mother stabbed . . . and then the rest is the truth. It would fit with her suicide note too.'

It was Tristan's turn to sit in a stunned silence.

245

That's the last thing he expected his straight up and down, law-abiding sister to say. And then another little kick of hope started his adrenaline flowing. Shit this might just work. Though he did have a few qualms, the more he'd thought about it, the more he wanted the same thing as Karen. He had to admit to himself that he was actually a moral upstanding pillar after all. Tristan had come to realise that both he and his wife wanted a complete clean slate and the past behind them . . . but this version wouldn't be the whole truth, would it?

'Bloody hell, Emma, that's a bit of a whopper. But if it works—'

'As I said, it might not, but her mother *did* have a well-known reputation for getting drunk and bringing lots of men home. This one was obviously not local, probably a sailor Karen reckoned, didn't you say?' Tristan nodded. 'So he'd be long gone nowadays,' Emma finished, taking a big swig of beer.

'But why aren't his prints on the knife?' Tristan said.

'Perhaps she attacked him just like she attacked Karen and he grabbed her hands just like Karen did.'

Tristan marvelled at her quick thinking. 'And motive?'

'They both were pissed as farts, her mother got nasty. That often happened as Karen said. Perhaps he wanted money, who knows?'

Tristan sat back and considered what Karen's response might be. She would probably be doubtful, but if he could put forward a logical argument in the way that Emma had, she might go for it. This would certainly be a solution, not the perfect one, but one they didn't have before he came here today, that was for sure.

'What are you thinking about?' Emma asked, putting her hand on his shoulder.

'Just that Karen would find it hard to not tell the whole truth I think—'

'Not bothered her so far has it?' Emma snapped.

Tristan looked at her flashing eyes and set mouth. Why had she always had such a downer on Karen? Emma had said earlier that her heart went out to Karen when she'd learned of her past, but this was the second time she'd said something a bit off. 'She lied before because she was protecting herself. This is slightly different don't you think? If she only tells half-truths I worry that she'll never be really free . . . that we'll never be free. Perhaps that will affect the person she is and that's exactly what she doesn't want to happen,' he said, searching Emma's face for understanding.

'Look, I'm sorry for being short with you, but it does seem to be all about Karen. Karen wants, Karen needs. What about how you and the children would be affected if she just blurted it all out to the police? She has to think about that, Tristan, and I'm *really* sorry for her, truly I am. But I care about you *more*. I couldn't bear it if your life was destroyed after you have come so far.' Emma's eyes moistened and she looked away.

Tristan could almost read what she was thinking.

They had been each other's anchor when they'd suddenly found themselves orphaned all those years ago. Yes, of course, there had been Aunt Helen who had been marvellous, but the bond that had been forged between them back then was something special, it had made them stronger. The lengths his sister had gone to for him today proved that. Emma was just being protective of him at the moment, over-protective he guessed, but he wouldn't have her any other way.

He put his arm around her and gave her shoulder a squeeze. 'It's not like that, Emma. I've realised I want the same thing too; it's not just all about Karen. She and I are one – we come as a package. And if you give her a chance you'll see how lovely she is.' He chuckled then and rubbed his knuckles on her head as he used to when they were kids. 'You daft bat, don't worry about me . . . It will work out, you'll see.'

Emma pushed him off and straightened her ruffled hair. 'It had better, Tris. And if Karen needs to chat to me, please let me know. I can be there in an hour or so.'

Tristan hadn't considered that Karen might like to share her worries with another woman. She did have Jenny, but of course she couldn't share this with her. In fact the more he thought about it, the more he thought what a great idea it was. Another perspective was always welcome and especially someone as knowledgeable about the law as Emma could only help the situation.

Yep, this was all good. At last he was starting to see a small chink of light at the end of a very long tunnel. Nodding at Emma he said, 'I think that would be a great idea. I'll talk to her and get back to you soon. And thanks so much for this, Sis.'

Emma gave him a peck on the cheek. 'Hey, that's what sisters are for.'

CHAPTER 28

If she sliced another sliver off that end, it should even up the general appearance of the cake. But would anyone have a real clue that it was supposed to be a lion wearing a flowery hat anyway? And why hadn't she encouraged Sebastian towards a simple round cake with his name and age on top? Why had she said, *what kind of cake do you want? Mummy can make anything.* Because she was an idiot, that's why. An idiot who preferred procrastinating with a cake for three days rather than tackling the Emma solution head on. And why, oh why, had Sebastian asked for a lion wearing a flowery hat? Because he's a three year old, Karen, that's why.

Karen sighed, picked up the knife and positioned it over the lion's rump. But if she cut more from there, wouldn't the liquorice tail look a bit too long? Oh bugger it. Karen put the knife down and folded her arms. The party was tomorrow, she'd dollop icing over the wonky arse and hope for the best. Enough was enough. Now for coffee and a sandwich while the kids seemed to be playing nicely . . . but weren't they a bit too quiet?

★   ★   ★

'Now watch CBeebies while Mummy makes her lunch . . . and no more crayoning on the wall, okay?'

'Okay, Mummy!' Sebastian and Bella chimed back. They were very pleased to be allowed to watch TV twice that day and gobbled their tuna pasta like it was going out of fashion. Karen normally limited their viewing to once a day and certainly never normally let them eat while watching, but she needed a break and caffeine after the lion cake fiasco. There it was on the counter, looking at her reproachfully from chocolate button eyes. Swiftly depositing it in the cupboard, Karen grabbed a crusty loaf, butter, cheese, pickle, tomatoes and a huge packet of Doritos. Comfort eating extraordinaire.

Half a sandwich and a big swig of coffee later, she began to feel more human again. She took another big bite out of her sandwich, chutney landing on her chin. And if Tristan thought she would speak to 'Emma Perfect Pants' he'd very much another thing coming. Tristan had told her what Emma had said and it had rattled Karen more than she'd let on to her husband . . . even perhaps to herself.

Trouble was her sister-in-law always thought she knew best. Not just about the law, but about every bloody thing. Karen sighed and wiped the chutney from her chin, where it promptly settled in her cleavage. Nice. And yes, if she were honest, what Tristan had explained about Emma's advice did make sense, but Karen had *so* wanted to get away from any more lies. But perhaps Emma's way was best . . . safer at least.

Her thoughts were upside down again. Yes it would be nice to chat to another woman about it, but Emma wasn't another woman, she was a Stepford wife except she wasn't married, and no wonder. How could any bloke compete with her ego? Successful lawyer, very smart, petite, impeccably dressed in her designer suits and heels you'd need a step ladder to put on, unusual amber-hazel eyes . . . a bit like a lion's.

God, she had lions on the brain. Thrusting her fingers into the bag of Doritos and rootling around in there she was disappointed to find only crumbs left. How did that happen? Sucking her fingers clean of salt and spice she conceded that perhaps she was being a little harsh on Emma. When they'd first met they got on quite well, but Karen had always felt that Emma hadn't completely welcomed her to her pert little bosom. And then there was the special relationship Emma and Tris shared after they were orphaned, no wonder really. Karen should have been pleased that Tris had her to rely on back then.

She took a sip of coffee. Perhaps Karen was just jealous, plain and simple. Emma was self-assured, confident, ambitious, and certainly hadn't screwed her life up big-time in the way that Karen had, despite being dealt a shit hand by her own awful mother. And the thought of 'she of the perfect pants' waltzing in and telling her what to do now was just above and beyond. Especially with what Karen had gone through lately.

Putting down her now empty cup and plate and scrubbing briefly at the brown mess the chutney had left on her light green T-shirt, she popped her head round the sitting room door to see what her cherubs were up to. Hmm, sitting as good as gold, food eaten, rapt. It was amazing what a dose of *Mister Maker* could do to tame the beast of mischief. Or was it *Justin's House*? The same guy seemed to be on all the shows.

In the conservatory, a two-foot cactus looked like it was on its last legs. Karen had neglected the plants in here dreadfully and the weather had turned decidedly nippy over the past few weeks. But it was fast approaching the end of November so what did she expect? The room was heated but it was always colder with all the glass and being exposed to the sea breezes.

A poke at the base of the cactus with a pencil revealed a glimpse of green through the brown crusty exterior and prompted Karen to look for that old fleece she'd used to protect the plant last year. Now where was it? Perhaps in the chest under the shelves in the sitting room. A smile of satisfaction played over her lips. Good, another little diversion to help her put serious thought out of her head.

Oh yes, procrastination was alive and well and living in the mind of Karen Ainsworth. Or should she call herself Melody Ainsworth? It had been so long since she'd thought of herself as Melody . . . well not in any real sense anyway. It was as if Melody was someone she'd left behind, was another person in fact. Someone who had been carefree, happy, singing and dancing along on the beach with her dad.

As she hurried through the hallway in search of the fleece the doorbell rang. Oh, who's this now? Didn't they realise she was on a cactus saving mission and had a lion's arse icing job waiting in the cupboard for her later?

Opening the door, a gust of icy wind wrapped itself around her arms while the caller's appearance on the doorstep dropped an icy stone into her heart. Bloody hell, why did it have to be *her* looking like she'd just stepped out of *Vogue*, while Karen stood there make-up-less and covered in chutney! Karen flushed and glanced at the stain again, on second thought it looked as if it might even be sh . . .

'Hi, Karen!' Emma chimed. 'I hope you don't mind me turning up unannounced, but I phoned Tris at the surgery this morning to ask what Sebastian would like for his birthday, and Tris said if I was free why didn't I pop down for a few days as I'd not seen you or the babes for ages.' A small frown creased Emma's otherwise unlined forehead and she pursed her peachy glossed lips. Karen was staring at her as if she'd got three heads and still hadn't asked her in out of the cold. Emma gave an uncertain smile and said, 'He said I'd be most welcome.'

Karen got a grip and stepped to the side, 'Yes. Of course, come in.'

Emma stepped inside and divested herself of her long olive-green mohair coat and her red scarf, and red beret. She wore a short woollen navy dress, offset with an art deco sparkly brooch at the shoulder and knee-high black patent boots with heels about the same height. She smelled of winter and expensive perfume and right at that moment Karen wished her far, far away.

'Would you like a drink?' Karen said over her shoulder, as she led the way to the kitchen.

'Ooh yes. A glass of red if you have it,' Emma said, dabbing a tissue at her delicate pink nose.

Karen raised a metaphorical eyebrow. She had meant tea or coffee. Blatantly obvious Emma was nervous then, why else would she ask for wine at half past one on a Wednesday afternoon? And why she had to put on this pretence about Sebastian's birthday when they both knew she was here to talk to Karen about her proposed plan, she had no idea.

She turned to face Emma and leaned against the worktop as nonchalantly as any person can with chutney stains spattered across their top. 'I meant tea or coffee, but I think we have a bottle of red . . . somewhere.' They had at least three, but Karen needed the moral high ground.

'Oh, silly me. No don't worry, tea is fine.' Emma's face flushed crimson and Karen licked an imaginary finger and drew it vertically down the air in front of her.

'I'll make it while you pop through and see the children, they're watching telly in the sitting room,' Karen said, turning back to the cupboards.

Emma mumbled something inaudible and tip-tapped away over the ceramic tiled floor.

A pang of guilt rose in Karen's chest; the woman was only here to help after all. Perhaps she should stop being so stand-offish. But then on the other hand, not trusting folk and putting up defences was par for the course with the kind of life she'd had, wasn't it?

Squeals of laughter greeted Karen a few minutes later as she carried the tea into the sitting room. Emma had taken off her ridiculous boots and was chasing Sebastian and Bella around the settee and tickling them. She looked a bit like Tristan when she laughed and *Vogue* cover girl image had given way to carefree fun-to-be-with auntie.

'I think they remember me,' Emma said, chuckling. She picked Bella up and spun her around.

'Of course they do, it's not been that long.' Karen set the mugs down on a high shelf away from the flailing arms and kicking legs of the kids.

'It's been five months,' Emma said, flopping down on the settee, her hair stuck up and she was out of breath.

Karen couldn't work out if that was a reproach or just a statement of fact.

'I wish I had been here recently. I can't begin to imagine what you and Tris went through when Andrea—'

'It was utterly vile, and I'd rather not talk about it now, Emma. Especially not in front of them.'

'Of course not. I'm sorry, I seem to keep saying the wrong things.' Emma sighed, lifting a hand to fend Sebastian off.

'Sebastian leave Auntie Emma alone now, she doesn't want you ruining her hair!'

Sebastian ignored his mother, climbed up beside Emma and proceeded to whack her round the head with a cushion.

'He's okay . . . certainly has lots of energy though!' Emma giggled as Bella joined in the assault with a cushion of her own.

'Hey, you two, do you want to play outside? Auntie Emma and I can have a nice cup of tea in the conservatory and watch you get rid of some of that energy.'

Emma shot Karen a grateful glance as she was beginning to look more battered than ruffled.

The two women sipped their tea and watched from the comfort of the sofa and behind glass, while the children, bundled in winter woollies, raced round the garden like a couple of hares. Before Karen knew what was happening, the neat pile of autumn leaves that Tris had gathered up on Sunday and weighted under a wooden crate was freed once more to float like lion's eyes on the chill breeze. Kicked by frenzied wellington boots they danced and twirled past the windows and settled in wide dispersal across the tidy lawn. Tristan's labours were undone in a fraction of the time they had originally taken.

'Great. Tristan will be thrilled when he gets back.' Karen smiled wryly.

'Yes, but aren't they just adorable. Look at their little faces. They are truly happy out there. Simple pleasures.' Emma's voice sounded wistful, sad even.

Karen stole a sidelong glance and couldn't be sure, but she thought that Emma's eyes looked damp. Surely not. Emma had never shown much emotion. 'Yes, we learn a lot from our children, I think.' Karen sighed and wondered how long it would be before Emma broached the elephant in the room. No further conversation seemed forthcoming for the moment however and her eyes alighted on the cactus again. 'Oh, I forgot that I was on my way to sort that poor plant out when you rang the bell. I'll have to do it when I have finished my tea.'

Emma drew her eyes from the children and followed Karen's gaze to the cactus as if coming out of a trance. 'Hmm? What's wrong with it?'

'It's feeling cold and unloved I think. Nothing a nice warm fleece can't sort.'

'I know how it feels. Have you got another fleece for me?' Emma tried to smile and then her face crumbled and her shoulders shook as silent tears poured down her cheeks.

Karen was horrified and embarrassed in equal

measure at the sudden collapse of the ice queen. Bloody hell, what on earth was wrong? 'Hey, what's up?' she said, hovering her hand over Emma's shoulder and then allowing it to rest there lightly.

'It's my bloke. He . . . he dumped me.' Emma wiped her nose with the back of her hand and Karen jumped up to get a tissue from the coffee table.

Blimey, this was the very last thing that Karen expected. Perhaps her sister-in-law didn't have the perfect life after all.

'Oh dear, I didn't know you were seeing anyone . . . well, not seriously anyway. What happened?' Karen passed the box of tissues and checked to see that the children were still playing and oblivious to their aunt's tears.

'It wasn't serious at first but all of a sudden I knew he was the one, you know?' Karen nodded sympathetically. 'And the other night we went to dinner and he said he had something to tell me.' Emma blew her nose and looked at Karen through mascara smeared eyes. 'My God, what a fool I was. I *actually* thought he wanted to propose. But no, he wanted to tell me that he was dumping me for a secretary. But wait for it, not his secretary, *my* secretary. Makes a change from the usual cliché I'll give him that.' Emma laughed humourlessly.

'But what went wrong, did he say?'

'Oh, yes, Robert, polite as ever told me the whole kit and caboodle. It seems that I'm very lovely, sexy, but too smart and independent. He wants to settle down and have children but he wants someone less ambitious, someone to look after, care for, be protective of. Yes, he actually said those words. Sexist shithead!'

Sebastian looked over from the Wendy house, a puzzled look on his face. Karen gave him a big smile and waved. He waved back and went inside.

'I know you're upset but try to keep your voice down, the kids are wondering what's up.'

'Oh, sorry. I didn't think . . . never do,' Emma blew her nose and tucked her hair behind both ears. 'Robert was so wrong about me. I put on an act because I'm frightened to be myself, in case myself isn't good enough. It's all smoke and mirrors. Inside I'm often scared stiff like a little kid. That's all down to the crap Mother dragged us through. She never praised us, or encouraged us at anything.'

Karen could relate to that big-time. And she felt kind of pleased that Emma had chosen to share her feelings. In fact, she felt herself really warming to Emma at last. She certainly looked like a vulnerable little kid at the moment.

'To be honest, Emma, I thought the same as Robert. You are a bloody good actress I'll give you that.' Karen smiled and gave her a little hug. 'And I can see similarities between our mothers. Perhaps you've been proving her wrong by being so successful and I'm doing the same in my own way. Lovely kids, husband, friends, lost half my body weight, and now soon to finally lay old ghosts to rest. My mother would be so furious if she could see me now.'

Emma giggled. 'And mine, vicious old cow.'

'So cheer up. Don't let her win, and to be honest if Robert said all that, then you are so much better without him.' Karen stood up and took Emma's half empty mug from her hand. 'Right, keep an eye on the kids. Time for a nice glass of red I think.'

An hour later Tristan popped in en route to a house call. He walked into the conservatory to find the two women he loved most in his life laughing like loons. 'Oh, you two seem to be getting on well,' he said, a big smile of relief on his face. He eyed the near empty wine bottle on the table. 'Ah. Should you be drinking when the kids are around?'

Emma flapped her hands at him. 'Oh, shush, Tris. You can be so stuffy sometimes! The kids are having fun. I promised to go out and play in the Wendy house in a minute.' Emma giggled.

'And I have a lion's arse to ice!' Karen guffawed setting Emma off shrieking like a hyena.

'Right.' Tristan felt like he was intruding on a girl's night out and was glad. 'Well, I have patients to heal, so I'll see you both later.' Tristan chuckled. He felt a weight lift from his shoulders as he walked to the door. Thank goodness things were good between his wife and sister. He'd half expected to come in and find stony silence and glares of anger from Karen, or worse. And it was Sebastian's birthday tomorrow, and his afternoon off. Yep, things were certainly on the up.

A little voice of doom came unbidden to his ear as he stepped out into the cold. *Yes, Tristan, just the small question of going to the police to sort out now.* The weight returned, settling across his shoulders like a black thundercloud ready to burst.

CHAPTER 29

'On November the twenty-second three years ago you had more to worry about than a lion's wonky arse,' Tristan said with a laugh.

Karen frowned and huffed again. The cake just wasn't working. She'd been up since six and two hours later after applying and re-applying the icing, the lion looked like it had some hideous inoperable growth on its rump.

'I had an easier time than this giving birth,' she said, sticking her empty mug under Tristan's nose and pointing to the cafetière.

'Oh, I think not,' he said, pouring coffee. 'I remember every painful minute of it.'

'Yeah, well this is painful too. I so wanted it to at least *look* like a lion.'

'It *does* look like a lion and stop fussing! Sebastian will adore it.' He kissed her on the cheek and headed for the door. 'It was made with love, just like the kids and that's all that matters.'

Karen waved him off to work with a lump in her throat. He said the loveliest things and really was the most wonderful man in the world. He was even going to dodge a meeting and pop back earlier than he should so he could see Sebastian blow the candles out on his cake. How on earth did she manage to bag such a fantastic guy?

And of all the toys they'd had that morning, Sebastian loved the farm Tris had got him a few weeks ago the best and he and Bella were busy playing with it in the sitting room.

'Mummy, look at the famer's smellingtons,' Sebastian said, holding up the little figure as Karen walked in. She hadn't the heart to correct him, and given the terrain a real farmer walked through, 'smellingtons' was probably an apt description.

'Hey, happy birthday, my gorgeous boy!' Emma said, entering the room in her pyjamas and slippers. Sebastian made a beeline for the big parcel she had under her arm nearly knocking her off her feet. As Emma knelt down amid paper and toys, Karen told her that there was a bacon sandwich with her name on it ready in ten minutes. 'Oh, you're a star!' Emma said, rolling her eyes at Sebastian's attempts to pack Bella into an empty box.

In the kitchen Karen smiled at the lion cake and put it in the cupboard until later. It was true what Tristan said about love. Love and a good family could get you through most things and last night, she, Emma and Tris had talked everything through again. They had eventually agreed that she would go with Emma's version of events, even if it meant another lie.

Emma's clincher had been that there was a good

264

chance that the truth could very well end up with the possibility of her losing everything. And hearing the facts in law-speak, cold, hard and in black and white had dropped a dollop of reality like a stone into her heart. Yes, Karen would be herself again if she told the truth, but what would the good of that be if she was in prison? So the lie had won. She hated it, but Karen figured it was a price she'd have to pay if she were to get her life back, keep her freedom and most importantly her family together.

They had also decided that Emma would take some of her long overdue leave and come down to stay with them for a few days next week. It would kill two birds with one stone for Emma. She would be able to go with Karen when she went to see the police *and* she would have some much needed time to get her head together away from Robert who worked in the next office.

Karen had suggested that she would talk to Buchanan too. He seemed decent enough when he'd come round to tell them about Andrea, and he would at least be a familiar face.

Emma had impressed upon her again that she might not get away with it completely, particularly if some bright spark somewhere decided there was enough evidence or doubt in her story to resurrect the cold case, do some investigation and bring it to court.

She had understood why Karen wanted to go ahead though. There had been a lot of understanding and forging of new bonds between her and Emma last night. It was just a pity that it had taken something as serious as this and the breakdown of Emma's relationship for both of them to realise that they'd really like to make a friend of the other.

A knock at the door saw Karen glancing at the clock with trepidation. Surely that couldn't be the first guests? It wasn't even ten o'clock. She wasn't anywhere near prepared and hoped it was just Kevin the postman as she hurried to the hallway.

On the doorstep, her face pinched and wearing an expression to rival any tragedy mask, stood Linda. The trepidation fell to the wayside, replaced by Karen's heart sinking to her boots amid a weight of guilt. Neither she nor Tris had given the poor woman a second thought since that day she'd come round to the house when they were racing out to meet up with Andrea. Heck, Tristan had practically shut the door on her.

Karen eyed a gaily-wrapped parcel under Linda's arm; obviously a present for Seb, and a flush crept along her neck and into her cheeks as she remembered how awful she'd been to Linda that day on the beach when she'd noticed her drooling over her husband. She really ought to have been more understanding, but because she was still reeling from the shock of meeting Andrea the night before, she hadn't been herself. In fact that was an understatement. Still, all that was to be expected given the circumstances. But now it was time to make amends.

'Linda, how lovely to see you!' Karen cried, as she stepped forward and enveloped Linda in a warm embrace. She felt the other woman stiffen and turn her cheek away from Karen's lips. Karen cringed. *Damn it, she must be really hurt.* 'I was only saying to Tristan the other day that we should invite you over for dinner or something.' Karen hoped her wide bright smile might soon be reflected in Linda's face, but the tragedy mask, though lifting a bit, still hung there.

'Did you? That's nice,' Linda muttered looking past Karen to the rumpus coming from the play-room. She sounded as if she believed Karen's words about as much as the existence of Father Christmas. 'I just popped over to bring Sebastian a present. It isn't much but—'

'Oh, that's so kind. Come in, come in.' Karen ushered Linda inside and led the way to the kitchen. 'Wait until you see my pitiful excuse for a lion cake, you will laugh your socks off.' Karen glanced over her shoulder at Linda and saw that she didn't look close to laughing, smiling or even smirking. Not even a little bit.

Linda placed the present on the counter and folded her arms tightly across her chest. Karen felt instinctively that it wasn't just somewhere to put her arms, it was a defensive gesture, a no-nonsense stance. The look in Linda's eye added to the feeling that she was here for a reason and it wasn't to bring Sebastian a present.

'I won't beat about the bush, Karen. I have

something to say and I don't think you are going to like it.'

Oh, great, more problems, not had many of those for a while. Karen took a deep breath and with it, a note of calm unexpectedly slipped into her psyche. 'That sounds ominous. Please take a seat and I'll pour you some coffee. I was just going to have some myself. I—'

'I'll stand thanks. It won't take long and then I'll be off.' Linda's navy-blue eyes had darkened to hard beads of anger but something else lurked behind their depths. Was it fear, uncertainty?

Karen gave a half smile and then turned her back to pour coffee for herself. 'Okay, I'm listening.'

'It's about Tris. I ran into him the other day and he said he was glad he'd seen me as he wanted to talk to me.' Linda's voice sounded strained – strung out.

Karen climbed onto a kitchen stool and sipped her coffee. 'So, what did he say?'

'He said that he suggested I get another GP because he . . .' Linda bit her lip and danced her eyes away from Karen's. '. . . Because he was very attracted to me and he'd realised it that day on the beach. He's fallen for me, Karen. And . . . I must say, I'm very fond of him too.' Her eyes danced back again, challenging, defiant.

A few weeks ago Karen – a frightened, scared, vulnerable and shell-shocked version of herself – would have crumbled into a heap and crawled away into the shadows upon hearing this. In fact, she had been suspicious that Tris *did* fancy Linda at the time, but today she just felt like laughing. Now that Tristan knew everything about her past and had stuck by her, bolstered her, demonstrated his love for her unconditionally, the whole idea of him falling for Linda was preposterous.

In that moment she realised that she trusted him implicitly, totally and forever. But looking into the other woman's eyes, which were now much more uncertain and fearful than defiant, the urge to laugh disappeared; instead her heart went out to Linda. Poor, poor, desperate Linda. How on earth did she think she was going to carry off a fib this big? Didn't she realise that Tris, when confronted would just tell the truth? Karen sighed but said nothing while she wondered what on earth she should do next.

Linda uncrossed her arms after a few moments and snapped, 'Well, say something then.'

Again an unexpected sense of calm thankfully prodded Karen into a response. She was pleased to find that when she opened her mouth, her voice sounded steady and compassionate. 'I think that you are upset at the way we, no, I treated you that day at the beach and rightly so. I had a lot on my plate and I took it out on you, which was inexcusable. And since then I haven't exactly tried very hard to see how you are. Though, as I said . . . I have had a few problems of my own.'

Linda's bottom lip trembled and she shook her head. 'But aren't you angry that Tris is in love with me?'

'If that was the case, then I would be more upset than angry. But I don't think it is.' Karen shifted slightly on the stool and swallowed hard. 'What I *do* think is that you are still hurting very badly, understandably so because of your rat of an ex, and because Tris is a good doctor and such a lovely man, you have formed an attachment to him.'

Linda opened her mouth, looked like she was going to say something but then remained silent.

Karen pressed on. 'I also think that you have a right to be upset with me. I haven't been a very good friend to you, and I think you are trying to punish me, perhaps?'

Linda sniffed, started to bite her nails and looked anywhere apart from at Karen. That sniff told her she was correct. Having run out of words, Karen just went with her gut, climbed from the stool and put her arm around Linda. 'Hey, let me try to make amends. Why don't you stay and have some cake, give the present to Seb. The kids would love to see you.'

'And they all lived happily ever after, huh?' Linda shrugged Karen's arm from her shoulder and dashed at her eyes with the back of her hand.

'That would be nice, but no, I think it will take quite a while for both of us to get a happy ending.' Karen sighed. 'But I'm willing to work at it . . . and I hope you are.'

Linda folded her arms again but this time the action seemed to be one of protection or comfort. 'I can't believe you're being so nice to me . . .

when . . . and you saved my life too . . .' Her voice trailed off and she dashed at her eyes again.

'Look, I know you didn't really want to say those things. You just felt trapped, desperate and hurt, so lashed out. I have been there myself in the past; it isn't a nice place to be.'

Linda ran her fingers over the brightly coloured paper on the present and blinked the last of the moisture from her eyes. She raised them to look at Karen, who was gratified to see that they held no defiance, anger or fear – just sadness. 'I won't stay for the party; I'm not in a party mood to be honest. But thanks for understanding.' She nodded once and walked towards the door.

Karen hurried after her and tentatively put her hand on Linda's shoulder. 'Promise you'll come for a coffee with me soon? We'll have a chat and catch up properly?'

Linda turned and shrugged. 'I will, but not for a little while. I need to see my counsellor – get myself straight. I missed the last couple of sessions.' A ghost of a smile played over her lips. 'And you know what?'

Karen shook her head and smiled back. 'No, tell me.'

'I think Tristan was right. You would make a good counsellor, Karen.'

Just as Karen was trying to get over the visit from Linda, her thoughts in a whirl, Jenny and five or six women from the choir piled through the door at ten-thirty to help make the food. An hour later, eleven children between the ages of ten months to three years filled the house with squeals, yells and the occasional wail. It was all Karen could do to make herself heard as she tried to settle them for the unveiling of the cake and she held her breath when Tristan carried it aloft, the candles lighting up his proud face as he set it on the table in front of Seb.

'You said it was a dandelion cake, Mummy!' yelled Sebastian.

'No, it's a lion with a flowery hat on, like you asked for,' Tristan said, grinning at Karen.

Karen put her hand to her head and frowned. Then realisation dawned and she collapsed into fits of laughter. 'After all that stress . . . you *actually* asked for a dandelion flower . . . not a lion with a flowery hat. God, what a palaver I had trying to get its arse right!'

A little girl of about three with a beetroot red face wriggled out of her mother's grasp and pointed accusingly at Karen. 'Bella and Sebastian's Mummy said ARSE!' There was an uncomfortable silence for a few seconds and then the whole room erupted into laughter.

The kitchen looked as if it had suffered a direct hit in the Blitz as the last of the children lined up to receive their party bags on their way out.

Jenny leaned against the counter and giggled at one child's attempt to swap hers with a reluctant little boy. 'They're all the same, Naomi,' she said, stroking the round of her tummy. 'Off you go now, Mummy's waiting for you!'

Karen smiled at her gratefully and poured a much needed glass of wine for herself and a fruit juice for Jenny. 'How's junior? Kicking up a storm?'

'Yep, he kept me awake half the night and today I think he wanted to join in with the other kids.'

'How long have you got to go, Jenny?' Emma said, joining them and helping herself to wine.

'First of January. Though I wish it were sooner. I'm knackered.'

'Just over a month then. Do you know what it is?' Emma asked.

'Yes, it's a baby,' Karen quipped.

'No, we didn't want to know. We like surprises,' Jenny said.

It crossed Karen's mind that perhaps Jenny wouldn't like the surprise she was about to spring on them. But then again, knowing Jenny she'd just take it in her calm and easy stride as usual. Perhaps she should broach it with her sooner rather than later. Jenny and Michael were their closest friends in Kelerston after all.

It wasn't until much later that Karen shared Linda's visit with Tris and he said that she'd done absolutely the right thing. He'd also echoed Linda's sentiments about counselling too. Karen was beginning to come round to the idea, but that was something that she might think about in a trillion years when the next mahoosive hurdle had been cleared, so she shoved it into a drawer of her mind labelled – 'one day maybe'.

The following morning she was pleased that she'd taken the bull by the horns and arranged to pop round to Jenny's. Emma had gone back to Exeter first thing, but would return on Sunday evening, and on Monday she and Karen had made an appointment to see DCI Buchanan at 2.00 p.m. Tristan had swapped his afternoon off to look after the children while they went.

In three days Karen would be Melody again. The thought filled her with excitement, but of course a huge amount of trepidation took the edge off. It could all go horribly wrong.

Watching a ship sail serenely past on diamond chipped water from Jenny's sitting room, Karen vowed to push her worries away and concentrate on the positive. Tris and his sister knew and they were both supporting her. Jenny had become one of her very dear friends and would surely understand too. Michael would do anything that Jenny asked and was a lovely guy anyway, if a bit impulsive where the choir was concerned. The choir . . . that was another huge positive. Once she came clean she could sing again! God, she'd missed that so much.

Jenny had just popped upstairs to bring the baby clothes down to show her, and when she came back, Karen would tell her about her past. *Then what, Karen? What if she reacts badly, shows you the door? What if she thinks you are a cheat, a liar and wants you far away from her family?* Karen sighed; the vow to push her worries away had lasted all of about two seconds.

'Who would have thought that one little human being would need all this?' Jenny asked from the doorway, her face flushed with happiness.

Michael helped her carry the mountain of clothes, nappies, toys, blankets and a baby bath into the room and dump it all on the two settees. Sebastian ran in next with a potty on his head, followed by Bella wielding a rattle and squeaky toy.

'This is just the beginning,' Karen said, chuckling. 'And we had that pile times two within thirteen months, don't forget.'

Jenny stopped and put her hand to her head. 'Oh my God, of course you did. How on earth did you ever . . .' She looked at the kids chasing Michael around the room. 'I'll rephrase that, how *do* you ever cope?'

'I have absolutely no idea.' Karen picked up a little lemon outfit and hugged it to her chest. 'This is making me feel broody. Take them all away!'

'Do you want more?' Jenny sat down and sorted through the nappies.

'I don't think so, it's not really practical. We have one of each and we feel complete as a family. It's just when I see pregnant women and baby clothes . . .' Karen smiled.

'Well Him upstairs will help out on the decision front. Now, do you want a cuppa?' Karen nodded, but kept quiet about Him upstairs. So far God hadn't been too helpful in her life, apart from Tristan and the kids of course, that went without saying. But her acceptance of God was very much in the dock and the jury didn't look like they were coming back any time soon.

A quiet calm settled over the old vicarage as the two women sipped tea and talked babies. The quiet was courtesy of Michael's trip to the beach with the children. Jenny said he needed the practice and that Karen needed a break. Just as Karen was wondering how to raise the subject of her identity, Jenny put her head on one side and said, 'So out with it. What's on your mind?'

Karen was amazed that Jenny was so in tune with her considering she'd not seen too much of her lately, but it made her feel more comfortable in what she was about to say. 'Blimey, how perceptive are *you*?' Karen smiled. 'I do have something to say and I'm not sure how to begin, so I'll just start at the beginning I guess.'

Unlike the silence Tristan was met with when he had told his sister everything, Jenny kept a constant barrage of sighs, platitudes and questions flowing at Karen. It was a wonder that she ever got to the end of the story with all the interruptions and also the tearful bear hugs she kept getting.

Jenny sat back and dabbed at her eyes for the umpteenth time. 'My God, how the hell did you stay sane with all that in your past? I'd be a proper mess . . . look at me.' Jenny pointed to her face. 'Blubbing like this and I've only been listening to you.'

'I only got through it because I told Tris . . . and I'm so sorry for upsetting you, Jen. I just felt that you and Michael should know before I went to the police.'

Jenny leaned forward and looked earnestly into Karen's face. 'Don't be silly. I would be even more upset if you hadn't told me and I just read about it in the newspapers . . . well, if something goes wrong.'

These words sank Karen's hopeful little ship of optimism. Jenny apparently thought that it could go wrong too and the word 'newspapers' jolted Karen upright in her seat. 'Bloody hell. I hadn't really thought about that. Do you think it would make the main news and headlines?'

Jenny sighed and shrugged. 'Um . . . like I said, *if* it went wrong . . . I guess . . . it would definitely make the local news. But in the end, it is just tomorrow's chip paper or budgie cage liner. You have to do it for your peace of mind and I'm sure it will all be fine.'

Karen wasn't so sure, but she knew that Jenny was right. There was no way she'd back down now, she couldn't. And Tristan seemed more determined that she should do it now than even she was. He had held her close last night and whispered that he was so proud of her and that he backed her a thousand per cent. 'Chip paper, when was the last time you had chips? They come in little polystyrene trays or just plain paper nowadays,' Karen said, pulling a face in an attempt to lighten the mood.

Jenny put down a teddy and held Karen's hand. 'Look, no matter what happens, no matter what the consequences, we'll be here for you, Tris and the children, okay?'

Karen nodded and hugged her. There was nothing else to say, and if there had been she couldn't have got the words out anyway. With friends and family like she had, surely everything would be all right, wouldn't it?

CHAPTER 30

For a woman who should be stepping lightly from the dark shadows of the past and into a bright, honest and hopeful future, Karen felt as if she was sinking in a quicksand of fear wearing the heaviest concrete boots in the world. Upon waking that Monday morning, a sickly portent had settled somewhere between her heart and her gut, insistently prodding doubt into her mind and undermining her confidence.

What if the *'something went wrong'* that Jenny had mentioned the other day actually went wrong? What if Buchanan looked across his desk and said. *Sorry, Karen. I know you are lying through your teeth. I'm going to arrest you, then the case will go to trial where you'll be found guilty, be sent to prison and they'll throw away the key.*

Karen looked at the reflection of a woman in a sober black suit, green shirt and no-nonsense flat shoes and couldn't help noting that she looked as if she was going to a funeral. She leaned forward and loosed a few strands of hair from the severe ponytail she'd scraped her hair into and applied more blusher to her pale cheeks. Then resting her brow against the cool glass of the bedroom mirror, she wondered for the hundredth time that day if it wouldn't be more sensible to just keep quiet and hope for the best.

Of course Tristan hadn't been privy to her disquiet, nor had Emma who had arrived the night before, full of good humour and optimism about the meeting with Buchanan. Karen knew that most of that was just for her benefit and both Emma and her husband were trying to support her the best they could, so even a suggestion of a mind change would throw a huge spanner in the works. Clearly the way she felt now was just nerves and no wonder – she needed to remain calm, strong and collected. *But really, Karen, is going to the police the right thing to do?*

'Karen, it's almost a quarter past one. You ready?'

'Yes, Emma, just nipping to the loo,' Karen replied, as she hurried across the landing to the bathroom. Closing the door and slotting the latch into place behind her, she immediately felt safer. Perhaps she could stay in the bathroom for the rest of her life . . . or until she'd made a firm decision. But she didn't have the rest of her life, did she? She had about five minutes.

Sitting on the edge of the bath she ran cold water into the sink. Her dad had once told her that putting his hands in cold water when he felt nervous or stressed always helped him calm down. Karen had tried it from time to time over the years and it had helped a little she thought. Or at least she'd imagined it had.

The icy water closed over her hands up to her wrists and flattening her palms on the white ceramic surface, she watched tiny air bubbles forming around her pale fingers and long burgundy painted nails. Why had she let Jenny paint them this colour the other day? It looked as if she'd dipped them in chicken livers or something. They looked wrong and didn't go with the suit and sensible hairstyle. Was it too late to take the polish off? She eyed the bathroom cupboard where the nail varnish remover lived, but then the handsome features of DCI Buchanan floated into her head.

In her mind's eye he looked impatient and cross, as if he'd been waiting for something, but then had been disappointed. Tough, if Karen wanted to cancel the meeting then she would and he could look as disappointed as he damned well pleased. A little bubble escaped the contours of her hands and disappeared. Why did that happen anyway? Did the bubbles come out of your skin or what? Very odd.

'Karen, we need to get going. It will take half an hour to get to the police station in Truro. You okay?' Emma called outside the door.

'Yeah. Just sorting my hair out.'

'There's nothing wrong with your hair. Are you having second thoughts?'

Karen detected a hopeful note in Emma's voice. 'Yeah, I thought I might go to the nearest airport and escape to Bermuda or somewhere for the winter.'

'Oh, hardee-har. Tristan's getting the kids ready to go out for a walk. I'll wait for you in the car, shall I?'

'Yep. Be down in a minute.'

Karen noted that there were little bubbles forming on the silver plug chain too. *Ah, so it must be the air in the water when it's run into the bowl, you daft mare.* She checked herself. What the hell was she thinking about bubbles for? She needed to get a grip and sort this, one way or the other. Wrapping her finger around the chain, she pulled the plug and patted her hands dry on a towel.

Being slightly pink now, her hands provided a weird contrast to the nail polish. Was she calmer for the cold water? She thought so. She also thought about Buchanan again. It wasn't usual for people to make appointments with the police because they wanted to discuss *something important* and then cancel at the last minute was it? He might suspect it was something they'd not told him about Andrea, so if she didn't go this afternoon he might come round to the house anyway.

In the end that scenario was just secondary, however. Karen could make up some viable excuse and be rid of him in no time. But could she be rid of her past quite so easily? Would she be able to shelve it and lock it away forever in some strong box like she had her journal? Her dad would have said no.

After a particularly awful row he'd had with her mother not long before he'd become ill, he'd held his distraught daughter tightly and whispered in her ear, *Problems and mistakes have a habit of growing bigger and uglier the more you try and paper over the cracks, Melody. Believe me, I know.* Karen had never been very good at papering; she preferred painting and now was her chance to start over with a blank canvas. Before she could change her mind, she slid back the bolt and ran downstairs.

Tristan had just about got the children dressed appropriately for the blustery November afternoon, but was having a tussle with Sebastian over his hat and gloves. 'No hat, Daddy. I'm hot.'

'Ah, but when we get outside you won't be. It's cold outside, Seb.' Tristan smiled encouragingly and pulled his son's hat on again. Sebastian immediately removed it and pulled a face.

Karen walked over and picked him up. 'Hey, you will be cold outside, like Daddy says. Look, Bella has hers on and Daddy will put his on in a second, won't you, Daddy?' Karen looked at Tris pointedly.

'Oh, yes. I love to wear my hat.' Tristan flashed a fake smile.

Karen knew full well that he hated hats with a passion. Perhaps that's where their son got it from.

'Now, where did I put it?'

Karen returned a second later with a woolly green hat in her hand. She grinned. 'Here you are, my dear,' she said, pulling it over Tristan's head.

He sighed and pushed it back from his forehead a little.

'Now, you're all set for a lovely walk outside. Wish I was coming, I could do with my cobwebs blowing away.'

'I wish you were coming too. It's not too late to do an about turn you know . . . if you are having second thoughts?' Tristan said, pulling her into his arms.

They had agreed last night that there would be no theatrical goodbyes or tears. Now here he was, holding her tighter than a Boa constrictor and reading her mind!

Karen extricated herself and avoiding his eyes, gave him a quick peck on the cheek. She was a bit shaky and very emotional, so saying more right at that moment would not be the best plan. 'Give Mummy a kiss you two, and have a lovely time.' She crouched down and gave her children a quick cuddle and then headed for the door before the tidal wave of emotion swelling in her chest threatened to break, drowning her good intentions and firm resolve.

As she stepped through the door Tristan called, 'See you later, sweetheart. You'll be grand. I know it.' The tremor in his voice increased the swell and the lump in her throat, so without turning around she just raised a hand in farewell and closed the door behind her.

The office of DCI Max Buchanan was as unwelcoming as a snow in harvest time. Grey walls, small dark wood desk. No photographs of family or even a framed picture or two lifted the dreary atmosphere. The one poster that did hang on the wall behind Buchanan's head was of a cartoon thief stealing from a car. The words *Don't be a victim – lock your car!* stood out in bold black type on a red background. The only splash of colour in the place drew Karen's eyes as she sat down in front of the desk next to Emma.

Buchanan followed her eyeline and turned around to look at the poster as if he'd only just remembered it was there. 'I hope you remembered to lock your car today, ladies,' he said, shuffling papers on his desk and picking up his pen.

'Oh, yes, Inspector. We are very vigilant on those matters.' Karen nodded, and then wondered why the hell she'd used the word vigilant. She never used words like that. It made her sound like some neighbourhood watch snoop, all twitchy net curtains and gossip. It was because she was nervous. She really needed to think carefully about what she said before she opened her mouth. Buchanan wouldn't miss a trick.

'Can I get you some coffee or tea before we get started?' Buchanan asked, his hand hovering over his desk phone.

'That would be lovely, Inspector. Coffee for me,' Emma said, gently poking Karen's ankle with her shoe as she was mutely staring at the poster again.

'Um . . . oh, yes, and for me thanks.'

★   ★   ★

Once the coffee was ordered, Buchanan folded his hands behind his head, leaned back in his chair, stretched his legs out and crossed one over the other at the ankle. He was clearly at ease with the situation and his body language suggested to Karen that he was relaxed, but she sensed that this was for their benefit. The sharp grey eyes deftly assessing both herself and Emma left her in no doubt that he was in control and ready to pounce at any second.

'So, what have you come to talk to me about, Mrs Ainsworth? You said it was something important, important enough to bring your solicitor along.'

Shit, he was already twisting things. Take a deep breath and answer him. 'It is important, but as I said, Inspector, Emma is my sister-in-law. She just happens to be a solicitor.'

'Yes, I'm her moral support today, that's all,' Emma said, flashing a gorgeous smile at Buchanan that would have had lesser men grovelling at her feet.

Karen noted that Emma's beauty had already made an impact, evidenced by the Inspector's double take when she'd walked into his office. But now Buchanan just nodded and allowed a tiny smile to briefly curl the corners of his mouth. He was obviously determined not to be influenced by Emma's stunning good looks. Part of his training Karen surmised. Something told her he wasn't married as she'd seen no wedding ring, but that didn't mean that he wasn't marri—

'Mrs Ainsworth?' Buchanan broke into her thoughts, his head on one side quizzically.

'Yes?'

'Well, are you going to tell me why we're here?'

Karen closed her eyes and imagined Tris and the kids out walking the lanes, kicking puffs of multi-coloured autumn leaves into the crisp fresh air, roses in their cheeks and giggles in their throats. She sent a silent declaration of everlasting love to them, sent a prayer to who it may concern, just in case, and then opened her eyes. Karen looked at Emma, Buchanan, the floor, and then focused on the red poster on the wall. She took a huge breath and began.

After about a minute, Buchanan abandoned his fake nonchalant pose and drew his chair close to his desk. He hunched over it, pen in hand, scribbling furiously on a large pad in front of him as if he were taking a crucial exam. His eyes darted to Karen's face and then back to the pad like he was watching some crazy tennis match every time she said something important.

Five minutes later Karen had told him her real name, where she was from originally, that she'd tried to kill herself aged sixteen because she was obese and depressed and that she'd assumed a new identity with Bob and Maureen. She still hadn't told him the whole story and he hadn't asked.

Her words dried up in her throat and she felt

Emma's hand slip into hers. Buchanan put his pen neatly by the side of his pad, gave her a sympathetic look – Karen suspected training again – and then he said, 'Right, I need to ask more about all this, Karen . . . er, Melody. You told me you were a depressed, troubled teenager. Why couldn't you go to your parents for help? Did you not get on with them?'

Karen felt tears forming behind her eyes and took a sip of coffee. How could she formulate the words and then say them out loud in this dingy little space? How could she say them to a policeman who would have no suitable expression of response in his training kit to the fact that she'd done all that because she'd found her mother dead? God only knew how he'd cope if she told him the whole truth. He'd probably fold his arms, unfold them, look sympathetic, frown, pace a bit and finally collapse in shock. Karen felt a smirk coming on. This alarmed her. For one thing, Buchanan would think she was winding him up, for another, why did she want to smirk in such a situation? She guessed that it must be because laughter and tears were often too close together. Right now, Karen couldn't slip a piece of paper between the two.

Emma squeezed her hand and said, 'Do you want me to tell him, love?'

Karen's heart thumped in her chest, she couldn't take enough air in and the grey walls seemed to be closing in around her. She grabbed at Emma's words as if they were the only lifeline in a storm at sea. 'Yes . . . yes, please, I do,' she managed in a trembling voice.

After Emma had finished, Buchanan stood and moved to the door. He kept his expression blank as he said, 'Okay. Now your request to see a DCI rather than a lower ranking officer makes more sense. In view of this latest information, I in turn will have to speak with my superiors. I must inform you that it will mean an interview and you'll have to make a statement. I'll be back in a while.'

Karen turned to Emma as soon as he'd gone. 'Hell, Emma, that sounds really serious!'

Emma patted Karen's leg and shook her head. 'I told you you'd have to make a statement, and an interview is routine in these circumstances.'

'Yes, but his voice sounded so stern. He suspects I killed her, doesn't he?'

'Calm down. He sounded normal to me, just doing his official duty, that's all.' Emma smiled encouragingly.

Karen felt anything but encouraged half an hour later in the interview room when she looked across the desk into the cold, shark eyes of DS Deborah Vessey. She hadn't asked many questions compared to Buchanan, but she never smiled or nodded her understanding in the way that he did. In her early thirties with short dark hair, thin mean lips and cheekbones you could slice bacon on, Vessey looked like she had been a hanging judge in a past life and wanted to revisit that incarnation in the future.

'So this man you say your mother was having sex with on that night,' Vessey said, knitting her perfectly plucked and pencilled eyebrows together. 'How could you be sure he was gone?'

Karen shrugged. What the hell did she mean? Did she think he was hiding under the bed? 'He wasn't in the house.'

'How could you be sure? Did you look around for him? Call the police?'

'No.'

'So immediately after waking and finding your mother killed, you didn't ring the police, just calmly found paper and wrote a note? If it were me back then I'd be scared for my own life, not knowing for certain if the killer had gone or not.'

Karen saw the other woman sneer at her down her nose as if she'd scored a point. Stupid cow. 'Well, DS Vessey, it wasn't you back then, it was me. And given that I was suicidal, why would I have cared if there *was* a killer in the house or not?'

Vessey twitched her nose and came back quick as a flash. 'Because I would suggest that it's a natural reaction. You wake up for a drink, come downstairs, find your mother stabbed and every instinct would tell you to run.' The dark, shark eyes latched on to Karen's blue ones and held them fast.

Emma leaned forward and said calmly, 'And I would suggest that people react in different ways to situations like this. Karen was distressed and devastated to find her mother dead. She was unhappy with her life already, as she's said, and this was the last straw. She thought she was better off dead.'

'And you said he sounded Greek?' Buchanan chipped in before Vessey could say more.

'Yes. Or Italian, something like that. Why?'

'That should help a little when we investigate. A faceless man wouldn't be much to go on, but an accent might jog people's memories,' he said, levelling a hard stare at Karen.

Karen sat back in the chair and absorbed the stare unflinchingly. She had hoped that they wouldn't investigate, that the case was too cold and would cost too much to spend money on, but apparently it wasn't to be. In her heart of hearts she'd expected it. And at least Emma had prepared her.

She had said they'd possibly go back to Penarthry and ask the locals in the Black Bull, where her mother had worked, about her mother's 'boyfriends' and her general character.

Luckily, Karen herself had kept a very low profile around the town so people wouldn't have a lot to say about her. They might have a lot to say about her mother though. It would soon become clear that Karen was telling the truth about the men.

Vessey doodled absently on the pad in front of

her with a pencil and then snapped her eyes on Karen's again. 'You say you didn't get on with your mother when DCI Buchanan asked earlier. What exactly did you mean by that?'

'I meant we didn't get on,' Karen said evenly. There was no way this woman was getting her to say more than she needed to.

'Can you be more specific? Did you hate her for bringing men home? And what about your father? You say he died of cancer. Did you get on with him?'

Karen's hackles were beginning to rise. Vessey kept saying *you say* as if she thought she was lying. How dare she imply that her dad didn't die of cancer? Why would she make that up?

'I did get on with my dad, yes.' Karen tried to keep an edge from her voice. 'I was devastated when he died. And I didn't like the company my mum kept, no. I could never seem to do anything right for her.'

'So you weren't too upset when she died then. In fact you might have been secretly pleased?'

'Of course she wasn't. Her mother had been stabbed to death for goodness sake,' Emma commented, barely concealing her contempt.

'I asked Karen.'

Karen had had enough of this. Why wasn't Buchanan saying anything now? Was it a game of two halves and Vessey was the bad cop? How very melodramatic. 'Are you trying to say I killed her?'

'I wasn't, but it's a question which has to be asked sooner or later.'

'Why does it?' Emma interjected again. 'Karen and I came here in good faith to set the record straight. Nobody forced her, she just thought it was time, and you question her here on tape as if she's a criminal.'

'Oh, please, Miss Ainsworth.' Buchanan steepled his fingers under his chin and looked disparagingly at Emma. 'You agreed to it, and you of all people must know that we'd have to ask a variety of questions in such a case as this, including some that might not be to your liking. We wouldn't be doing our jobs if we didn't.'

'And assuming another identity and faking official documents is a crime. Some therefore would say Mrs Ainsworth *is* actually a criminal,' Vessey said.

'That wasn't her doing. Bob and Maureen did that for her. She was a minor at the time, as well you know,' Emma replied heatedly.

'She *was* a minor, but she's not now. *Now* it could be seen as fraud.'

'You know as well as I do that *intent* would have to be proven. Karen did not *intend* to defraud anyone. She was just a frightened young girl who had suffered a huge trauma.'

'Let's get back to the main issue here, shall we?' Vessey muttered. 'Did you kill your mother, Karen?'

Karen looked at both police officers unblinkingly.

293

'No, I did not.' Even though there had been no hesitation in her voice, the words hung in the air brittle and shrill. To Karen's ears her voice had sounded like someone else's – someone who was a guilty as sin.

Vessey seem to detect it too and cocked her head to one side. 'Not even in self-defence?'

'No.'

'Did your mother ever hit you? In my experience I have found that when people make a habit of getting drunk regularly and have the kind of life-style your mother seems to have had, violence is never far behind.'

'From time to time she did, but not in the time leading up to her death,' Karen said quietly. A flame crept along her neck and she sucked the inside of her cheek in between her teeth. Vessey was *really* making her feel uncomfortable now. Why the hell had she done this? Why, oh why, hadn't she listened to Tris at the outset?

'Really?' Buchanan asked, rubbing his fingers over his five o'clock stubble.

'Yes, really,' Emma answered. 'And now I think you have quite enough. We've been here a very long time.' She narrowed her eyes at Buchanan. '*Volunteered* to come here might I add, and now we're leaving. I'm sure you'll be in touch shortly.' Emma stood and tipped her head, indicating that Karen should do the same.

'We're not done yet,' Vessey growled and looked up at Emma from hooded eyes.

'Oh, I think we are, unless you want to charge Karen with something?' Emma glowered back.

'No need for that, Miss Ainsworth, but rest assured we will start investigations shortly.' Buchanan leaned forward and spoke into the tape recorder. 'Interview terminated at four fifteen p.m.' He turned it off, walked to the door and held it open.

'What investigations will you do?' Karen asked quietly, as she shrugged on her coat.

'Well, like I said before, we need to interview people who remember your mother to see if they can place the man she was with that night. We'll also see what we can find out from the folks in the wider community, school, shops et cetera.'

Karen slipped her arm through Emma's, who was saying something to Vessey and leaned heavily against her. The word *school* kicked so hard into her gut that she could have cried out. Somehow she didn't though, and instead she said, 'I honestly didn't think that you'd be so suspicious of me.'

'We're not necessarily, Mrs Ainsworth, but you *must* understand we have to ask these awkward questions of you. And we must also do a proper investigation. After all, there might be a slight possibility that we can catch your mother's killer even after so many years. Surely you would like there to be justice for her, even though she wasn't the most perfect parent?'

Karen nodded and stepped out into the corridor after Emma. 'Yes, of course.' And then her mouth went into overdrive and she could have slapped herself immediately after she said, 'I suppose you're going to say *don't leave town* like they do in the corny movies?'

Buchanan attempted a weak smile, but the atmosphere was cold and there was no humour behind his eyes. 'Something like that,' he said, glancing at Vessey who had joined them, arms folded, face deadpan. And when Karen saw the hostile look in her eye, the atmosphere turned from cold to way below freezing.

CHAPTER 31

On the drive home Karen barely spoke, just leaned her head against the cool of the window and tried to stop herself from collapsing in a quivering heap. If Karen was quiet, Emma was the opposite, trying to fill the silence as if she were trying to win gold for the prattler's Olympics. Karen nodded from time to time and shrugged at various questions tipped her way. Eventually Emma said, 'Come on, Karen. It isn't *that* bad, you know. They had to ask those questions, Buchanan was right there . . . and after all I . . .' Emma's voice tailed off.

If she says I told you so I'll not be responsible for my actions. Karen buzzed down the window and took in big gulps of the wood-smoke, damp leaves and manure. Manure was appropriate given the situation. Even though it could have been worse, as Emma kept saying, Karen didn't see how. They'd practically accused her of murder and Vessey especially had been a prize bitch about it all. Still, that was her job she guessed.

'You okay? Do you want to stop, take a walk and get some air?'

'No. I just want to get home and then never leave again. I don't know how much longer I'll be allowed to stay there after all.'

'Oh, Karen. Let's not get the whole thing out of proportion. They have very little to go on, very little. They've got to go through the motions of investigating, but I'm betting my last pound they won't have enough for the CPS to make a case. Don't forget the cost of these things is an important factor, especially nowadays.'

Karen barely heard. She focused on the first few words. 'Out of proportion? I wonder how *you* would be reacting right now if it *was* you in my position, Emma? Would you be sitting here laughing your head off, full of the joys then?'

Emma tutted. 'No, of course not. But I really think—'

'You know what? I don't want to know what you really think at the moment. I'd just like some head space if you don't mind.' Karen buzzed the window back up and closed her eyes. She felt rotten for snapping. Emma had been bloody fantastic after all. But they were going to need more than platitudes and positive mental attitude to get through this.

Emma would not be as cheerful if she had latched on to the extra big grub of information in the whole putrid maggoty apple of a mess. But Karen wasn't sure she'd heard everything Buchanan had said, as she'd been talking to Vessey. This extra big grub went by the name of Andrea Stanton.

When Buchanan had mentioned investigating Karen's old school, her whole world rocked, teetering precariously on the edge of a precipice, just like the big boulder in the famous cartoon about a coyote and a roadrunner.

If Buchanan or cold case detectives got wriggling around in her school records, then the boulder would tumble to the canyon below. Then she, Tris, the children and their lovely life would be squashed flat under it. *Meep, meep.*

When they arrived home she apologised to Emma for being such a cow, kissed Tris, Sebastian and Bella and went straight to her bedroom. Even though it was only six o'clock, Karen couldn't bear the strain of pretending to be normal for the children and keeping her chin up. Tris hadn't asked how it went. Her face said it all as she'd walked in the door and more or less collapsed into his arms. Emma had filled him in while Karen had been in the loo trying not to be sick.

It was Tris who had suggested that she went upstairs and he'd bring up a meal later for them both. The very thought of food turned her stomach and she doubted that Tristan would be eating much either when she told him her fears about Andrea. Karen lay on the bed swaddled like someone having a duvet day. The quilt felt warm and comforting, but not nearly as comforting as her husband's arms would feel. She bit back a sob. God it had been so awful today, she felt violated.

It didn't seem fair. How had it happened that Karen was painted as the bad guy, when it had all gone pear-shaped in the first place because her mother had been such an evil witch?

All of a sudden she needed Tris more than life. She was about to call him when he popped his head around the door. 'Chicken casserole for Melody Ainsworth,' he said, and then his face fell as she burst into tears. Running to her, he set the tray on the bed and scooped her up into his arms. 'Hey, honey, I'm sorry. I thought you'd want to be called Melody now it is all out in the open.'

'It's not that, Tris. I do want to be called Melody again, but God, what a price I'm paying for it.'

Tris looked like a fish in a bowl of water full of algae after she'd told him why she was so worried. He opened and closed his mouth, apparently trying to find the right words but finding none. Eventually he lay down next to her and she placed her head on his chest, comforted by the steady beat of his heart.

'No wonder you were more upset than you should be, Melody,' he said eventually.

Hearing him speak her real name like that made her feel slightly weird, but in a good way. The timbre of his voice carrying the name her father had given her sparked a tiny bit of hope in the darkness. Everything was still a bit too dark to lift her spirits much at the moment, however. She held him tighter and said, 'I can't believe neither of us thought that the police might go to my old school. Not even Emma mentioned it.'

'Yep. It stands to reason that they would want to get a handle on the kind of girl you were. I guess we were just too wrapped up in all the frenzy to look at it objectively. Why didn't you ask what Emma thought?'

'I don't know. She didn't latch on, not sure she heard everything he said, and I just wanted to pretend it wasn't happening, I guess.'

After a few more minutes of silence, and concerned that Tris wasn't trying to bolster her morale and think of ways round it, Melody propped herself up on her elbow and looked into his eyes. 'So, you think that's it then? I'm up shit creek?'

Tris blew heavily down his nose. 'I think that if the police are told by the school that you were bullied, and that Andrea was expelled because of it, only an idiot would miss the connection between her death and you. Buchanan is no idiot and this Vessey sounds even sharper. You were seen talking to her in the kitchen a few days before by the verger, for God's sake. And then when her death was announced you never admitted to knowing her at all when you were at school together. It doesn't look marvellous, does it?'

Melody lay back down again. Her limbs felt leaden, her blood chilled. If Tristan was voicing her worst fears, not even trying to pull punches, there was no hope for them. Silence sat between them as wide as a canyon. There was nothing to say. Melody felt a fat teardrop slip from the corner of her eye and trace a hot path down her cheek and onto the pillow.

Then from a spark in the darkness, a thought kindled. 'Believe me, I know how it looks. Ever since they mentioned going to school the whole thing's been whirling round my head. The thing is, Tris, she was an addict. They must have found needles and stuff in her house? Of course it looks suspicious that I never told anyone that I knew her, and that's why I think they'll dig further into my case, but murder? How could they possibly try to pin her death on me?'

'Isn't it obvious?' Tris sighed. 'I'm a doctor. I could easily have got heroin and done the deed. I'm your husband, you were being blackmailed, your whole past was about to be blurted out so I got rid of the problem.'

Melody's heart hammered up the scale and a cold wind of fear snuffed out the spark. 'But how could they know that she was blackmailing me? And how could they prove something that never happened, anyway? You weren't involved with her death, hell, neither of us were there!'

Tristan sat up and put his head in his hands. 'It isn't rocket science. And I don't know, Melody, but I think they'll have a bloody good go. Wouldn't you if you were Buchanan and found out about Andrea?'

Melody sat up and started to bite the skin at the side of her nails. She didn't reply, there was no need. *What the hell were they going to do?*

'Which teacher knew you best at school? Mrs Goodsale?'

'Goodhale, yes. She was my Head of Year too, so they would definitely question her. Oh God, Tris. This looks terrible. And as you said, you might get drawn into it too now!'

Tris took her into his arms and kissed her tears away. 'Shh, calm down. I just presented the worst case scenario. I'm sorry, I was thinking aloud, really. We'll find a way round this. I promise.'

Tris got up to check on Emma and the kids, but before he went he offered to give her something to make her sleep. She gratefully accepted. How wonderful it would be to slip into oblivion, to sleep but never wake up. Today she had become Melody again. And at that moment, she felt firmly back inside her sixteen year old self on that fateful night by the side of the moonlit sea.

CHAPTER 32

It feels good to be writing again. Well, as good as I can feel at the moment with the worry of the police investigation plaguing my every waking hour. Tristan asked me at the start of all this why I needed to 'confess' now that Andrea was dead and he knew all the story. I told him but I'm not sure he got it, not really. I get it, of course, but I think I need to see my reasons put down in black and white, order my thoughts to give me the strength and conviction to get through this awful time.

If I kept quiet I couldn't be true to myself. If I continued to be Karen from Swindon, I would deny my origins, my dad, what made me, me. Could I ever truly rest, live a normal life, fearful that at any moment someone else from my past might recognise me, go to the police, and blow my world sky high? I wouldn't have had time to prepare Tris, the kids? I would have looked SO guilty. The press might have got hold of it, savaged me, splashed photographs of the old 'singing whale' over the news. If that had happened, I don't think I could get through it, not again. The chances of me going to prison would have been higher, too, I reckon in that situation – if I'd been 'outed' instead of coming forward myself.

Also, Tris helped me to make the decision. He was angry at first, of course he was, me lying to him about the agoraphobia – though in the latter stages I feel I did get depressed and fearful of leaving the house more than usual when Andrea was taunting me – about the coming from Swindon, stealing the drugs for Andrea, the whole thing. But then he showed his unconditional love, pure and simple. I didn't deserve that, still feel I don't, but because of Tris, I felt strong enough to come forward, with him beside me I felt invincible . . . even, righteous.

Of course, I didn't tell the whole truth, even though I desperately wanted to. The whole truth and my conscience being salved wouldn't tuck the kids in at night, watch them grow, be there for them, be a wife to my husband, while I was in prison, would it? And as Emma said, the likelihood of that would have been greater if I had come completely clean. How my mother would have loved it if I ended up in a cell somewhere. That would have been the icing on the cake. Obviously I know she is long dead, but she'd have still won.

I sometimes think I should have stayed in Swindon, saved myself all the heartache. Of course I could have been recognised, sprung there, too, but very unlikely. And I would still be living a lie. I ached to come back to my beloved Cornwall with its open spaces, sense of freedom, windswept beaches, rugged coastline and homely people. I could see Tristan itched to come back, too, and when he got promotion he almost became a different guy. More hopeful, less stressed, more young and carefree. He was so excited when he got the call to say his application to be a GP in Kelerston had been successful. How could I rain on his parade? I didn't want to rain on his parade; I needed it as much as he did. But how could I pull it off without getting recognised? The answer came when I read an article on agoraphobia in one of Tristan's medical journals. It would be hard to keep up the pretence, but it would be a chance . . . so reluctantly I agreed to move.

And how do I feel? Do I regret the decision to return here – to try for a real shot at a normal life in the place Tris and I love, to be singing again, to have met some lovely people like Jen and Michael – now that the police are digging their clever little snouts into my past? I don't know, is the answer. I'm erring on the side of no regrets, because of everything I have just written, but . . . oh God, please let it end well. I need a happy ending, and with everything I have been through in my life, I think it's overdue.

CHAPTER 33

After surgery the next afternoon, Tristan sighed and shook his head as he typed an address into the GPS. Why the bloody hell had he promised that they'd find a way around it to Karen – or Melody rather, it was taking a while getting used to that. She had refused to get up today, even to see her children.

When he'd left this morning she had barely spoken to him, just stared out of the window across the grey drizzle soaked garden, wrapped up in a duvet. Emma had thankfully extended her leave until Friday because Tristan was struggling to get cover at the surgery. She had insisted that she didn't mind staying as she wanted to make the most of her time with her niece and nephew. Emma was concerned, however, that Melody was disproportionately upset at this stage. The time to worry would be if the police decided they'd found something.

Tristan explained to her that they probably would, once they'd been to Melody's old school. Emma's reaction to that hadn't been at all comforting. She couldn't believe that she'd not put two and two together, but at the time Buchanan was talking to Melody, she had been talking to Vessey and was only listening with half an ear. She then said that if she hadn't made the connection, then perhaps the police wouldn't either. Both Tristan and his sister knew that was a load of baloney, but he knew she was just trying to pull even a tiny vestige of hope out of the bag for him. At the moment though the bag seemed well and truly empty.

The only straw left to clutch at was a half-baked idea that had been floating around his head since last night. In the course of the few weeks since she'd divulged her identity to him, Melody had told him that Mrs Goodhale had been lovely to her throughout her secondary school years. She'd been a lone shoulder to cry on when Melody's dad died and had always encouraged her to share her beautiful voice with the world.

When Melody had piled on the pounds, Mrs Goodhale had been a counsellor and a huge support. His wife had remembered that some days she'd been allowed to stay in her Head of Year's office when it had all got too much and she couldn't face a lesson or a break time. This open door policy had been a lifesaver. According to the school website, Mrs Goodhale no longer worked there, but Tristan had found her easily in the phone book. There weren't too many Goodhales listed, funnily enough, and it was to her address that he now drove.

Penarthry was so much like Kelerston that Tristan had to do a double take as he trundled the car up through the narrow streets, even down to the lookalike butcher's shop, though instead of Jackson's this establishment was called Corney's. It had been years since he'd actually been here, though he'd been near it hundreds of times, of course, on the A30 bypassing the town.

A thought occurred to him that he could have walked past Melody on the street back then and he wouldn't have known. Not to know her was unthinkable to him now. Apart from the kids, she was his whole world. When she walked into the room his heart still danced at the sight of her and sometimes after a long day at the surgery, he'd only to picture her waiting at home and his spirits would lift in anticipation of the welcoming kiss she always planted on his lips as he came through the door.

Tristan slowed the car and turned into a narrow country lane just past the village border. The ocean hugged the coastline to his right, seabirds danced in the blue sky and he wished he could get out and explore, just go for a walk. He couldn't though – he had a mission to complete.

The arrow on the map told him he would reach his destination in one minute. He hoped that the visit would bear the 'we'll get round this' kind of fruit he had promised Melody the night before, or their future destination would be decidedly bleak. Though Tristan didn't see himself as the strong hero type character of romance novels, he knew that he'd do anything for his wife. And what he was about to do was pretty heroic he thought, because if it went pear-shaped, it wouldn't look good for him at all.

Barbara Goodhale opened her door and shot a questioning smile in Tristan's direction. He immediately warmed to her; she just had one of those faces. He judged her to be about sixty, youthfully dressed in jeans and a checked shirt, wore her salt and pepper hair in a ponytail and her brandy coloured eyes assessed Tristan intelligently.

'Good afternoon, Mrs Goodhale. I'm Dr Tristan Ainsworth. I wonder if I might have a few moments of your time?'

Barbara frowned. 'Oh, so you're not selling anything?'

'No, certainly not.' Tristan gave her his most reassuring smile.

'Um, I don't know. What's it about . . . and do you have any ID?'

Tristan nodded and held up his plastic ID card that he always wore around his neck when he was working.

She read the badge carefully. 'And what's it about?'

Tristan was tongue-tied. He was about to tell a giant fib and it didn't come naturally to him. Barbara's eyes narrowed and he could almost read her mind. *She thinks I'm a bit shady and who can blame her. Stood here on her doorstep at the end of a country lane, just staring at her and if she's on her own . . .*

'Well?' she asked, folding her arms.

Now she sounded just like a schoolteacher, but then that wasn't surprising. He took a deep breath. 'Sorry for hesitating, but I think you might be in shock when I tell you. Do you remember teaching someone called Melody Rafter?'

Barbara's eyes widened and she nodded. 'Yes, I do, very well. Why?'

'Because I'm her therapist and she's having a tough time at the moment. I'd just like to ask you a few questions about her school life.'

She leaned against the door frame and gasped, 'My God! She didn't drown then?'

Tristan shook his head and grinned. 'No. She's very much alive, Mrs Goodhale.'

In the lemon, white and olive themed sitting room, Tristan waited for tea. The decor cheered him a little and through the French doors, the small walled garden framed by blue agapanthus, red skimmia, and yellow strelitzia thrust their colours defiantly against the grey of the November afternoon.

Barbara had almost cried with relief when he'd explained that Melody had been rescued and assumed another life. Tristan had told her that she was in therapy and haunted by memories of her school life at the moment. He wanted to see if her old teacher could shed any more light on it than he already knew. Tristan hated himself for lying to such a lovely woman, but that's what he had to do until he was absolutely sure if he could trust her or not.

A moment later she came in carrying two mugs of tea and a packet of biscuits under her arm. 'I just can't get over it, Doctor. My husband, Terry, won't either when he gets back.'

'Please call me Tristan. He knew her too?' Tristan smiled, taking the offered mug.

'No. But I used to often break my heart to him about her after I thought she'd taken her own life. I broke my heart about her when she was alive, too. Her mother wasn't the best parent.'

'Right, yes. Melody did mention that. She also mentioned that she didn't really tell anyone at school about her home life, though.'

'She didn't. But I expect you know she put an awful lot of weight on very quickly?'

Tristan stirred his tea and nodded.

'Well, unbeknownst to Melody, I phoned her mother and asked her to come in and see me. I wanted to talk about it with her. Melody was comfort eating because of her dad's death and I hoped her mother and I could discuss ways to help.' Barbara shook her head sadly and took a sip of tea.

'So I'm guessing she didn't come?'

'You guessed right. In all my years of teaching, and there were many,' she rolled her eyes, 'I just retired this year, I have never spoken to a more foul-mouthed, uncaring parent.'

'She didn't want to know?'

'That's putting it mildly. Do you know, Tristan, I've kicked myself many times over the years for not taking further action, but I thought social services would just make things worse for poor Melody. I heard stuff about her mother and men too – gossip around town, you know?' Tristan nodded again. 'But I chose to let things lie. So stupid. If I hadn't, perhaps she wouldn't have tried to kill herself.'

Tristan put his mug down and leaned forward. 'No, really you mustn't think that, Barbara. Melody told me that she was more worried about social services than staying at home. She was just planning to hold on until after she did her exams and then she would get a job and leave. She also told me that she couldn't have coped as long as she did without your kindness, encouragement and open door policy.'

Barbara's eyes misted over. 'Thank you for that. It means a lot.'

Tristan sat back and steepled his fingers. Just how should he tackle the next bit? How much did she remember about Andrea and were there still records about what happened? They were the sixty-nine million dollar questions. But he needed her untainted recall, not autosuggestion from him. He looked at her intently. 'Barbara, do you remember a girl called Andrea Stanton?'

She nearly choked on her tea. 'Do I? How could I forget! If there was ever a young woman who was actually evil, I swear it was her. She bullied Melody and other kids something rotten, but she was so sneaky, got her entourage to close ranks. We couldn't pin anything on her until the last year. Her parents were lovely, so you couldn't blame them. And yet poor Melody's mother was so vile – there's no justice sometimes, is there?'

This gave Tristan the perfect road in to the reason for his visit. 'No, there isn't, Barbara, but perhaps you could help Melody there.' He leaned forward again and rubbed his hands together, they felt clammy and a nervous rash had started on his neck. He'd not had that for years. Shit, this had to work or they were dead in the water. The irony of that thought, given Melody's past, wasn't lost on him.

'Barbara, Andrea died recently . . . a drugs overdose.'

She raised her eyebrows slightly and sighed. 'I'm not surprised. I suspected she dabbled, even at school. And if I'm honest, I'm not sure if I'm really sorry – like I said, she was vile to lots of kids. I'm sure she contributed to Melody trying to take her life, especially after the incident on the stage. No, there was no getting through to Andrea. Most wayward kids have some redeeming features, but not her. Not Andrea Stanton.'

Tristan swallowed hard. 'You see the thing is, Barbara, Andrea found out about Melody being still alive and blackmailed her, said she'd tell her family about her past and that she'd killed her mother if she didn't pay up.'

Barbara banged her mug down on the table. 'Such a bitch! I'm definitely not sorry that she's dead now! As if Melody could have done such a thing. The gossip round the place was that one of her mother's many drunken men had done it.'

Tristan encouraged by this response said, 'Yes. Well, after Andrea died, Melody decided that she couldn't hide any longer, never knowing whether someone else like Andrea would crawl out of the woodwork—'

'Huh, no chance of that, she was a one off,' Barbara spat.

'I think you're right there. But the trouble is, now she's told the police her real identity, they are investigating how Melody's mother died.' Tristan cleared his throat and rubbed the rash on his neck. 'Melody is terrified that when they come back here to Penarthry to talk to people who knew her back then, Andrea's name will come out. She didn't disclose to the police that she had known Andrea before, or that she was blackmailing her.'

Barbara leaned back and pinched the bridge of her nose between forefinger and thumb. 'I'm a little confused, Tristan. First you tell me you're here because Melody is having troubled memories. Now you say that the police are investigating her mother's death and then all this blackmail stuff about Andrea.'

'Yes, sorry. I didn't know how to approach it really. It is pretty huge, so I thought I'd start gently.'

315

Tristan knew this sounded lame but couldn't think of anything else.

Barbara's brandy eyes fixed on his and Tristan knew they wouldn't miss a trick. Any sliding around the truth he might try would be seized on like a hawk's talons upon a field mouse. Then she gave an encouraging little smile as if he were a pupil in class who couldn't express himself properly.

'Okay, let's get this straight. Melody has told the police who she really is and they are investigating how her mother died, presumably because they think Melody might have had a hand in it?'

Tristan nodded and rubbed his neck again. Barbara sighed, stood and walked over to look out at the garden. Tristan stared at her back feeling like a naughty schoolboy in her office.

'I see. And Melody hasn't told them that she knew Andrea years ago or that she was recently being blackmailed by her. Andrea is now dead. Melody is worried that when they find out from people who knew her, such as me, that Andrea bullied her rotten, the police will become suspicious about Melody keeping quiet. They might begin to think that Melody killed Andrea *and* her mother, too?' Barbara turned round to face Tristan.

'Um, yes, that's about the size of it,' Tristan said quietly, trying to avoid the hawk glare.

'Hm, well, I can tell you now,' she wagged her finger, 'and I'll tell any investigating officers, that Melody could *not* have done such a thing. It wasn't in her.' Barbara shifted her gaze from Tristan and stared at the wall, lost in thought. Presently she said, 'The only way I think Melody *could* have killed her mother, was if it were in self-defence. I can quite picture a scenario where her mother, roaring drunk as usual, had attacked poor Melody. Anyone would have done the same . . . but as for Andrea, no way. And how could she have killed her? Didn't you say it was a drugs overdose?'

Tristan began to feel like a nodding dog on the back shelf of a car. When she'd said the bit about self-defence he'd looked at the carpet to hide his flame-red face and now he daren't say anything, as he was scared his voice would sound like he'd borrowed it from Mickey Mouse.

'You *did* say drugs, Doctor?' Barbara apparently was getting fed up with a nod as a response.

'Yes, but Melody thinks that their suspicion might lead them to all sorts of false conclusions,' Tristan managed to say, sounding more like James Earl Jones now than Mickey Mouse, as he'd over-compensated for a possible squeak.

'Right . . . I can see the logic in that I suppose.' Barbara pursed her lips and then came to sit opposite Tristan. 'I have a plan,' she said, her eyes sparkling like polished conkers. 'The records I had of Melody will have been destroyed by now. They are kept for ten years only. Back then records were kept mostly in tutor group files on paper. Some were computerised, but our Head was a bit old-fashioned and not big on computers. And even if they go to the school and see the new Head, and he manages to find them on the school system, our policy was not to write the name of the bully on the records anyway. They might say something like, *an incident with a pupil from the same year group: action taken – parents contacted, or no blame approach used.* Things like that.' Barbara helped herself to a biscuit and nibbled thoughtfully.

'And if they questioned the other teachers they will draw a blank there, too,' she continued. 'Most who taught her have moved on to other jobs. And she only really had a strong relationship with me anyway. As you know, Melody kept herself very much to herself.'

She then fell silent and studied him closely. Her words had lifted his spirits. If there were no records to speak of, then apart from Barbara's testimony, there would be very little for the police to go on. Under her continued scrutiny, Tristan felt extremely uncomfortable, however. Barbara seemed to be weighing him up extremely carefully. And after a few moments he could stand it no longer.

'All that is very encouraging, Barbara, but what's your plan?'

'That depends on you. Who are you to Melody exactly? I can tell that you're more than a therapist by the way you talk about her. You are extremely fond of her. My years of experience tell me that you are a good man, but nevertheless you're hiding something. I knew that after the first ten minutes.'

'Um . . . I—'

'Don't even bother denying it. You flush beetroot, won't look me in the eye for more than a few seconds and have a nervous rash on your neck. I have seen a few of those, but normally on teenage boys who have been found smoking behind the proverbial bike sheds, not on thirty something medical practitioners.' Barbara chuckled, but Tristan wasn't fooled. She would stand nothing but the truth and he felt as if he had no option but to tell her. But could he totally trust her?

'I guess, you might be right,' he said with a sheepish grin. 'I'm not exactly her therapist. But can you give me a hint at your plan first, before I tell you . . . I am in a *really* tough spot here.'

'I knew it. *Busted,* as the kids would say!' Barbara said, her eyes shining triumphantly. She then drained her mug and sighed. 'Okay, my plan would be to keep shtum when plod comes calling. I would be as vague as I could possibly be; say I didn't really have anything to do with her beyond routine pastoral stuff. Say that her home life was poor, that she was a little withdrawn, but that nothing really terrible happened to her, yada, yada. I'm quite a good actress when I have to be, Tristan. All good teachers are. They can never be them-selves in front of a class of unruly teenagers.'

Tristan's heart thumped in his chest as he looked at this remarkable woman opposite. He couldn't believe his luck. This was more than he could have possibly hoped for, as she'd said exactly what he'd wanted to ask her to say in the first place! God, if

319

she were fighting their corner, perhaps they could really find a way through like he'd promised.

'That would be fantastic! Melody will be overjoyed that you'd be willing to do this for her—'

'Hang on.' Barbara shook her head and held up a finger in warning. 'I said I *would*, not that I *will*. Until you tell me the whole truth about who you are to Melody, then I'm promising nothing. And I don't have to remind you that I won't be satisfied with half-truths.'

Tristan nodded yet again and stood up. He didn't quite know how to begin, so from the inside pocket of his jacket he pulled out his wallet, shook out the concertina photo section and handed it to Mrs Goodhale. She looked carefully at the three photos of the Ainsworth family. One was of them all on the beach, one of them last Christmas, and the most recent one of the children either side of Melody as she and Bella helped Sebastian to blow the candles out on his lion birthday cake.

She looked up from the wallet, her eyes moist. 'My God, she's beautiful now, and the children too. Is Melody your wife, then?'

'Yes, she is. I'm *so* sorry for lying to you.'

'So why did you?'

'I had to be sure that you would react like you have. If you knew I was her husband right away, you might think I was biased and covering things up somehow—'

'So your name isn't Tristan Ainsworth?'

Tristan frowned. 'Yes, yes it is, why?'

'Well, what would you have done if I had reacted differently? I could have told the police that you had been round here, pestering me, trying to pervert the course of justice. Then Melody's case would look even bleaker, wouldn't it?'

He groaned inwardly. What an idiot he'd been. 'I guess so, I wasn't thinking straight. I knew if you reacted badly it wouldn't look good for me . . . but it never occurred to me to change my name. Melody doesn't even know I'm here; I just went on gut instinct because of the kind of person Melody said you were. I knew I had to act fast in case the police came to interview you in the next few days.' He shrugged and fell silent.

Barbara stood up and to his surprise put her arms around him. 'You and poor Melody have really been through hell, haven't you?' she said, and released him.

Tristan felt his throat thicken with emotion. 'Yes, we certainly have. But if you say you'll do what you said you would for us, and providing the police don't find anything else, I think at last things might be starting to look up.'

Barbara patted him on the back. 'I will help you all I can; now I'm certain that you're telling the truth.'

A few minutes later after they'd exchanged phone numbers, Barbara showed him to the door. 'Now don't forget, I'll ring you as soon as the police have been to fill you in on all the details,' Barbara said with a mischievous smile. 'I'm quite looking forward to it actually. I miss my drama.'

Tristan took her hand in both of his. 'You are a real lifesaver, Barbara. I don't know how I can ever thank you.'

'Anything I can do, I'm glad to help. It's about time that wife of yours had a happy life. God knows her early life sucked big-time. And tell me, does she still sing?'

'When she can, but not recently, of course. She's in the choir and I hope she'll be able to get back to it soon.'

'Well, if she does book me a pew, won't you? That voice is a sound for sore ears.'

CHAPTER 34

The miracle that Melody had prayed for all day but never thought would come to fruition appeared in the shape of Tristan, charging upstairs and bursting in to the bedroom brandishing flowers and champagne. He shook them at her nose, the only bit of face she allowed to protrude from the cocoon of a quilt that she'd fashioned for herself.

At first Melody pushed them away, and stared at Tristan, baffled. It would take a damned sight more than that to make her feel better. But the story of Mrs Goodhale proved to be exactly the damned sight more she needed. And fifteen minutes later, she squealed with happiness and pounced on him pulling him down on the bed with her. Tristan laughed, popped the cork and put the bottle to Melody's mouth. 'Quick, take a drink before it goes everywhere. And we're definitely not out of the woods yet, but I thought we needed to celebrate this victory. They've been far and few between lately.'

Melody gulped down the bubbles and coughed as some went down the wrong way. 'Oh, Tris,' she said, once she'd got her breath back. 'You are *so* clever! I would never have thought of going to Mrs Goodhale's house. And I certainly wouldn't have had the nerve to tell her the truth . . . well, most of it.'

'It could have gone *so* wrong, though,' Tristan said, sighing with contentment as Melody's cool fingers massaged the knots out of his shoulders.

'But it didn't, thanks to you, my love.' Melody looked at Tristan's soft green eyes smiling up at her and planted little kisses all over his face. And for the billionth time since she'd know the man she thanked her lucky stars for his love, loyalty and steadfastness. Then unexpectedly given the situation, the smell of his skin, feel of his stubble on her cheek and warm breath on her neck caused a flicker of passion in her belly. Smiling she slipped off her robe, along with the remnants of darkness that had surrounded her all day, and pushed him back to lay naked in his arms.

Instinct, six sense, something told her that things were set to get better and she had an uncontrollable urge to feel him inside her. It had been too long. Forget champagne and flowers, she'd rather celebrate by making love to her beautiful husband.

'I know it might sound corny, but you're my real-life hero and I think you need to stay in here for a while before you go and see Emma and the children, don't you?' she said, unbuttoning his shirt and running her tongue down his chest and circling around his navel.

'A real-life hero? Gawsh, I don't know about that,' he said, cupping and caressing her breasts with cool strong hands.

'Well, I do,' she muttered huskily, twisting her hand through his hair and pulling his mouth roughly to hers.

The sixth sense or whatever it was proved to be accurate. Melody was overjoyed to discover that things did get better and almost immediately. Two days later she spoke to her old teacher and mentor over the phone. It was so fantastic to be in touch with the only anchor she'd had in a raging storm that lasted nearly three years after her dad had died.

Barbara Goodhale had told her that the police had been to her old school first but had drawn a blank. They had told them that Barbara was the person to speak to and they'd gone round to interview her. 'Oh, Melody I was in my element! You would have been so proud. I waffled on for England! I said that I couldn't remember that much about you, but that you were very quiet and kept yourself to yourself. You once told me you were a little depressed after your dad died and about your weight problem, and we chatted a few times about it, but that was all. I also said you were fab in the choir and musicals, but apart from that, I couldn't tell them much more.'

'Oh, thank you Mrs, Goodhale! What did they ask about my mother?'

'Forget Mrs Goodhale, call me Barbara for goodness sake!' She laughed. 'They asked if I had any dealings with her over the years and I told them that she didn't care much for school meetings. I said that I had heard that she was a bit of a floozy, and had a temper, but again, I couldn't tell them much more.'

'Fantastic! And did they ask about my disappearance, what people thought?'

'Yes. I said that people were shocked, and had no clue as to why you would have committed suicide. I also said that nobody ever imagined you had killed your mother as rumour had it that it was a foreign sailor passing through.'

'Oh, thanks, Mrs . . . Barbara. How can I ever thank you?'

'No charge. The policewoman interviewing me more or less implied that I was negligent in my pastoral care of you. You were very overweight, upset about your dad and told me that you were depressed. And why hadn't I done more to help you? She was right. And as I said to your husband, I never forgave myself for not insisting your mother talk to me, particularly as I knew you were being bullied as well by she who shall remain nameless. If I had, you might not have tried to . . .' Barbara's voice trailed off.

'Hey, don't say that. You did more for me than anyone else at that time. And no matter what you tried to do, you couldn't have stopped the way my mother was with me. You told Tris that you thought

Andrea was evil. Well, so was my mother. It was a shame that we couldn't have swapped parents.'

'Thanks for that, Melody. And talking of parents, you have two kids now, wow! They look adorable from the photos.'

'They are! And you must come and see them when all this is over.'

'Oh, you can count on it.'

Over the next few weeks the investigation turned up some evidence, but in Melody's favour. She was asked to meet at Buchanan's office so they could discuss the findings. He'd hinted that things looked better for her, but no details. Tris accompanied her rather than Emma and although a butterfly storm whirled in her belly, she felt so much more hopeful than she had the last time she'd walked up the stairs to his office.

The battleship-grey decor and chilly atmosphere didn't strike depth charges of uncertainty into her confidence anymore either, as DCI Buchanan and DS Vessey faced her and Tris across the desk. Vessey still looked like someone had stuck a spike up her backside though. Perhaps that had disabled her smile.

Buchanan gave a ghost of one now and said, 'As I told you on the phone, Mrs Ainsworth, we interviewed people from the community of Penarthry and from the statements we have of those few who remembered the events of fourteen years ago, there seems to be more evidence in your favour than

327

against.' Buchanan scanned the papers in front of him. 'The landlord and landlady of the Black Bull where your mother worked, a Mr and Mrs Reardon, who at the time were bar staff, said they remembered a foreign sailor with your mother that night, though she had been with many.' He stopped and looked at Melody. 'We don't normally divulge all this, but you did volunteer to come to us after all.' He glanced at Vessey who clamped her jaw as if she were ready to explode. 'I can read it to you if you wish, but it might be upsetting.'

'Please do, Inspector. There's nothing that could upset me about my mother anymore.'

'Okay, this is the landlord speaking,' Buchanan said. '*That night, Sandra was sitting in the corner where she normally sat, with this sailor. Greek I think he was. She was drunk as usual and I saw her slap him across the face and he slapped her back. I thought, here we go, another brawl, but next minute they were all over each other. I never saw him again, and it wouldn't have surprised me if he'd done her in. He was out for trouble, barging past customers and glaring at folk as he came to the bar, a right nasty character in my opinion.*'

Buchanan looked up again. 'His wife added the following. *Some folk said that Melody had done it because she ran off and killed herself . . . but now I find that she didn't and I'm right glad about that. I felt so sorry for her. I knew she hadn't done it. And like my Harry, I think it was the sailor. He gave me the creeps. Poor Melody had a right old life with*

Sandra. She used to tell us how she tormented her, called her names. She drank more than she sold, too. But old Fred, the previous landlord, wouldn't sack her because she kept him sweet, if you know what I mean?

'So, this corroborates your story and elsewhere we have drawn blanks, really. There isn't enough evidence for the CPS to warrant prosecution.' Buchanan gave a warmer smile this time and Melody felt her heart do a somersault. *Was this it then? Was it all over?*

'However, there is the issue of false documentation.' Buchanan nodded at Vessey, who visibly preened at her chance in the spotlight.

'Yes, I need the surname of this Bob and Maureen that took you in and falsified documents. Intent to defraud on your part would be difficult to prove, as your sister-in-law intimated last time, but *they* do have a case to answer.'

Melody sighed and shook her head. Was this woman for real? 'I told you they are in Australia now.'

'Nevertheless, their surname please?' Vessey poised her pen over a small white pad.

Melody guessed there was no way she would waste time and money trying to prosecute Bob and Maureen at this distance and they both knew it. Vessey was just fuming that the investigation had fallen flat and wanted to score a point. Melody would certainly not help her if she was even half-serious. 'I can't remember. They were just Bob and Maureen to everyone.'

'You really can't remember?'

'No.'

'No matter. You say you lived in a Traveller camp in Swindon. Did they have relatives there?' Vessey arranged her mouth into a supercilious sneer.

Melody nodded. Damn her, was she really going to snoop around up there?

'Which site was it?'

'I have no idea. Things were a bit of a blur back then.'

'Never mind, I'll go and see what I can find out. There can't be more than half a dozen up there.'

'I think you are making a bit of a mountain out of a molehill on this one,' Tristan said huffily. 'These people only had the best intentions.'

'A lot of people who are in prison have the best intentions, Dr Ainsworth. Obtaining a false birth certificate, false name, place of birth et cetera is against the law, as I'm sure you know.'

Tristan tutted and stared with contempt at Vessey.

To Melody's surprise, Vessey then pulled a sympathetic expression out of her training toolkit and said, 'I'm not sure if you're both aware, but I have reason to believe that because you used a false name on your marriage certificate, you might not be legally married.'

Melody felt the room spin. Just when she thought they were free of misery. She looked at Tristan and swallowed a lump in her throat. Was this lovely man not really her husband?

He shook his head and squeezed her hand. 'Not to worry, love, Emma has already looked into this and I'm happy to say that we are legally married. Your surname was the right one and Karen was one of your middle names, so it's cool,' he soothed, then glared over at Vessey. 'And you can wipe that false concern right off your face, madam.'

Vessey recoiled, her dark eyes flashing. 'I beg your pardon?'

'You heard me perfectly well,' Tristan growled. Then he turned his attention to Buchanan. 'Am I to understand that we are free to go now and there will be no charges against my wife?'

Buchanan put the top on his pen, ignored the woman fuming by his side and smiled, genuinely this time. 'Yes, you are.' His sharp grey eyes settled on Melody's. 'I really hope that you will be able to put the past behind you and enjoy your future now, Mrs Ainsworth.'

Melody felt the strain and tension of the last few months starting to melt away at last like snow from a sun-warmed roof. 'So do I, DCI Buchanan. It's been a long time coming.'

CHAPTER 35

Tristan ended the call to Emma and went in search of his wife. He found her in the bathroom amidst suds, shrieks of laughter and two far from sleepy looking children. 'Hello, gorgeous,' he said, skimming a handful of bubbles from the bath and placing it on Melody's chin. 'Look, Mummy has grown a beard.' He pointed and covered his mouth as if in shock. Sebastian and Bella giggled and made their own bubble beards.

'Thanks, Tris, I always wanted a bubble beard. But can we try to wind the kids down instead of up? It's bedtime in half an hour.'

'Certainly, my sweet. Then later we can have a cuddle on the sofa with a nice glass of wine . . . toasting our toes by the roaring fire . . . watching the snow fall thick and fast outside our window.'

'Snow?' Melody looked at him in surprise. 'It didn't forecast snow.'

'I lied. I just thought it would make a nice image.'

She gave him a withering look. 'Did you tell Emma the good news then?'

'Yep. She shrieked loud enough to burst my eardrums. She said we were very, very lucky and that she agreed with you that Vessey wouldn't pursue Bob and Maureen at such a distance. Vessey was just trying to scare you.'

Melody poured a jug of water over Sebastian's hair. 'I wonder why she is such a cow? Must have had a witch for a mother.' Melody grinned. 'I hear that kind of thing makes a person weird.'

'Well, it's certainly true in your case.' Tristan received a handful of soapsuds on the arm in response. 'You know when you fibbed about not remembering Bob and Maureen's surname?'

'Yeah.'

'What was it?'

'I think it was Heron, though it was true that they didn't use it much. Why?'

'Well, I thought we might try and trace them, send a Christmas card, you know?'

'No. It's a nice thought, Tris, but a few months before I met you I bumped into Mary, one of their daughters. It was her who told me they'd emigrated. I was hurt and sad that they'd not said goodbye, but I could understand why.' Melody chucked a towel to him and they set about the task of drying the kids.

'When I left the camp to work at the farm they said I needed to have a clean break with the past, start a new life. They were the only tie between my old life and my new and, though it hurt like hell, I knew they were right. Of course they said come back and see them sometime, but we all knew that it would be best if I didn't.'

Sparks crackled and whooshed up the chimney as Tristan poked the open fire. Melody was getting the children to sleep and then she'd be down for that cuddle. In the unlit room, a yellow glow warmed his face and the thought of Melody in his arms warmed his heart, as he stared into the flames lost in thought. It was over then. At last the whole horrendous nightmare had passed and they could look forward to sweeter dreams. Thank God. He wasn't sure how much longer he could have coped with it all – on the surface appearing strong for Melody and the kids, while underneath feeling like he was sinking into the depths of despair.

Moving to the window to draw the curtains he thought about how lucky they were to have good friends and family too. Without his sister, Barbara Goodhale, Jenny and Michael, he was certain that it would have been a very different story for them. It would definitely have been a story without a happy ending.

He put his hand on the curtain and noticed the full moon suspended by stars in the black December sky. How magical it looked. Tristan always loved this month. And how much nicer it was to be back in his beloved Cornwall, with the promise of Christmas just a whisper away, the shop windows cheered with decorations, the ice-blue skies under-lined by the grey of the sea and white horse waves gusted by a chill wind. Then came New Year, a celebration of the old and a welcoming of the next twelve months.

A smile crept over his lips as he pulled the curtains shut and poured out two glasses of wine. That's what they needed, a special celebration to mark the end of worry, fear and despair and the start of hope, happiness and laughter. That bloody romantic trip away never did get booked, unsurprisingly; there had been one or two obstacles in the way of that. But a gut feeling told him that something a bit grander than that was now needed. He thought for a few moments and then Tristan took a sip of wine and chuckled to himself. He'd suddenly had a fantastic idea of *exactly* how to celebrate.

Under Melody's hand a perfectly defined foot moved and she squealed with excitement. 'Oh my goodness, it's a real baby in there!'

Jenny laughed and pulled her top back down. 'What did you expect, a stuffed cushion?'

'No.' Melody giggled and picked up her coffee cup. 'But I can't quite believe you only have about three weeks to go. It's flown past, hasn't it?'

The two friends were catching up in Jenny's sitting room a week after the Ainsworths had been given the great news by Buchanan. Melody had mostly spent that week being out and about in Kelerston with her children, just to experience the sheer joy of walking around in complete freedom, with her head held high, and no fear of her past catching up with her for the first time in fourteen years.

One of the highlights of the week was telling old Harold the butcher that her name was really Melody and the reason behind her 'agoraphobia'. She didn't go into details about exactly why she'd left her past life behind and changed her name, but he'd reacted as if she'd told him that she'd actually come from Mars. Harold shook his jowls and his eyes popped as if he had suffered an electrical current somewhere that Melody preferred not to think about.

'Eh? . . . What? So, you have been hiding out here then so to speak . . . under a false name and that?' he spluttered.

'Er, yes, Harold. I guess you could say that,' Melody said, trying to keep a straight face. He made her sound like a cold-war spy.

'Bloody 'ell! 'Scuse my French, but who'd have thought it? You being a doctor's wife, an' all.'

'I know! You'd never guess to look at me would you, isn't it exciting?' Melody giggled.

Harold's eyes narrowed and then he gave one of his classic kookaburra laughs. 'You're pulling my leg, aren't you?'

Melody extracted a plastic sausage that Bella had snatched from the display and gave it back to Harold. 'That's for me to know and you to find out, Harold. Toodle-pip.' Melody shooed the children out of the shop and laughed out loud in the street. God, that had felt so good.

Jenny had howled, too, when Melody had told her about it just now. 'Oh, I so wish I could have been there to see it. Harold is such a pompous old sod,' Jenny said, wiping tears of laughter from her eyes.

'He is that. It will certainly give him something to puzzle about.'

Serious all of a sudden, Jenny said, 'I am so pleased everything worked out for you, Melody. I have been on tenterhooks since you told me about it all.'

'You and me both, hon. There was a chance it could have gone horribly wrong, and I mean horribly. Worst case scenario I could have ended up in prison.'

Jenny wrapped her cardigan more closely about her bump and shuddered. 'I know. It doesn't bear thinking about, the poor kids . . . and Tristan, of course.'

Melody nodded. 'Talking of Tris, he's been acting a bit odd these past few days.'

'Odd?'

'Yeah. He was vague about why he wasn't spending his afternoon off with us, something about a computer overhaul at work, but he wasn't home until gone eight. And when I have walked in on his telephone conversations a few times he's ended the call.'

'Oh, well it's obviously a surprise for Christmas, isn't it? It is only a few weeks away after all,' Jenny said.

'But we don't normally make a big fuss at Christmas for each other. It's Bella's second birthday next week, too. We concentrate on the kids at this time of year,' Melody persisted, noticing that her friend had a rosy flush creeping along her cheeks.

'This year is different though. You have something to celebrate after the awful time you've had.' Jenny picked up a baby magazine and fanned her face. 'Look at me, I'm a furnace – must be my hormones.'

Melody doubted it. She could tell from Jenny's shifty eyes that she knew something about Tristan's strange behaviour, but wasn't letting on. Melody opened her mouth and leaned forward on the sofa, preparing to grill her further, when Michael stepped in, bringing with him the smell of winter on his coat and the children charging in behind. She noticed how Jenny looked at her husband with relief, obviously glad he'd interrupted before Melody could pin her down.

'Shall I get them a bite to eat? All that playing outside in the chilly air has made them ravenous,' Michael said with a grin, pulling off his woolly red hat and allowing his blond curls to tumble to his shoulders.

Melody thought that if his female parishioners could see him now, all pink-faced and sparkly blue eyed from being out in the cold, they would swoon dead away like characters in a Brontë novel. 'They only had lunch a couple of hours ago, but if they insist and you don't mind, thanks, Michael. That would be lovely.'

'Okey dokey, and can I ask when you might be gracing us with your lovely voice again? We would love to have you in the Christmas choir, now things are getting back to normal for you.'

'There's nothing I would like better, Michael. But I don't want to be involved in a TV programme. As you say, getting back to normal is what I need.'

Michael looked sheepish. 'Don't worry, that's definitely very much on the back-burner until further notice.' He stepped forward and kissed Jenny on the head and rubbed the round of her tummy. 'Once little junior is here, there'll be no time for breathing, let alone TV appearances.'

Melody felt relief and excitement arrive all in one heart thumping little package. A Christmas choir! Just what she'd hoped for that day back in September before Armageddon had struck. She smiled, 'Ah, Michael, at least you know what's about to descend on you then . . . no, I'll re-phrase that. At least you *think* you know.'

'So, will you be in the choir?' Jenny said, looking hopeful.

'Just try to stop me,' Melody replied with a huge grin.

Tristan kept up his odd behaviour for the next few days, whispering on the phone and snapping the computer shut when she walked into a room. Melody had just decided that she would challenge him about it that evening, when he came in and confessed that he was organising a surprise celebration meal for her at the weekend.

He explained that he'd been whispering on the phone as he'd been booking a nice restaurant and talking to relatives by email. Emma would be there, so would his Auntie Helen and Jenny and Michael, too. Now at last it was all organised and Audrey, the receptionist at the surgery, had offered to babysit.

Melody couldn't understand why he'd blown the secret two days early, but he'd said that he knew she was becoming suspicious and didn't want her to be stressed again. It made sense she supposed, and it would explain Jenny's shifty looks, too. But something she couldn't put her finger on didn't quite ring true.

The day of the 'surprise' celebratory meal dawned bright, blue, crisp and cold. Melody opened the conservatory door, sniffed the pine-scented air and walked down the path. The iced leaves crunched underneath her slipper boots and still in her fluffy turquoise dressing gown, she hugged her arms tight around her chest. A contented smile grew on her lips. Just the thing on a perfect winter's day like this was for them all to have a brisk walk on the beach wrapped up like Michelin men in their puffer jackets.

'Tris!' she called, as she came back into the warm and started to clear away the breakfast dishes.

'Tris! Shall we go to the beach in a bit? It's so lovely out there!'

'No need to shout, I'm only here,' he said, wandering into the kitchen.

Melody turned round and looked at him. 'So, can you get the children ready while I clear up?'

'Yes, but not just now. They're happy playing at the moment and I have something very important to ask.'

Her stomach flipped over. He looked so serious, what the hell was he going to ask her? She couldn't bear any more bad news. Melody put down the plate she was holding and pushed her trembling hands into her dressing gown pockets. 'What's up?'

'Nothing's up, my love. For the first time in ages. Isn't that great?' He smiled and she saw his eyes moisten. Then from the back pocket of his jeans, he pulled a small box and went down on one knee before her. She noticed his hands trembled too as he opened the lid to reveal a platinum band rimmed with diamonds.

Melody gasped and her hand fluttered to her mouth. 'Oh my God, Tris, it's beautiful.'

'It had to be. Look who's wearing it,' he said, taking her left hand and slipping it onto her third finger.

Melody looked at it sitting next to her wedding ring and shook her head in bewilderment.

Still on one knee, Tris cleared his throat and looked into her eyes, his own reflecting the deep love they had for each other. 'Melody Ainsworth,

I love you more than life. Would you please do me the honour of renewing our wedding vows in a blessing I have arranged for us today?'

Melody sank down in front of him laughing and crying with happiness. She cupped his face in her hands and kissed him, her salty tears on his lips. At last they drew apart. 'So *that's* what you've been up to!' she said, laughing again. 'A surprise meal indeed.'

'Yep, and you haven't answered me yet,' he said, furrowing his brow in a pretend frown.

'Of course I will, my darling!' But then her smile was wiped off her face by a barrage of thoughts pummelling her brain. 'But what the hell will I wear? I have nothing suitable. What time is it happening and where will it be?'

'The attire is all taken care of courtesy of Jenny. The time is noon, the place is the beach. And Michael is doing the honours.'

'Jenny? The beach?'

'Have you lost the ability to string a sentence together? Yes, you heard right.' He got up from his knees and clicked his fingers under her nose. 'Now, get in the shower, wash your hair and make it look presentable for a beach blessing. It looks like a birds nest at the moment. Jenny will be round in half an hour and I'm taking the kids down to Michael. I have to make myself look beautiful too and we only have . . .' he craned his neck to see the microwave clock '. . . two and a half hours.'

Flabbergasted, Melody's brain refused to compute. 'But this is a blessing, right? We are still legally married?'

'Yep. But the news that we might not be gave me the idea. I just thought it might be nice to do it again for our friends and family to witness our love and also to hear you declare at last who you really are to the world.'

Melody stood up and hugged him tightly. 'It's more than nice. It is absolutely bloody fantastic,' she said, kissing him again.

CHAPTER 36

The woman in the mirror must be somebody else. Melody, stunned, stepped forward and peered more closely at her reflection. In just an hour or so, Jenny had transformed her from a frantic woman in a dressing gown with a bed head, into a radiant beauty. The warm copper-brown eye shadow Jenny had applied, accentuated the light blue of Melody's eyes, and a brush of subtle blusher added warmth and definition to her cheekbones. After that, only a touch of soft rose lipstick was necessary to finish the look.

Parted down the middle, tresses of her golden hair had been gently twisted from her temples and secured at the back of her head into a clip Jenny had fashioned from holly leaves and berries. The rest of her hair had been left long and it spilled over her shoulders and down her back like a shimmering golden cape.

A gasp had escaped Melody's lips when Jenny had pulled the dress out of its protective cover. They had seen it once when they had been shopping in Falmouth together a while ago in a shop selling incense sticks, candles and very unusual clothes. Melody had remarked how lovely it was but that she would never have an occasion to wear it. It was made of the deepest emerald-green velvet, had long medieval tapered sleeves with delicate embroidered white flowers along the edges of the cuff and deep neckline.

Admiring the way the sumptuous velvet clung to her curves and then flared out like a daffodil trumpet to the floor, Melody marvelled at the way the day was turning out. Then she felt Jenny lift her hair and secure a silver chain around her neck, and from the chain, a single pearl was suspended that settled in the hollow of Melody's throat. She turned from the mirror and hugged Jenny. 'Oh, this necklace sets the whole thing off perfectly!'

'I wore it on my wedding day, and these matching earrings will complete your transformation.' Jenny smiled and hugged her back. 'I feel like a fairy godmother.' She giggled.

'You *are* a fairy godmother!' Melody said, turning round and round in the middle of the room. 'And I don't know how to thank you. When I got married I had nobody to help really. Emma did her bit, but because of my circumstances I had no real close girlfriends.'

Jenny's eyes welled up. 'You are very welcome. My thanks is to see you happy.'

Melody smiled and then wrinkled her nose. 'Now, let's see. I have something borrowed, I need something blue and something old . . . or is that just for a wedding? I'm not up on vow renewals and blessings to be honest.'

'You can do whatever you please, but I think it would be nice to be traditional. I thought you could wear your taupe boots with the wedge, so that could be something old. You need something that you won't fall over in on the sand and nobody will see them under the dress anyway.'

Melody nodded, her eyes shining with excitement. 'You have thought of everything . . . and something blue?'

'Ah, that's been sorted by somebody else.'

'Somebody else? Who?'

'Never you mind,' Jenny said mysteriously, and led the way downstairs.

Melody tugged the heavy woollen black pashmina more closely about her shoulders as she stepped out of Jenny's car at the foot of the dunes. The wind had got up slightly since that morning, but after a few moments the winter sunlight stroked warm fingers over her face and soon, in the shelter of the dunes, the temperature became quite comfortable.

'Now, my instructions are to make you promise to close your eyes until we get over the dunes and onto the beach. Tristan wants the setting to be a surprise.'

Melody laughed out loud. 'Well, make sure I don't tangle my feet in the marram grass and fall on my arse!'

Arm in arm, the two women made their way

carefully up the path through the dunes and down the other side. A snatch of familiar music came to Melody's ears on the breeze, but then was tugged away again before she could place it. She wanted to open her eyes but Jenny told her to keep them shut a little longer. The sand underfoot was replaced by what Melody guessed was material of some kind, and the music became louder, until she knew exactly what it was.

'Okay, open them,' Jenny said, removing Melody's pashmina and placing a bouquet of flowers into her hands.

Upon doing so, Melody saw that the flowers were white roses, and she stood upon a red carpet aisle just inside the entrance to a small marquee. To either side of this aisle were seated a small group of friends and family and the backs of heads of a few she couldn't place. She did recognise a tumble of amber hair though and when Linda turned and waved with genuine warmth in her eyes, Melody waved back swallowing to dispel a huge lump in her throat.

At the end of the carpet, Michael stood behind a table festooned with flowers, and in front of him, Tristan, in his best suit, turned around, his brilliant green eyes shining with love. Overwhelmed by emotion as Bobby Darin sang her dad's favourite song, *Somewhere Beyond the Sea,* she walked down the aisle towards the most wonderful man in the world.

Tristan took her hand and kissed her gently on

the lips, and then, before all there, they spoke the beautiful words Michael had prepared and re-affirmed their everlasting love for each other. After a while, Sebastian and Bella struggled to join their parents, but managed to be restrained and entertained by Audrey, until after their final kiss cemented the end of the blessing.

Emma had appointed herself photographer in chief and snapped away while the couple looked into each other's eyes. Melody had barely glanced at anyone else apart from Tris since she'd stepped into the place and was quite happy for the moment to never end. It was only when Emma called her name and asked her to look toward her up the aisle, that Melody recognised the faces of the strangers she'd noticed at the beginning.

If Tristan hadn't been there she knew she would have collapsed, as her legs had become two strings of jelly. Leaning against her husband she struggled to staunch the flood of emotion welling up behind her eyes. Because there, sitting in the middle row, were Bob, Maureen, and Barbara Goodhale.

A sob escaped her and she took a step towards them, but just then Michael announced that drinks and a buffet were waiting at the vicarage and everyone started talking at once, taking photos, and milling around. Then from the hubbub, Bob and Maureen were suddenly right there in front of her.

Maureen, not looking in the slightest bit older,

cleared her throat and nodded at a dark blue ribbon around Melody's bouquet. 'I 'ope that brings you luck, love.' Melody, puzzled at such an odd greeting after so many years, looked at the ribbon. 'It were on my bouquet when me and Bob were wed.' Maureen's eyes moistened, mirroring Melody's. 'Somethin' blue for you.'

'It brought us luck, that's for sure. We are just as 'appy now as we were forty year ago,' Bob said, blowing his nose nosily on a big white hanky.

Melody handed the bouquet to Tristan and flung her arms around them both. 'Oh my lord, you are *such* a sight for sore eyes! I missed you so much.'

Bob chuckled. 'We missed you too, Bobby!'

Melody released them and took a step back. 'But how on earth did you get here . . . and how did you know about this?'

'Well, it's not that far from Swindon, and your smashin' 'usband asked us, of course.' Maureen grinned.

'But I thought you were in Australia?'

'We were there on an extended 'oliday for a few months, but then there was a cock up with immigration. They didn't take kindly to us bein' Travellers and that, so we came 'ome. Glad we did, couldn't cope with those bloody spiders the size of yer 'at,' Bob said.

Melody, bewildered, turned to her husband. 'And how did you know all this, Tris?'

'I didn't,' he said, slipping his arm round her waist. 'I went up to Swindon on my afternoon off to see if I could talk to their relations. I thought it might be nice to get back in touch despite what you said. And you'd given me the surname, so I soon found their camp.'

Maureen gave a wheezy chuckle. 'Mind you, he nearly fell over backwards when our Harley told him we were still right there, just two caravans down.'

'It was a shock, but a nice one.' Tristan grinned. 'And just think, Melody, Sebastian and Bella have a couple of oldies to run ragged now.'

'Oi, less of the old!' Bob said.

Melody laughed and hugged them both again. 'I know we're not related, but you were like parents to me when I thought my life wasn't worth living,' her voice broke with emotion and she took a deep breath. 'I would *really* love you to be honorary grandparents to our babes. Little one's need them.'

Bob and Maureen nodded and kissed her on both cheeks. No words were necessary.

As everyone made their way out, Melody looked for Mrs Goodhale. She'd been there in the background when she was talking to Bob and Maureen, but now she'd disappeared. She asked Tristan if he'd seen her and he said that Barbara had mentioned that she might not come to the vicarage as she felt Melody needed space to take everything in and also to catch up with the Herons.

'But surely you told her she *must* come?'

'Yeah, but she said that she'd meet up with you properly another time.'

Melody felt her heart sink with disappointment. Although she had spoken to Barbara over the phone, she would have loved to have thanked her in person for everything she'd done for them. Still, there would be another time. And Linda . . . where was she?

Casting her eyes around, she suddenly spotted Linda by the door, talking to a guy that Melody hadn't seen before. He was tall, mid-thirties, longish dark hair and had twinkly blue eyes that were attentively dancing over Linda's. She looked away from the guy when Melody walked over and put her hand on her arm.

'Melody, congratulations! I was hanging on here to speak to you when you'd finished chatting to that older couple.'

Melody shot her a warm smile. 'Thank you so much for coming. I am so pleased that you did.' She gave Linda a quick hug and kissed her on the cheek.

'And I am so glad that Tristan invited me; I wanted to show you how much I appreciated . . . what you did for me.' Linda's eyes welled up and the guy put his arm protectively around her.

'Oh, don't be daft.' Melody flapped her hand dismissively and inclined her head towards the guy. 'Aren't you going to introduce us?'

'Oh, sorry!' Linda grinned. 'This is Jed. We met at a therapy session and . . . I guess we just hit it off.'

Jed nodded and shook Melody's hand. 'Nice to meet the woman who my Linda speaks so highly of,' he said, with a shy smile.

Melody smiled back, hugged Linda again and whispered into her ear, 'My Linda, eh? That sounds promising.'

Linda grinned and turned an interesting shade of crimson.

'So will you join us at the vicarage, you two?'

'Yes, please. We can perhaps have a bit of a chat later, too?' Linda grinned again.

'Oh, you can *so* count on that, missy,' Melody agreed.

A few minutes later as she and Tris walked arm in arm up to the top of the dunes, the children scrambling along in front, she spied Barbara waving goodbye to Jenny by the car. Hoisting up her dress Melody sped down the other side so fast that she thought she'd go flying. 'Barbara, wait!'

'Careful, you'll break your damned ankle, girl!' Barbara warned, her teacher's head firmly back on.

'Tristan tells me you won't come to the reception,' Melody said panting, and placing her hand on Barbara's arm.

Barbara sighed and shrugged, 'Well, I—'

'You must, you *really* must. Without you we wouldn't even be here today.'

'Oh, I don't know about that—' Barbara began.

'Well, I do. Please say you'll come!'

'Okay, don't get your knickers in a knot.' Barbara chuckled and hugged her.

Melody and Tristan, after making love for the second time, lay entwined in each other's arms, still wide awake in the early hours. Though the day had been long and emotionally exhausting, they both had a feel-good buzz in their heads and were unable to sleep.

'And guess, what, Tris?'

'Er . . . your real name isn't Melody but actually Daisy May and you want to pull on some cowboy boots and do the hoedown right now?'

Melody thumped his shoulder playfully. 'Yeah, how did you guess? No. Barbara was chatting to Jenny about the choir and said how much she missed directing musicals. Jenny actually persuaded her to help out with the choir while she had time off with the baby! She also said she'd like to join the Christmas choir. Isn't that great?'

'It certainly is. That means that you'll be in the Christmas choir with your favourite teacher. It will be just like old times for you,' Tristan said, giving her a squeeze.

'No. It will be much better than old times; things were pretty grim back then. And guess what else?' Before Tristan had time to make up another daft answer she said, 'Barbara said that I would make a brilliant counsellor.'

Tristan propped himself up on his elbow and

353

looked at her. 'Er, I think you'll find *I* said that some time ago, and so did Linda.'

Melody giggled at the indignant look on his face. 'Yes I know. I told her that you'd said it and that I might think about training when the kids are bigger. She said I should deffo go for it.'

'Good. I'm glad she talked some sense into you, even if I couldn't. Now I think we should try to get some sleep, the munchkins will be on the warpath at six-thirty.'

'And guess what else? Bob and Maureen said they'd come down to stay for a week in the New Year. Isn't that brilliant?'

'Yep, now shush,' he said, snuggling down next to her.

'And guess who's the most perfect man in the universe and I want to thank him for the billionth time for making this day perfect, well almost, and sharing the rest of his marvellous life with me in perfect perfectness?' She giggled.

'Hope that's me. And why was the day only almost perfect?'

Melody gave a sigh and swallowed down an unexpected lump of emotion. 'Because my dad should have been there . . . should be here to share our life . . . our children's lives.'

Tristan turned her to face him. 'I know he should, my love. And I wish I could have made that happen for you, but he's gone, just like mine.' He kissed her on the tip of the nose. 'But both of them live on in us, and in the kids. And I know they would be so proud.'

Melody nodded and kissed him. 'God, I love you so much, Tristan Ainsworth.'

'I love you so much too, Melody Ainsworth.'

'And guess what?'

'What?' Tristan groaned.

'You're babysitting tomorrow morning while I go to choir practice. Jenny said I need extra as I've missed so much.'

'Oh, marvellous. Right, turn the damned lamp off and say goodnight, Melody.'

Melody flicked the switch and snuggled down. 'Goodnight, Melody.'

The church – with its stained glass windows brightly lit with flickering candles, and snowflakes drifting through the night sky and settling on the path under Melody's feet as she hurried towards the entrance – felt like something out of a Disney Christmas scene, but without the cheesiness.

Melody walked down the aisle towards the assembling choir and remembered that back in September, the church had had a Christmassy feel somehow. Now it was only a day away. Her nostrils were filled with incense, cinnamon and the breath of winter on everyone's coats as they shrugged them off to make ready for the final rehearsal of the Christmas concert tomorrow.

'You ready for the big day?' Michael asked her, as they all took their places.

'Just about. Sebastian is so excited I think he'll pop!' Melody said, waving at Jenny, Barbara and Linda. 'Bella is excited but she's not quite as up on Father Christmas as Seb yet.'

'Jenny looks ready to pop, too.' Michael grinned and pointed at his wife struggling to lower herself into a chair at the front. 'For different reasons, obviously. Hope junior waits until after I've done the service tomorrow at least.'

'I can hear what you're saying, my dear. I'm preggers *not* deaf, you know,' Jenny admonished. 'Right, you lot. I might not be able to stand during this forty minute rehearsal, but I'm still conducting, so mind you keep an eye on me, okay?'

'Yes, miss,' Barbara said, which caused a giggle to do the rounds.

Jenny smiled back. 'Okay, Melody, we're starting with your solo, *Silent Night*, yes?'

'Right you are, skipper,' Melody said, and noticed a wiggle of emotion in her voice. It suddenly hit her that this was the first time that she truly felt like Melody since she'd revealed all. People had started calling her by her real name for a few weeks or so now, but it had seemed a little strange. But right here, in this place, on Christmas Eve, about to do what she loved so much; it felt like she had come home. She hoped she wouldn't feel too moved to actually get the notes right, but after a few seconds Melody forgot her nerves and saw instead that she'd moved Jenny to tears . . . and most of the choir from the sniffs and dabbing of eyes going on around her.

On Christmas Day itself, however, she nearly did lose it big-time when she noticed Seb brush a tear away from his dad's eye as they watched her singing from the front pews. Bella waved and then clapped her hands as best she could when the audience erupted in appreciation at the end, and Melody beamed with pride wishing for the thousandth time that her dad could have been there to see how happy she was now.

Even though she was exhausted after the concert, the cooking of Christmas lunch for the four of them, Emma – and a new man, Nate, early days, but seemed nice – and Auntie Helen, then playing with the children and all their new toys, the early hours found Melody wide awake and staring at the ceiling. Thoughts of the past, the future, and the present filled her mind and if her heart were a jigsaw, it was clear that a 'dad shaped' piece was missing. He would have been so proud to see her sing solo today. But he was gone and that was it.

Melody closed her eyes, but the sound of the Atlantic Ocean whispering on the wind outside the window made her open them again. Suddenly she knew what she must do.

Dressed in pyjamas and a dressing gown, Melody wrapped a thick blanket around her, tiptoed downstairs and shoved her feet into Wellingtons. She took her warmest coat from the hook and then wrapped the blanket back over that.

It wasn't snowing now, but it was freezing outside. The yellow beam of her torch picked a clear path through the dunes and then at the top the moon took over, slipping out from behind the sliver clouds, hanging cold and serene in the navy sky.

Melody's heart flipped and began a steady beat in her ears. The scene was so reminiscent of that night fourteen years ago when she'd offered herself to the ocean, broken, her life beyond repair. But this time it was different. This time she was mended, strong and ready to live life to the full again.

She ran down the dune and onto the beach kicking off her Wellingtons as she went. Though it was cold, the sand felt good between her toes, she felt free, her heart racing, the wind whipping her hair across her face. On the shoreline, she slipped off the blanket. She didn't need it, the adrenaline coursing through her veins kept her warm.

Melody looked out to sea, its dark rolling waves glittered here and there with a sprinkling of moonlight, and she said, 'This is for you, Dad.'

With her heart full of joy, she spread her arms wide, tilted her face to the sky, took a deep breath, and lifted her voice in song.